Tina

K THE COP ILLER

A NOVEL BY
DARRELL DEBREW

Publisher's Note

Edited by: A. Slye
Proofing: Marion Dixon Bey

Chapter 1

"Get her," Clyde hollered to his men when Tina walked out of Alexander's. They were on the Grand Concourse in New York City. The borough of the Bronx to be specific.

For fourteen months, Clyde has been tracking Tina. There was a warrant for Tina's arrest for murdering a DEA agent who happened to be Clyde's father and hero. Clyde was on leave from his job as an Ohio Deputy Sheriff and to catch Tina, he was having to spend his own money. The men with him were bounty hunters for hire. By instinct and luck, Tina saw Clyde before he hollered and ran back into Alexander's. With the five o'clock rush hour, she hoped that all the people in the store and the streets would provide ample cover. At six-foot-two, hiding in a crowd was rather hard for Tina. She ducked behind a clothes rack so she would be able to see him when he walked through the door. She figured that Clyde had other cops waiting at the front entrance.

Suddenly, two bounty hunters burst through the rear door and went deep into Alexander's. Tina saw Clyde wasn't with them. It didn't matter to them that they didn't know where they were going. What mattered was who they were looking for.

Clyde called for back-up. Local authorities were always willing to help catch a cop killer. Clyde had tracked Tina from Louisiana, Delaware, New Jersey, Atlanta, Florida, and finally, he caught sight of her in New York. She seemed to stay in a place for about a month. The letters she wrote her boyfriend in federal prison provided the trail.

Tina had to think fast. Sitting still wasn't an option. Going out the back door wasn't an option either. Clyde was probably prepared and ready with the desire to start shooting. She headed for the basement where she worked on a part-time basis. She had to come in to get her paycheck because the address she had given them was bogus. Having a real address was an easy way for the cops to find out where she laid her head. Her boyfriend, Tyrone, had given her this guidance.

Less than ten minutes after Clyde made his call, Alexander's started being surrounded by police. Even the S.W.A.T. team had been called in. Clyde had been speaking with them for several days.

Clyde had seen Tina a few times in the vicinity and one of the letters had eventually led him to Alexander's. There's a theory that a criminal only gets one chance to slip. Tina had written to Tyrone about a suit she wanted to purchase for him and this letter also said something about getting back to work.

On his first sighting, he knew that he only had a few weeks to nab her. He moved slowly and cautiously to keep from spooking her. One night he followed her to a building in Brooklyn but she never came out. Another night he followed her to a building in Queens and again, she didn't come out. Getting at her had proven to be a difficult task.

Once he determined that Tina worked at Alexander's he set up his trap for payday,. Asking too many questions of store personnel might prove to be rather risky, especially if any of them notified her and then, he would have to start all over. He was certain she would show up to get her paycheck and faked a job inquiry over the phone to confirm it. He did it not know what part of the store she worked in, and he didn't want to take a chance by walking around the store.

Tina

They had sighted her going in Alexander's at eleven-thirty a.m. Clyde had six bounty hunters with him. and Alexander's had four entrances. There was a bounty hunter at each entrance and two were with Clyde at the front. One of the hunters that went in looking for her had the intention of killing her. He had orders to arrest, with the ulterior motive of killing her which would be justified later. For two hours, they looked for Tina but found no trace. She still had to be in the building. Half of the precinct was on the scene searching, including two helicopters, one of which belonged to Channel Seven News.

As darkness settled, people were being let out of stores, one by one. As people were coming out, undercover cops were going in.

In the meantime, Tina had made her way up from the basement and was on the top floor looking out of the window. She was wondering how she had been found. That night she was planning on heading to Chicago. *What do I do? Where do I go?* Jumping out of the window was not an option. There were too many cops on the ground. There was no other building for her to jump to and hiding on the roof was out of the question. All she could do was to get inside the hiding spot she kept for just such an emergency.

By six-thirty, a hundred cops had searched Alexander's, but Tina was not to be found. It was completely dark outside and the TV cameras were rolling.

"This is a live broadcast of the chasing of a cop killer. Tina Thompson is somewhere in the Alexander's building. As you can see, the place is surrounded. The police seem not to be able to find her." The reporter started walking. "Here we have the man that started this event. Would you tell us who you are?"

"My name is Clyde Atkins. I'm a deputy sheriff from Youngstown." Tina's picture suddenly came across the screen.

"I've been tracking her for fourteen months, ever since she's been charged with murdering my father.". Clyde admitted to himself that Tina had played the cat-and-mouse game like a champion. Just because she was a black girl from the projects didn't make her dumb. His task had proven to be much more complicated than he thought it would be.

Because of the blood relationship with the victim, they wouldn't let him take part in the manhunt. He accepted that to a degree but on the side, he did his own investigating. The police's manhunt proved to be fruitless. They just put it on the back burner. Clyde put it on his front burner.

"Did you say she killed your father?" the reporter asked with interest, thinking, *great stuff for the ratings.*

"Yes, she killed my father. I conducted my own manhunt and I promise you, she will be found tonight". An idea suddenly popped in his head and he brusquely said "I have to go."

Clyde walked over to the officer-in-charge. "What's up? Y'all can't catch one country female in a building?" Clyde hated not being part of the action. His father's killer was just inches away from being arrested.

"We got this, country boy. Just relax. She can't disappear into thin air. We have a hundred men in the building. We'll have her in a minute."

Clyde was debating if he should tell him that Tina had found a good hiding spot. "If you don't find her in an hour, let my people and me go in after her."

"This is my jurisdiction," the Sergeant responded. "We got this."

"Listen, my people are professional bounty hunters. We'll find her in fifteen minutes."

Sergeant Knowles just happened to be the highest ranking officer at the time. "I'll meet you halfway. I'll let y'all go in in an hour if she isn't found. But not just y'all. I'm not

Acknowledgement

Naturally my publisher, Tiah Short, has to be first for being far more relentless than I would be, which is quite rare.

My best friends Felecia Belcher and Harriet Davis have made so many things possible that if I get rich they get rich.

Toy Styles: Thanks for the information on Triple Crown.

There are many others who I'd love to mention and many I would fail to mention by mistake. "Why didn't you put my name in the book," is the question I'm always asked. This is my way of being fair. If we have love for each other we don't need it in writing.

Get at me at facebook/mrdarrelldebrew
or: facebook.com/authordarrelldebrew
or: facebookcom/darrelldebrewfanpage

Dedications

For all my beautiful black sisters who do all they do for their loved ones and our race this book and all my other books are dedicated to you all.

"I Thank God For My Sisters" – Darrell Debrew

going to let you kill her in my city." His eyes slanted distrustfully at Clyde.

"Sounds good to me." Clyde ignored the last comment.

Meanwhile, Tina was hiding in the ceiling on the fifth floor over the offices. She could hear what all of them said when they walked in the offices. If they gave up, she could hold out for a day – then leave the next day. It was the only chance she had.

It was eight-fifteen when Clyde and his bounty hunters entered the building, fully equipped. They all had on goggles that detected body heat but the sergeant wouldn't let them carry in their M-16's. His officers would make the arrest, that was the deal.

Methodically, they covered every part of the first floor and then went on to the second floor. Then the third and fourth floors. .

"Okay fellas. She has got to be on this floor. Let's get her." Clyde had dismissed the possibility that Tina had somehow slipped by him. "Tina, you might as well come out. We are going to find you."

Tina prayed the silence meant the police had given up on her. It had been at least thirty minutes since she had heard a voice. Her nerves were making her want to urinate. Clyde was the first one to get a reading. He pointed up at the ceiling to let the officer that was with him know that she was up there. They walked back out of the office and radioed that she had been found. The media celebrated on the outside and the reporter called in a newsflash. "We have been notified that the cop killer hiding in Alexander's has been found." Being on the FBI's Most Wanted list was the only thing that could make Tina look any more infamous.

Clyde was the man in charge on the inside. "I got a simple plan that'll make her come out of there." His bounty hunters were listening. Bounty hunters are similar to mercenaries. If the money is right, they will try to pull off a justifiable homicide. If only the New York police officers weren't around.

Clyde would not give up. It didn't matter that his father was a bad cop. He still wanted justice for his father and his mind had been made up a long time ago. It was time to get Tina out of the ceiling.

"What's the plan?" an officer asked. One of the bounty hunters replied, "We can make her come out of there with mustard gas. Do you have any suggestions?"

After arguing for about ten minutes, it was decided to use the gas.

Tina heard them arguing, but couldn't make out what was said. Their close proximity had her feeling uneasy. If the son was anything like the father, there was no telling what Clyde was capable of. No matter how hard she tried, she couldn't get her heart to stop beating fast and fear was causing her to sweat profusely. *How did he find me? How did I slip up?* She was terrified. Too terrified to do anything. Having to piss wasn't helping either; she prayed that her silence would save her.

Clyde was still watching her with his thermal imaging goggles. He was so glad that he had come fully prepared. It was time to gas the place up. "Whump, whump," the cans sounded as they were hitting the floor and exploding, filling the office up with tear gas. The New York cops had to retreat for lacking gas masks.

Tina heard the cans as soon as they landed. She closed her eyes and shook her head. The "shoooo" sound told her that they might be trying to gas her out but she prayed that maybe it was a bluff.

Clyde figured the tear gas would flush her out in a matter of minutes, like three to five and he was counting.

After a minute, the tear gas had the room almost consumed and Tina started feeling the affects. She covered her eyes with her t-shirt and refused to move. She planned to hold out as long as she could. She kept telling herself that she had to make it for Tyrone.

Two minutes passed and Clyde was surprised that she hadn't moved from the spot. Now it was time for the mustard gas. "Go to Plan 'B' boys."

"Whomp, whomp," the cans sounded as they hit the floor. Yellow smoke began to quickly fill up the room.

Clyde looked at his watch as he backed away from the room. Mustard gas was known to get past a gas mask.

Tina had used up all of her strength handling the tear gas. She didn't know if she could handle the new smell. Her insides started bubbling and she puked before she knew it. Now she had to get up. Luckily there was little food in her stomach so she only puked so much. It was the uncontrollable coughing and the feeling that she couldn't breathe that made her come out of the ceiling. She had to get away from the gas. All of her insides were about to come up out of her.

Clyde smiled. "She's coming out of the ceiling. Damn, she's tough." The object was to get her in the open to see if she had a weapon. There was only one way to find out.

They blinded her with flashlights and yelled, "Get on the ground!" Her coughing and gagging didn't mean a thing to them. It was her fault that they had been there this long.

Clyde was satisfied, but he could have been happier. He knew in the morning, his picture, along with Tina's, would be flashed across the world's media and publicity was the last thing he wanted. If she ended up dead while in his custody, he'd be the number one suspect.

Clyde was what people called a gangster-slash-cop – a cop that used his badge to act like a gangster. His father had taught him how to be this way. It was a power thing, especially over black people. His father had started teaching him how to deal with them since his adolescent years. The power and prestige that came with a badge was irresistible to Clyde. It was natural for him to join the Sheriff's Department after he served in the Marines. Being in law enforcement was never to him about serving the community and upholding the law. It was about making it look good and taking and stealing to live the best life possible. Just like with any other gang, there was a code of silence. As long as things didn't get out of hand, a cop could use his badge any way he liked. Clyde's father used his badge to get all the fringe benefits that he could. Poor blacks and poor minorities were his main targets and Clyde had been taught to do as he liked with them.

Clyde didn't care that his father was wrong with many of the things that he had done but he was still his father. Blood is thicker than right and wrong.

"Cuff that bitch," Clyde hollered to his men. The smell of mustard gas was still in the air and several of the New York cops had left the area.

Tina was desperately trying to get all the air that she could. Some relief came from the fresh air but she still could barely breathe. While Tina was coughing and gagging, they wrestled her to the ground and cuffed her.

"You are under arrest for the murder of DEA Agent Larry Atkins." Clyde announced, read her rights and took her outside.

******

By now, you know my name is Tina. Tina Thompson, that is; better known as Big Tee Tee. This clown of a cop just bagged me up for a murder.

I'm from the Westlake Projects in Youngstown, Ohio, and I ain't had nothing but one thing my whole life and that's my man. Although he's been in federal prison for five years, he's still my motherfuckin' man. I'll tell you some good shit about him later.

Let me tell you how I look so you can get a good visual. I'm that dark-skinned Amazon chick . For a big girl, I'm fine as a super-model. People be telling me all the time how they

Tina

love my pretty eyes. They also talk about the dimples in my cheeks and my high cheek bones. Most guys talk about my big ass and big titties. All my shit is big, but none of it is sloppy. I'm what they call a shapely big girl – like Jayne Kennedy. I don't talk about my weight and height because it scares men. Just use your imagination.

Really, many men around my way are scared of me because I've whipped a few of their asses right in the street. That's the good thing about being naturally strong and fast. My mother taught me not to take any shit from any man. We all know how some black men be trying to treat their woman or women. They be thinking they pimps and gangsters. Tina ain't with it. Fighting didn't make me the most chased-after girl. I just waited my time until Tyrone came along.

It was like Tyrone and I were meant to meet each other. We met at a shoe store in the mall while he was buying a pair of Nikes. He offered to buy me a pair. There was no way I was going to let a stranger buy me anything. We talked a little bit and exchanged numbers. He was acting like a true gentleman, though he was looking like a drug dealer.

Fo' real, he had a thing about him that just turned me on. That dark skin of his made me think about a Zulu warrior. When he smiled, I thought I could just melt and go to heaven. Him being tall, dark, and thick, with a set of big, broad shoulders made him just my type. My imagination stripped him naked before I even knew his name. To make the look totally on point, he had a low hair cut that looked like he just stepped out the barbershop. Oh yeah, I almost forgot those luscious lips. They looked like plums, ready to be plucked and sucked. He just needed to have something on his mind to have me wrapped up.

Judging from his jewelry and clothes, he had plenty money. My mother had taught me to look past these things, and all I really wanted was a man to be a man to me. "Just because a man has money doesn't mean he'll treat you right."

my mother would say this all the time. Let there be no confusion, my man has to be about getting and having something. When I say having something, I mean getting it the right way – the legal way, so they can't take it away.

When I met Tyrone, he was hustling. He wasn't what I call a baller. He was making enough money to take care of his son, Keith, and to stay looking fresh. He had quit school when he was fourteen to run the streets. I didn't try to get in his business until things started to get serious. He had me open like a 7/11 and was spoiling me like a baby. We went to shows, concerts, and events all over the country. One night, when we were in Alabama, I asked him about his plans for the future.

When he told me that he wanted to be legit so that we would never be separated, I knew then that I would do anything for him. It was like a ghetto love story. He had been saving his money so he could survive until he found a really good paying job and got a college degree. He had to get his G.E.D. first and then he started going to community college with me. My man and I were going to school together. God had blessed me. I had a man that was dedicated to our relationship, dedicated to me, dedicated to his son and mother, and dedicated to making it legitimately. We had the perfect relationship.

The sex was so good that it scared me. At times, I wanted to get mad at him for treating me so good. I was scared that it might end one day. At times, I did spaz off. Females do that at times. He would just listen to me until I finished. He knew that he hadn't done anything wrong. It felt so good to be listened to and to be understood. I can't think of a time that he wasn't there for me. He even let me tell him how to touch me, talk to me, fondle me, lick me, and stroke me.

I could hardly believe that although I have a ghetto attitude, a man was in love with me and loving me for me just being me. I had no choice but to totally give myself to him.

Tina

He made me feel safe and liberated. He made me understand the difference between having sex and making love. I'm talking about the kind of making love that makes a woman cry tears of joy. Every time I heard Erykah Badu's song, "You Better Call Tyrone," that's exactly what I did. When I called, he came. When he called, I went. I'll never stop loving my man.

It was all good until Tyrone and Atkins met. Atkins is what we called a crazy-ass-dirty cop. Atkins used to terrorize the Westlake Projects. He did things to people just because he knew that he could get away with it. Who do you get to press charges against a DEA agent? When I say he did like he wanted to, I mean it. He bought pussy, sold pussy, and even took pussy. Yes, he came to the projects and took pussy from several females. There was no one for them to run to. He even had cats in the projects selling drugs for him. Many people avoided him like the plague when he came around.

One night, while Tyrone and I were chillin' in his Impala, Atkins came up and knocked on the driver's window. It was three in the morning. I was in shock.

Tyrone gave him a look that could kill. Atkins started asking Tyrone a lot of questions that were pure harassment. My pleas for Atkins to stop went totally ignored. I could see that Atkins was getting to Tyrone, it was understandable. Atkins made a lot of racist comments and accused Tyrone of selling drugs in *his* projects. When Tyrone talked back , Atkins got mad and pulled him out of the vehicle with his gun placed to Tyrone's head.

My heart was beating so hard and fast, I thought I was going to have a heart attack. I couldn't believe it. Atkins didn't stop there. He made my man spread eagle on the ground and I kept begging Atkins to leave him alone. Meanwhile, Tyrone wasn't saying a thing. I knew he was mad and I was just as mad, if not madder.

Atkins promised Tyrone that he would go to jail before

11

the month was up. Somehow two kilos of crack were found in Tyrone's Impala and that called for a fourteen-year sentence in the feds. Atkins taunted Tyrone the whole time, trying to make him a rat.

A few years later, Atkins ended up getting murdered in the projects, right in the middle of the street. When they put out a warrant for my arrest, I had to get ghost. Now I have to deal with Atkins' son.

Chapter 2

Clyde was beside himself. In a few hours, he would have Tina in Youngstown's federal detention center. Because of the cameras, Clyde made sure Tina wasn't coughing and gagging when he took her outside. The only thing that he hadn't calculated on was all the press. If it weren't for them, he could have faked her escape or something. No matter, he had big plans for her.

Youngstown was a ten-hour drive. Clyde's adrenaline was flowing so hard, he could have driven to Texas, if necessary. Getting past all the media was the hard part. He was practically forced to grant an interview and most cops would have been begging for an interview, especially after conducting such an ingenious manhunt. Showing off just wasn't Clyde's style.

By his appearance, Clyde looked like the average, young white male, with boyish looks – blonde hair, blue eyes, and simple charms. He was expected to do well in the military and law enforcement. Deep inside, he was mad with the world because his mother died when he was ten. He hadn't taken it well nor had his father.

So they both ended up becoming renegades. Atkins had taught his son how to be negative in all ways possible. Whenever Clyde got out of line, Atkins would beat him with a stick. A *cop* committing child abuse! Atkins also taught his son how to drink and get high. Although the relationship looked rough on the outside, they were actually very close with each other. Other people couldn't stand to be around them for long periods of time.

All of their negativity and abusiveness isolated those two. They even worked alone at their jobs with no partners.

These things caused Clyde to be an underachiever in many respects. Because of his talents, he was chosen for many solo missions. This is where he was stuck at in his life. Without his father, he didn't have much of a life.

In less than forty-eight hours, after his father's death, he was accusing Tina of his murder. It took a few months for him to convince his superiors to press charges against her. He worked on the case as much as he could, both, when he was doing his job and when he wasn't doing his job.

Because of the father/son relationship, Clyde's superiors had tried to make him leave the case alone. However, they knew their words were being wasted from past experience. They were actually concerned that Clyde would kill Tina but it wasn't her that they cared about. They'd rather see Tina in jail than Clyde.

Clyde pressed the situation as much as ppossible. A week didn't go by that Clyde wasn't harassing Tina. Tina had to leave town to get away from him. Somehow Clyde got an indictment with a minimal amount of evidence.

"Wake the fuck up," Clyde hollered at Tina as he poked her in the arm. They had just crossed the Pennsylvania state line.

Even though Tina had tried her best to stay awake, the gases had taken too much out of her. Since talking with him wasn't on her wish list, she was hoping he would think that she was still asleep.

He poked her in the arm again. This time he used enough strength to make her hit the passenger door. "I know you ain't sleep. I'll punch you in the jaw next time."

Tina

"What's up with all the police harassment? You just tried to kill me with those cops back there." It didn't take Clyde long to find out that Tina spoke what was on her mind.

Clyde started laughing. "If you had died back there, it wouldn't have mattered. You are going to get the federal death penalty."

Tina fell quiet. Asking about what he had just said would open the door to a full blown conversation. He wasn't on her current favorite person list.

"You can be quiet if you like, but you might as well talk to me. After all, we go way back. If I weren't sure that I could get you the death penalty, I'd kill you myself and go on the run."

"So you really are crazy?" There was no faking in his voice or his past actions. "So why didn't you kill me while we were in Ohio?" She was talking to make sure he didn't change his mind about killing her now. After all, he *was* Atkins' son.

"Don't think that I didn't think about it. But I figured a witness would come forward sooner or later." Generally, when a murder occurs, the streets know who did it. It would be a matter of the police finding a witness to testify and it was all just a matter of pressure. *So,* Tina thought, *he lied about having a witness.*

"So you are going to convict an innocent female of your father's death? How can you have a witness for something that didn't happen?" The thought of him stopping and blowing her brains out was a real possibility; showing fear and antagonizing him weren't good options. She also wanted to know how good a case he had.

He looked over at her. "I know that you did it. I also know why you did it. I know you so well that I could prosecute this case myself. Believe me, I know." His confidence told her that questioning him further might start an argument.

"So how did you find me?"

Clyde smiled. "That was easy. I have copies of all the letters that you and Tyrone wrote to each other. I know the both of y'all very well."

Tina had an expression on her face that said he really *is* crazy and obsessed.

"When you sent him money, I kept track of where it was coming from. It didn't matter the name. Western Union is the easiest. I'd get a specific location, so when you changed cities I changed cities. I always knew that you had to be in the vicinity and with a little luck, I managed to find you."

During all that time, Tina had been thinking that she was playing the game perfectly. Now, she couldn't think of a thing to say. It seems she had been placed in a no-win situation. She had to write Tyrone and she had to send him money whenever she could. That's what lovers do for each other. She also had to get letters from him. Just accepting his phone calls on a burnout wasn't enough. She settled for the thought that she couldn't have done things in a different manner or in a different way. Not communicating with Tyrone would be like death itself.

Clyde had a grin on his face. Revenge couldn't have felt better and the look on his face told it all. "I took things to the point of tracking your mother's mail and I tapped her phones. That's how bad I want you to get the death penalty." Clyde wanted her to show signs of fear. From there, he could try for a confession but for now breaking her down a bit was the first step. Things seemed to be getting there.

Unfortunately, these were things that Tina hadn't thought about either. The taste of fear began to culminate in her mouth. Knowing that he was that serious put cold fear in her heart. She wanted to say something but no words would come to her. She wanted , no she *needed* to hear from Tyrone.

"If you make a confession, I'll be able to get you a life sentence. At least you and Tyrone will still be able to keep y'all's relationship going." He added a sarcastic laugh.

Tina

She lookined at him incredulously when he said life. She knew that life in the feds meant *life*. She also knew it would also be a federal case. Saying something – *anything* – was a must.

"So you are just as mean as Atkins was?" She was making an attempt to findi his soft spot.

"I would like to think that I'm the new and improved Atkins." His father's approval meant the world to him. Being mean was part of the package. They were doing seventy-five on a country road and Clyde tightened his grip on the steering wheel.

"So what makes you thing that I did it?" Tina's mother had taught her many things about handling men. Asking good questions was one of the basic lessons.

"When it happened, I knew that you had done it. Most of the people in the projects don't have the heart to kill a police officer. When you saw that you couldn't get your boyfriend out of jail, you killed my father." Before Atkins' death, he was being prosecuted for being a dirty cop, along with several other officers. Many defendants tried to overturn their convictions on the grounds of new evidence and failure to provide discovery. Clyde made sure he attended the hearings that were granted and Tyrone's case was connected to Tina's projects. Clyde went to the courthouse to read all the minutes. It was just a process of elimination.

Although Atkins had been convicted of being a dirty cop and terminated from his job, he still terrorized Tina's projects.

Tina was a little touched by what Clyde had just said. He said it as if all life had left him because of his father's death. Tina thought to herself that she would have felt the same way about Tyrone if he had been murdered.

He cut his eyes at her to see how she was feeling. She was looking out the window, but he could tell that he had touched her.

Darrell Debrew

"What if I told you that I didn't do it? What would you do?"

Clyde laughed. "You might as well had done it. I'm making sure that you wear it."

Tina asked him all the questions that she could think of to keep his mind occupied. He made all kinds of comments, threats, and promises. She wanted to keep him from stopping the car and killing her. She knew he wanted to scare her.

******

I just saw my girl, Tina, on CNN. It's about to be the fourth time that I've watched it.

When I went to sleep last night, I felt that something wasn't right. My bunky Steve told me that I was doing a lot of tossing and turning. This tells me how strong the feelings between Tina and I are.

Steve was the one that told me Tina was on CNN, after he got me out of the bed.

FCI Loretto has been my home for the past five years because of Atkins. That dirty cop straight set me up for practically no reason at all.

When I met Tina, I was doing the stolen car thing. Being that I had a few dollars, I didn't mind spending a few dollars on a female that I wanted. I knew that I wanted Tina the first time I set eyes on her, but she played hard to get. Well, she made me wait to get the pussy. I started to say the hell with her. I might have just left her alone if she hadn't kept calling me. We used to talk about all kinds of things. She was really interested in what I wanted for the future for me and my son, Keith.

Somehow we ended up going places and finally making love. A lot of cats said that after that she had me pussy-whipped. I was in love and I wasn't ashamed to admit it. For once in my life, I knew that I was on the right track. Life to her was about getting an education, getting a good job, and having a family. Without her, I wouldn't have given up the street life and illegal hustling. She

18

didn't set her standards by material things – cars, rims, clothes, and jewelry. She wanted a long-term relationship and I was feeling all of this.

Tina is a down chick that has a lot of slick things to say. She told me something that really impressed me. Once, It was like the fifth time that we had a phone conversation, she just bust out and said, "Vanity kills." She was straight up playing head games. Well, it worked because I had to ask her a thousand times about what it meant before I got an answer. She told me that my way of trying to be pretty all the time would come back to haunt me. I couldn't argue because what she was saying made a lot of sense. That statement and Tina changed my outlook on my life because I could see my behavior in the bigger realm of things, being counter-productive and self-destructive. She was the first female that I met that didn't mind struggling to make it for the long term.

I decided to give the legitimate life a try. We've been like soul mates ever since. I don't regret one thing.

When Atkins' murder went down, a lot of cats asked me if Tina did it. I knew these cats were looking for a way to get back into court. I just looked at them like they were crazy. His murder occurred two weeks after my Rule 33 hearing. I just knew that I was going home and so did Tina. At the time of my arrest and trial, Atkins was under investigation for Racketeering, Conspiracy to Commit Murder, Prostitution, and a bunch of other things. When I went to trial, under Rule 16 of the Federal Rules of Criminal Procedure and Brady v. Maryland, I was entitled to this information for my trial.

At the trial, it was my word against his that the drugs were in my car. I couldn't believe that a cop could set me up that easily and get away with it. I still can't believe that I'm doing a fourteen-year sentence for some drugs that were planted on me. It's even harder for me to believe that I didn't win my Rule 33 hearing. Evidence concerning his credibility meant everything in my trial. Now my girl is about to get tried for his murder in the same courthouse.

I'll be writing her and sending her cases the entire time. There's no way in the world I'm going to let a public defender sell my baby out.

While I'm at it, I might as well tell you how the entire thing got started. One Sunday night, about two a.m. in the morning, Tina and I were just kicking it in my pimped out Impala, when I heard two taps on my driver's window.

Atkins was using the barrel of his gun to get my attention. Naturally, I was smoking.

"That's a cop,, baby," Tina told me to warn me to keep my mouth shut.

I just looked at him with a look that said, "You got to be crazy." With his finger, he told me to put the window down. Need I tell you how mad I was?

On sight, Atkins looked like a beach bum that had been drinking all his life. He had this long hair that looked oily. It was a shade of gray that looked dingy. Acne covering his face made him look disgusting.

Before the window was even cracked, he was hollering, "Get the fuck out the car."

"Atkins, he ain't did shit to you. Why the fuck you bothering us?" I hate to admit that I was scared that this crazy cop was going to blow my brains out.

"Get the fuck out the car," he hollered in a gravelly old man's voice, sounding like he was about ninety years old. He even opened the door for me.

He had me standing up against the side of my Impala and that's when my fear had subsided and turned into anger. Then it started to rain. I knew I was in a nightmare when I heard the thunder and saw the lightning strike.

Atkins began looking me up and down. He was the first person I've ever seen who had black, beady eyes. With a black hat, a broom, and a black dress, he would have made a perfect witch.

"Are you trying to sell drugs in my projects, boy?" He kept waving the gun in my face.

Tina

"No, he isn't. He ain't from these projects." Tina was defending me from the other side of the car. It seemed that the rain kept coming down harder and harder.

"I keep seeing this car in my projects. Atkins!!! That's me. I run these projects. Don't a gram of anything go through these projects without me getting a cut. You ain't trying to deprive old Atkins of his cut?" This was like some shit out of a pirate movie. It halfway sounded like he was inviting me to sell drugs for him.

"You ain't goin' answer me boy?"

"He don't sell drugs Atkins." Tina was doing plenty of hollering. She was now on the same side of the car as he and I. Something was keeping me from opening my mouth. It could have been my anger or it could have been my pride. It could have been the embarrassment I was feeling because it was happening in front of my future wife. Then again, it could have been a combination of all three. I've never figured it out.

"Fuck that. Get the fuck on the ground, boy." He had the barrel of the gun right in my nose. I think I was sweating, but with all the rain that couldn't be a possibility. I know for sure that my temperature was up 'cause I felt surges of heat running through my body. At that moment, I could have murdered that cop.

"That isn't necessary, Atkins. He ain't a drug dealer."

"He had better say so. Say something, boy. I'll blow his brains out." The entire time I couldn't believe that this was really happening. This man was about to make me get on the ground because I wouldn't say anything. I had on a brand new suit at that.

He fired two shots at my feet. Tina screamed, "He ain't done nothing to you Atkins!" At night, shots tend to sound really loud. He almost shot me in the foot, so I was definitely scared. I still couldn't move and no words would come out of my mouth.

"Boy, you had better answer me," he hollered at me. I was looking at how close he had come to shooting me in the foot.

I ended up on the ground after he hit me in the back of my head with the butt of his gun. The last thing I heard was, "I'm going to get you, boy." That's when I blacked out. I could still hear the rain *and Tina hollering and the sight of the street lights down the streets in the projects. This event is a recurring nightmare for me.*

Although now he's dead and gone, I'm still suffering. I can't let my girl end up in prison. I'm going to make sure she beats this case, whether she did the crime or not. I can do the fourteen years.

After that night, I haven't been the same. I feel like part of my manhood was taken. What he did to me was uncalled for and extremely embarrassing. No matter what Tina did or said, there was no way for her to repair my ego. I tried to suck it up, but I just couldn't. The only thing to me that would have made his death satisfying is if I had pulled the trigger. How other way should I feel when I'm living proof there is no justice in this country, especially when it comes to a black man.

******

Several police cars met Clyde as he entered the outskirts of Youngstown, Ohio. The cop killer was being brought in and they wanted to make as big a deal about it as possible.

Youngstown was a town of about eight thousand with a high murder rate. A real high murder rate for a city that didn't have any apartment buildings that were over two stories. There was the North, South, West, and East sides. Getting caught in a part of town that you weren't from wasn't the wisest thing.

Clyde wasn't satisfied with just catching her like many of his fellow officers were. He was cynical because he had seen many criminals walk and get away with murder because of corruption. Although it was unlikely because Tina didn't have access to lots of cash, Clyde had intentions of keeping his eyes on the ball until it went through the hoop. It wasn't exactly an open and shut case.

Tina was shocked by all the attention that they were giving her. To give her any more attention, they would have to give her a parade. Three camera crews were there to film her being taken into the Youngstown County Jail.

Tina

The last twenty-four hours had seemed like the longest of Tina's life. She was most relieved to be out of the presence of Clyde and away from the eerie feeling that he gave her. Instinct told her that the cameras and publicity had saved her from him. She also knew he had to be as deadly as his father. They had the same facial features and wicked smile.

She had kept them from questioning and interrogating her by asserting her Fifth Amendment right. This was one of the things that Tyrone had talked about in his letters. She liked the idea that he stayed in the law library and was learning about the ways of the legal system. As a fugitive and a totally down chic, she sopped it up like it was an oasis and encouraged him to keep it up. She knew he was going to help her fight this case, just as if it was his life on the line.

Before getting arrested, she thought she had the game on lock. She figured that if she kept moving from place to place, there was no possible way for them to catch her. Having to be on the run hadn't mattered to her. When her man had been sent to prison, it was like they had taken her heart out of her chest. She still felt that way.

Facing the death penalty didn't matter to her that much, either. When they wouldn't let Tyrone out of prison, even after it had been proven that Atkins was a bad cop, she felt that her life had been taken away.

After the denial, she stayed in her room for two days without eating. *It just wasn't fair* was all that she could think. The entire community was shocked that Tyrone hadn't been set free. Tina understood enough about the law to know that the decision wasn't right. Since then, her entire being had been changed.

Tina had been placed in isolation with all the other murder defendants. A small section had been set aside for the females. Joann was the only other female that was there with her. She was a crack head from the South side and had been charged with killing her boyfriend. Their cells were directly across from each other.

"So if it isn't Tina, the cop killer. Girl, you the biggest thing in Ohio right now." Joann figured she had enough time to get settled. All Joann did was smoke cigarettes and watch television.

Tina was a little surprised to hear another voice. She had been thinking that she was in there alone, though she noticed there were four other cells, all with bars on the door. Showers had been installed specifically for the female prisoners.

"So who might you be?" Tina stepped to her cell door. It did feel good to be having a conversation with someone in a similar situation.

"My name is Joann. They say I killed my man." The sound of her voice told that she didn't care about much. She had been paid an ounce of crack to kill two people. One was a stick-up kid. The other was her boyfriend. The both of them had robbed the wrong set of drug dealers. They were taking care of her to make sure she kept her mouth shut. She also knew they would kill her mother and the rest of her family if she ratted.

Tina smiled. "They say I killed a cop for my man." Tina said, imitating Joann's tone. Though they had that in common, and had no choice but to socialize, something was telling Tina to not trust her.

Six months of incarceration had done Joann a lot of good. At one-hundred-and-ten pounds, she was weighing more than she had in years. The most that she had been able to get her hands on was some weed. Joann would do anything to get a hit. There wasn't much that she hadn't done to get high. She was known in the streets for how well she could give a blow-job. At the age of twenty-four, there wasn't a drug or a combination of drugs that she hadn't tried. If the right guard came along, she'd give him some pussy or a blow-job to get her a taste. The only thing that she wouldn't do was tell on the drug dealers that had paid her. It would be a few more months before she went to trial as it was a common practice to hold a murder defendant to make him or her break under pressure.

"I don't know if you like it or not, but you are famous." Joann took another drag off her cigarette.

"Yeah, they're treating Clyde like he's some kind of hero. He was talking about killing me and some more shit. What part of Youngstown are you from?" Tina's body began telling her to lay down and rest . She would in a few moments after she satisfied her need to talk to someone.

"I'm from the South side. I already know that you're from the North side. I've been watching you on the news all this morning. You can get somebody to send a television. It helps the time go by." Joann had no plans of telling Tina that she was a crack head on the street. She felt good that she finally had another female to talk to.

"Look here girl, I need to get some rest. It's been twenty-four hours that I've been up."

"Okay girl."

Joann was feeling Tina's style. She wanted to know if she had really killed that cop. Her experience in the street had taught her there are certain things that you just don't ask. This had been learned from the attitude of the mostly male gangsters she knew. In her heart, she knew Tina had done it. Her feelings didn't have anything to do with what the streets said. She wanted to know from the source and if she really did it because she loved her man that much.

It took about an hour for Tina to go to sleep. It was the first time she had ever been locked up. She started wondering if Tyrone was going to maintain his end of their relationship now that she was locked up and couldn't do things for him. Just letters from him would be enough to keep her going. She felt guilty about questioning him because he had never shown any sign that he was using her or done anything that called for him to be doubted. The death penalty wasn't a factor now. She couldn't help but to think that she might end up in the chair for him. Her love for him was that deep and she would never feel any regrets. Since the day that they had met, she hadn't felt alone. To her, the value in that was immense.

There was a certain relief in not having to run anymore. She didn't see there being any possible way for them to convict her. Beating the case would mean she could go back to living a normal life and waiting for her man to get out. She had to think that way, though she had no idea of how things would go. Tina was the kind to only feel scared when it came to a man hurting her feelings.

Exhaustion finally put her out for the count.

Chapter 3

Tyrone and Steven were the first ones in FCI Loretto's law library on Sunday morning.

Steve was doing a sixty-five-year sentence for robbing three banks. Fifty-seven of those years came from using a gun while committing the crimes. For the first bank, the gun got him seven years. For the second and third, he got twenty-five years apiece. All of his sentences had to be served back to back.

Steve was super-smart, super-lazy, and loved to get high. Being a wavy- haired, brown-skinned, pretty boy that had been spoiled by his mother and father and females, added to his demise. He was used to having his way and finding females to get him out of trouble, usually his mother. Nobody could help him when it came to the feds. He had no choice but to learn the law to try to get himself out of jail. He had filed every motion that he could think of, but to no avail. After ten years of fighting, the feds had sucked most of the life out of him. On a daily basis, he did whatever to pass the time and make it through the day. Seeing people going home and to halfway houses and to camps added to his depression. With the legislature steadily making it harder on gun crimes, he knew that he would be past the point of being a senior citizen by fifteen years. At that point in the game, he felt it would be best for him to stay in prison. On many days, he hoped that he would die in prison. He had the longest sentence of anyone there. Steve did just enough law work to keep his locker full and to keep a nice sweat suit and sneakers. Most of the time, he had to be begged to do a case. Tyrone kept Steve going by being his best friend. Plus, Steve had a thing about dirty cops. The small amount of weed that Tyrone provided him with didn't hurt the situation, especially in a jail that had so little drugs.

In a snitch camp, like FCI Loretto, the police know about things before they get started good. Knowing is so easy that even some police start to hate the snitches. Snitches will also tell on the police. Many snitches had reported that many cops didn't do enough shake downs of inmates' lockers. Snitches want to have the security that comes with manipulating the police. If the police aren't on their jobs, they don't feel protected. As crazy as it sounds, that's the way it is in many federal prisons.

"Okay Steve. Where do we start?" Tyrone's first goal had been completed. It was hard to get Steve in the law library.

"First of all, we have to think about the evidence and the elements of the offense." They were sitting across from each other by the window, enjoying the heat coming from the radiator. They were the only ones there besides the clerk.

The law library was a small room, about thirty feet by thirty feet. It looked even smaller with book cases on all the walls and another twelve in the room, with books on each side. The two tables in the middle and chairs on each side left little room. Of course there was a desk and a section for the law clerk to function from.

"Well, there is no evidence. Without any evidence, there can be no way to prove the elements." This is something he had heard Steve say before.

"Okay, if that's the case, we can push for a speedy trial and the discovery. We both know that they can make up a case." Steve wanted to ask him if Tina really did it and if he knew how much they probably knew. It's hard to litigate something that you know so little about. He would have asked if he felt that his man wouldn't trip.

"That sounds good to me. Let's do two motions for the both of them." Tyrone's thing was to do something, anything.

"Pass me the Federal Rules of Criminal Procedure. The Annotated version and the Sheppard's books. While I'm reading, you can write down the Sheppard's for the Sixth Circuit." This was how they operated. Tyrone would even be there when Steve worked on other people's cases. He had learned a lot. He just didn't know how to write a petition.

******

Tina had slept so hard that she missed her dinner and breakfast trays. If it wasn't for the visit, she would have slept past ten o'clock and maybe even past lunch. It was the first night that she had without having to think about getting caught. A year without peace of mind takes a toll on the soul, spirit, and body. The guard had to holler at her to get her to wake up.

An hour later she was taken to a small private room. Before she entered, she had gotten really excited about seeing her mother, whom she was expecting to see. She was surprised when she didn't see a glass petition or her mother for that matter.

The guard's body language indicated he was confused as if he didn't know whether to leave or stay. The surprised look on Tina's face caught his attention. It was his job to make sure Tina wanted to see her lawyer.

Shadika Jones interceded. "It's okay. I was retained by her family. Please have a seat, Tina. She was not expecting to see me.", she added to the guard.

Hesitation wasn't even an afterthought when the guard heard the authority in her voice. Besides, he also liked the face and figure. Her voice was just the style he had heard from so many confident lawyers, some of them cocky.

Shadika Jones was in her mid-forties and one of those older sisters that knew everything about the civil rights movement, mostly firsthand. She had participated in marches and demonstrations all across the country. She had personally shook hands with Malcolm X and Dr. Martin Luther King, Jr., and many more. She had started out practicing criminal law and felt like she could make a difference in the lives of many of her people. However, a lot of fighting in vain had taken a massive toll on her and she decided to practice civil law instead, as had happened to so many lawyers. She had to accept that there really wasn't 'justice for all'.

In California, she had prospered in an up-and-coming law firm, and even made partner. She could retire on a day's notice, which is exactly what she did. She had to have the privilege of coming home and fighting Tina's case.

"Listen Miss. I don't –"

"It's Shadika Jones." She extended her hands and offered Tina to take a seat. The guard had locked the door.

Tina shook hands with her as she began to sit down. "Shadika Jones. Ms. Shadika Jones, why are you interested in my case?" Tina took note that Shadika looked and sounded like a lawyer .

"I'm from the city. In fact, I'm from the same projects that you are from." She said this to make Tina feel like they had something in common, which made her more comfortable. "I don't feel like you killed that cop."

Tina started shaking her head from side to side.

"And if you did kill that dirty cop, he deserved it and you deserve to get away with it. They've gotten away with plenty." Her thoughts went to all the police brutality that she had seen.

A smile that Tina couldn't hold back suddenly came across her face.

Tina

"I'm pretty sure they'll convict you if you let them appoint you a lawyer. Clyde is going to push all the way."

"One thing though, Ms. Jones, how am I supposed to pay you?" A lawyer just popping out of nowhere to represent her just didn't seem right, especially an older one that looked rich.

"Listen young lady. Shadika Jones loves to fight the system. I'll be sending you a few dollars to make sure you keep your spirits up. Do we have a deal?" They shook hands.

"Okay lawyer lady, what is the first thing that you are going to do? My life is in your hands." What Tina saw in her eyes made her feel she was in the best hands possible.

"The first thing that has to be done is to find out what evidence they have. You didn't make a confession, did you?"

"I asserted my Fifth Amendment right. I just gave them enough information to book me. My boyfriend in prison taught me that." Her boyfriend teaching her about the law inclined her to believe Tina did it. He had done a good job. However, she only cared what the evidence showed.

"From what I've read in the papers and heard on the news, they have very little evidence."

"So that sounds like a really good sign." Tina had become a little excited.

"Yes it is, but Clyde may have a surprise." They talked only a little while longer so that Tina could also visit with her mother.

It felt good to Shadika to be back where she was from and raised. Since her college days, she had been back only three times. Twice when her mother and father had died and when she had graduated from law school. Shadika had dramatically changed during her college years. She learned a lot about her heritage and the struggle while she attended Howard University in DC. Her entire life had been changed after that. The struggle and the betterment of her people had become her main priority and driving force.

31

After she got her law degree, she headed back to Youngstown, Ohio, to make a difference. She had as much trouble fighting with her people as she did fighting the powers that be. Many of her people would call her a too-high-saddity, yellow bitch – on many occasions, to her face. When it came time to file a lawsuit or to fight a criminal case, she was the first one they called on. Also, they called her when there was something that they needed a demonstration held for. It was as if they hated her as much as they loved her. No matter how much she helped them and encouraged them to better the community, they still disregarded her like a doormat.

Because of her light complexion and long black, semi-curly hair, many mistook her for a white woman that loved to help blacks. Though she had won many small battles and a few people showed their gratitude, the one-woman crusade took a toll on her. Everybody wanted to benefit, but few wanted to do the work. One day, she felt like she had had enough and left to make a life for herself.

For years, a feeling in her gut kept nagging at her to go back. It wasn't guilt, for she had felt that she had done plenty and had helped many. She just wasn't satisfied. Beating Tina's case would make her feel complete. In a way, she felt like she had abandoned her people when she left.

******

"What happened baby? How did they catch you?" Sonia Thompson wasn't the kind of woman that cried easily but she couldn't help it when she saw her daughter.

Tina had tears in her eyes also. "I'm not sure what happened Mama, but I have some good news."

Sonia was seventeen when she had Tina. At the age of forty-three, standing next to her daughter, they looked like sisters. "Please tell me something good. These people are trying to hang you."

Tina

"A lawyer came to see me. She said that she's from around here and wants to fight my case. She just left." Tina wiped the tears from her eyes.

"What's her name and how much money does she want?" Sonia had plans to do all that she could to save her daughter's life.

"She doesn't want any money. She's paying me to take the case."

Sonia leaned back from the glass. "Are you sure about this? What's her name?"

"Her name is Shadika Jones. She says that she's black and from around here, but she kind of looks like a white lady."

"Are you sure that she said Shadika Jones? She's a living legend."

"She said that's what her name is. What did she do in the past? Tell me something."

The guard hollered that the visit was over. "I can only tell you that I heard a lot of good things about her. You may be in great hands."

"Okay. Bye Mama."

"Bye baby. Call me when you can."

******

Damn, I was a free female just forty-eight hours ago. This is the first time that I've ever been locked up. I don't feel too bad because this lawyer named Shadika Jones said that she feels that they don't have a case. Still, I have to wonder if it's going to be that easy. They're talking about putting a young, black sister to sleep forever. I'm talking about that lethal injection shit that happened to Timothy McVeigh.

From what my mother said, I may have one hell of a lawyer. My man had a hell of a lawyer and still ended up getting convicted and got fourteen years. I saw this first hand with my own eyes, on more than one occasion. When the case first popped off, Tyrone's lawyer tried to get the evidence thrown out of court. Atkins claimed that he had an anonymous tip from a reliable informant that drugs were in the car. That was supposed to have been the probable cause to get the search warrant. Just from listening to Atkins on the stand, it was obvious he was lying. The only person they could tell anyone anything about Tyrone was me. He would drive from Pittsburgh, Pennsylvania into Ohio, strictly to see me. Tyrone's lawyer said it was the worst decision that he had ever heard.

At the trial, the lawyer presented the defense that Atkins was out to get Tyrone. Tyrone and I both testified. Though the prosecution had worn us out on cross-examination, I thought we had the trial in the bag.

I really knew that Tyrone was going to win his Rule 33 hearing. Atkins himself was about to go to trial for everything under the sun. It was the biggest thing on the news in Ohio and Tyrone was right on top of it. His lawyer had a motion into the court before the clerk closed the office that day. I just knew my man was coming home. It was supposed to be a simple matter of arithmetic. If we had known that he was indicted, we would have presented this information to the jury and any credibility would have been crushed. The only thing that got crushed was my feelings.

About two weeks later, Atkins was found dead in a pool of blood. It happened on an off street in the projects. Clyde and the police hounded the projects. A few days later, Clyde stated that he was going to put the murder on me. Everybody, including my mother, told me to run. It seems that they were right. Three weeks after I left, a warrant for my arrest was put out. A rather close call.

If all of what I just told you isn't enough for anybody to be scared of getting the federal death penalty, I don't know what is. Clyde is trying to see me die if it's the last thing that he does. That blonde-headed, beady-eyed, white boy is dangerous. I mean dangerous.

Bad ass that I am, I don't mind admitting to you that I'm scared. These people that run these courts can be as dirty as can be. You also have to remember that I'm accused of being a cop killer. They just can't have folks going around thinking that they can kill

Tina

cops and get away with it. Part of my attitude is to keep it realer than real.

If I have to die because of my man, so be it. That's just how much love I have for him. I have no choice but to feel this way about Tyrone. He didn't use me, abuse me, pimp me, or try to beat on me. The true, unconditional love that I've experienced with this man is worth whatever price I have to pay.

All I ask of him from here on out, is that he stick with me and support me the way I did when he got locked up. It's been more than a year since I got a letter from him. I need to read how much he loves me and cares about me. With his letters, I'll be able to make it through this no matter what the results.

I guess for the next few months, this place is going to be my home. No getting my hair done, no shopping, no going to see my man, and definitely no getting my freak on. I guess that crack head across from me and I are going to get to know each other real well. She better not talk but so much.

I might as well get as comfortable as I can. It is about to be a fight to the death and I do mean to the death.

******

Shadika rode around Youngstown reminiscing. It had been twenty-five years since she had uprooted. When she saw the Elks Lodge, memories flooded her mind. She had done most of the talking for these meetings. She had no idea if meetings for everything were still being held at the Elks Lodge.

When she walked through the front door, she didn't see any familiar faces and didn't expect to. Even at the age of twenty-one, she was one of the youngest to attend the meetings. Now the place is totally different. It looked more like a bar than a community center. Nobody exactly paid her any attention. She doubted that any of them knew her because they were all in their thirties at best.

She went up to the bar to buy a beer. With all the televisions, she figured that it was a sports bar.

"Hello ma'am. May I help you?" The male bartender happened to be the owner. The Elks Lodge was Marcus Milton's pride and joy. Born and raised in Westlake Projects, he considered himself to be a community leader.

"Let me have a light beer and some kind of chicken wings." She reached for her wallet, which was inside of her large shoulder bag. "How much will that cost?."

"That isn't going to cost you a thing." Marcus had a big smile on his face and didn't care how silly it looked.

"Excuse me, sir." She looked at him wondering if he was playing a rather bad joke.

"I couldn't even think to charge you for a thing. All of your drinks and meals will be for free as long as you are here. I know who you are." He was loving the fact that he had her baffled.

"Young man, I'm sure you don't know me. I just came from California. What kind of game are you playing?"

"Turn around and look up."

She did so slowly, just to humor him. What she was looking at amazed her and almost took her breath away. It was a portrait of her in her younger days, when she first got her law degree. She didn't know what to say or do. She put her hands in front of her mouth. "Oh. I'm so flattered." For several seconds, she stared up at the portrait.

Many of the patrons had stopped what they were doing. They were looking at the portrait and looking at her. Soon, all eyes were on her and the painting.

When she got back to the bar, she took a sip of her beer. "Why is my picture up there?"

"You were the one that kept them from kicking so many people out of the projects and you made them bring the buildings up to code." He was speaking like it had all happened yesterday.

Tina

"How old were you back then?"

"I was seven years old then. My mother used to tell me stories about it all the time."

"What is your mother's name?" Shadika had filed a lawsuit against the owners of the projects. It was a time when many couldn't keep up their rent payments because of high unemployment. Many blacks were the last to be hired and the first to be fired. Shadika had filed the lawsuit to buy time.

"Her name was Mother Milton. She passed away about ten years ago. Where have you been all this time?" Many people had gathered around.

"I went out to California and couldn't make it back." She knew that the next question was going to be why she hadn't come back. "But I came back to defend Tina Thompson."

"I used to tell my mother that you'd come back if we really needed you. God works in mysterious ways."

It was just like Shadika Jones to come home. All those years she had felt so unappreciated and disrespected, not knowing that she was considered a hero. They started telling her about the bad things that Atkins had done to the people in the projects. It meant the world to them to find out that he had been murdered in the streets of the projects.

They also told Shadika how great Tina was. Shadika was glad to hear that Tina was great and loved by her community. That would make a big difference when it came time to go to trial. Maurice did most of the talking.

She resisted asking any questions. To them, Tina was a hero. She sensed it the way they talked about her. They wanted to see her beat the case as if they also were on trial. Interestingly, none of them gave any details to place her some place to give her an airtight alibi. Tina didn't do that either. To Shadika, this meant that if she did do it, there could be an eyewitness. As a lawyer, she always had to think with the end in mind. For now, she would just enjoy the fame that had been bestowed upon her.

******

"Damn girl, you had an extra long visit." Joann waited until they had both finished their dinners to start a conversation.

"The first visit was from a lawyer. I guess I got a little lucky."

"Girl, your people got money like that? That was quick. You just got arrested." Joann fired up a Newport.

"Nah, girl, I'm from the Westlake Projects. She's taking the case for free." Tina commented.

"Well, I can see that you are a celebrity around here. What is the lawyer's name?" She was smart enough to keep her jealousy in check.

"She said her name is Shadika Jones. She acts and talks black, but she looks like a white lady. She says she can beat the case." Tina was starting to get a little excited.

"My mother used to talk about Shadika Jones.", Joann interjected.

"Say what? Stop lying."

"Yes. Shadika used to fight for the people, no matter what the case. My mother says that she just got up and left one day." She took another drag on her Newport. She was also eyeing Tina suspiciously.

"Are you serious?"

"Yeah, my mother said that she only came back two times for her parents' funerals. There was a gas leak in their house." She was happy to be able to tell such a significant story to her.

"Why is she so famous if she abandoned the town?" She didn't know if she should be glad or sad.

"She used to fight for the people like Thurgood Marshall. They talked her into being a legend after she left. I guess they missed her. I know my mother talks real good about her." She lit up another Newport. She chain smoked to get a buzz.

Tina

"Well, she did act rather feisty. I don't want a public defender. They want to give me the death penalty."

"So Tina, tell me something."

"What's up?"

"Did you kill that cop like they said you did? Right in the back of the head with a .22?"

The look on Tina's face said *what the fuck?* Nothing in the world was going to make her say "yes." So she definitely had to say "no." Tina, also, didn't want to hurt her feelings since they had to be together. Her instincts said it was best to check her lightly.

"I think that you are playing me a bit too close. You must think we're really friends." .

Joann copped an attitude also. "Well sister, I'm woman enough to admit that I did it."

Tina just stepped from the door. She was reminded of all the snitches that Tyrone told her about in FCI Loretto. The game being played was easily recognized.

Chapter 4

Clyde had been celebrating all weekend. Now that he had made the arrest, it was time to make sure that she didn't get away. He wouldn't be satisfied until he saw her strapped to that gurney and pronounced dead. Before that happened, he had to make sure the trial went right.

"You didn't have to show up at my office to let me know that you were back in town." Allan Coppedge was the Assistant Prosecutor that handled murder cases in federal court. Bringing him to the feds from the state of Ohio, with fifteen years of experience with capital cases, was mandatory when he applied. So far, in his five years with the feds, he hadn't lost a case.

"Coppedge, you need to stop it. You are about to be a famous prosecutor." Clyde stood up to shake his hand. They shook hands then walked into Coppedge's office.

Coppedge had begun months ago to feel like Clyde's therapist. "I hope that you are about to tell me that you have a good witness or a weapon with some prints on it and ballistics." Coppedge sat behind his desk.

Clyde sat directly in front of him. "Listen, man, I understand your concerns. We have to work with what we have." They had been planning the prosecution a few weeks after Atkins had been murdered. Each one kept saying the same thing with the words changed up a little bit.

"What we have is a bunch of letters that aren't concrete evidence that she did it." He knew that he could try the case and possibly win it with circumstantial evidence if the defense attorney didn't defend with vigor.

"The whole town knows that she killed my father. What jury from these parts isn't going to want to convict her? All we have to do is take her to trial." As simple as he saw it was as simple as it could be. He was ready to gamble on it.

"I wish one of you cops would try a flimsy case in front of a jury just one time. We need a good eye witness. It happened in the middle of the projects. Somebody is always in the street in those projects." Calling him incompetent for not being able to find a witness was extremely tempting.

"A witness, a witness, a witness, is all that you keep talking about. We don't have time to find a witness. Let's get this thing on the road." Before he had gone on his one-man manhunt, he hadn't been able to find a witness. Nobody in Westlake would talk to him about the murders. It had been pretty much the same thing for the other officers.

Coppedge stood up. "Listen to me. If you want a conviction as bad as you act like you want one, you had better find a witness. You have plenty of time. It'll be at least six months before we go to trial."

"Six, damn that's a long time." He stood up also, but not in a manner to be disrespectful or challenging.

"You are not listening to me at all. She's already locked up. She isn't going anywhere. What the hell is the rush?" They had been speaking so much for the past two years that he was starting to feel like they were relatives. Clyde had called every week that he was chasing Tina.

"I don't care about her being locked up. I want her dead." Nobody would ever be able to make him see that his emotions were in the way.

"Another thing, don't let the press hear you say that. This is a cop killer case. They are going to be watching everybody's moves." He was glad that Clyde wouldn't be taking the stand. His neurotic, aggressive behavior could hurt the trial like his father almost had on several occasions.

Clyde knew there was no need to argue with Coppedge. Coppedge was dedicated to getting convictions. That's what mattered. "I'll have you a witness in a few weeks. I'll talk to you later." Clyde was about to do whatever he had to do to get a witness. He had made plans before he caught Tina.

Coppedge was one of those lawyers that couldn't excel at defending clients, though that's where the big money was. As a prosecutor, he could pick and choose the cases that he tried. He would work with the police until there was enough evidence to ensure a conviction. With murder cases, he would wait for years, if necessary, because there is no statute of limitations. If he had to be dirty, he didn't have a problem with doing that also. At times, he had gone out in the field himself to interview witnesses. He wasn't able to do that in the feds because of his heavy case load.

The case meant as much to Coppedge as it did to Clyde. A cop killer conviction would make him famous, especially if CNN covered the trial before the entire world. Losing this one was out of the question. No matter what he did, he had to make it look professional. He had no intentions of missing out on the benefits – talk shows, book deals, speeches, consulting, etc. – that would come his way for winning the trial.

At the age of forty-two, there weren't going to be a lot of other opportunities do to something big. He saw it as a now-or-never situation. Coppedge planned to handle the case in a manner that would keep all eyes on him. If Clyde didn't find a witness, he would. He had done it before, with very few people knowing about it. A little dirt doesn't hurt if no one knows.

******

When Tina woke up at ten-thirty, the reality of the

situation came at her from another angle. She had been scared out of her sleep by a nightmare. It was a vision of her hanging from a tree with a noose around her neck. She had just fallen through a hole in a platform. Clyde was standing above her with a cigar in his mouth and a great, big smile on his face.

Sweat was all over her. Fear had made her sit straight up. It didn't help that this was her first time being locked up. Reaching out to someone to get some comfort wasn't a possibility. She was experiencing a moment that makes it seem like the walls of the cell are getting smaller. She was in one of those cells that didn't have a window and was only big enough for her to walk twelve feet in one direction. A fourteen-by-ten is basically a big closet to most people.

The excitement of meeting Shadika Jones, talking to her mother, and hearing about Shadika's reputation weren't enough to help with the desperateness that she was feeling. Only hearing from Tyrone would make her feel like she could make it through this. She started to wonder if he had written. Did he have the address? She was pretty sure that he knew where she was because her mother said her arrest was on CNN. Did he still care about what happened to her? Was the love still there? She knew that part of what she was feeling was paranoia. Tough as she was, she still had feelings.

At two-thirty, that same feeling came back at her. It was her first appearance.

"How does the defendant plead?" Judge Alice Grumpfree asked. Judge Grumpfree had been on the bench for almost fifty years. At the age of eighty, she had no plans of retiring until she hit the grave. As a native of Youngstown, Ohio, she was familiar with all of the town's history. It surprised her to see Shadika Jones. Judge Grumpfree was one of those white people that supported the civil rights movement. But, she was still pro-government, unless it was a case of severe injustice.

"The defendant pleads 'not guilty' your Honor." Shadika was happy to see Judge Grumpfree. She knew that if she was caught at the right moment, that a fair decision would be rendered. At times, her decisions defied logic – then she would act arrogant.

"Your Honor, it just came to my attention that Ms. Shadika Jones may not be able to practice law in this district." Coppedge had his assistant searching to see if Shadika was a member of the bar in Ohio. Her name hadn't been found. Usually defendants didn't have an attorney show up at the preliminary hearing, unless they were wealthy. Coppedge wanted to see an attorney from the area to be the lead in the case so they could work something out.

"If I know Ms. Shadika Jones, like I know Ms. Shadika Jones, she can practice in this district." It excited Judge Grumpfree that she was about to see a good battle. She threw in the statement to let Coppedge know to stir up the pot.

"Your Honor, you are absolutely right." Tina started smiling. The sound of Shadika's voice and style made her feel good. "I put in the necessary paperwork this morning. As I'm a former attorney from this area and have practiced in this court – several times before your Honor – I think there isn't a problem. If Mr. Coppedge has his assistant check with the bar association in the morning, I'm sure my name will be there." She cut her eyes at him to see if he had something to say.

At the moment, Coppedge wasn't sure of what to say. "The government has nothing else to say." He would be checking the court records to see about Shadika Jones.

Judge Grumpfree leaned back on her chair and asked, "Are there any other motions that I need to hear at this time?" She leaned back in her chair expecting to hear the usual requests for bail and change of venue.

Out of respect, Shadika looked towards Coppedge to invite him to go first.

"The government has no further requests." He looked towards Shadika, making sure that his manners were as on point as hers.

Tina

Judge Grumpfree looked towards Shadika to put the mike back in her hands. She wondered to herself how bad they would be talking to each afterwards. From the look on Shadika's face, she knew that she had something on her mind.

"Your Honor, I have a very simple request, something that Coppedge will agree with. We would like a speedy trial." As expected, she hadn't asked for the usual. Shadika skipped the usual motions that she knew she'd get denied on. There wasn't going to be bail for a defendant that was on the run; and there wasn't enough evidence to get a change of venue.

All Coppedge could do was shake his head in acquiescence, though that was the last thing that he had wanted to hear.

"Let the record reflect that the defendant has asserted her right to a speedy trial." Only the most corrupt of judges would deny a defendant the right to a speedy trial. There's a big difference in making a request and asserting a right. Judge Grumpfree touched her glasses as her means of saying 'touché.'

Most defense attorneys don't – don't even think to – put the pressure on the government for a speedy trial. They just let it be, especially in the feds, which is natural because most cases are decided by guilty pleas. In fact, most defense attorneys don't understand the nuances that accompany speedy trial rights. Not Shadika Jones.

Shadika Jones was the kind of attorney that played aggressively when she saw a weakness in the opposing side's case. If she allowed them to, they would have the trial start a year later, with the hopes of breaking Tina down. She also knew from Clyde's testimony that they desperately needed witnesses to the crime. Allowing them time to find one would be the worst thing that she could do. The people at the Elks Club, who mostly lived in the projects, seemed to have a code of silence about the subject. Before someone changed their mind, she had to get an acquittal.

Filing for discovery is the only motion that she intended to file. Discovery motions don't stop the speedy trial clock because these motions don't have to be ruled on by the court. Nor does it require a hearing. Even if she hadn't elected to file for discovery, the government was required to provide it in full. Police reports and pictures were all that she expected to see. If there was more, she'd change her course of action.

Shadika had set the tone. The next case was called. Shadika told Tina that she'd be visiting her later.

"What is she trying to do? What is this speedy trial stuff? Why didn't you do something?" How Shadika was acting and handling herself had Clyde more worried than what she said.

Coppedge looked at his assistant and started heading for the side door. At the moment, he didn't feel like he could tolerate Clyde. Maybe Clyde would get the message if he kept walking, Coppedge hoped.

Clyde waited until they got in the back to continue. "You can't ignore me. I asked you a question."

Coppedge stopped and turned around. "Let me tell you what it means Mr. Atkins. It means that we have to go to trial in seventy days. In those seventy days, you had better find a witness or she's going to get acquitted. Do you understand that?" The way he said it made it sound like a death threat.

"You act like this is something that I caused to happen." He was reacting on instinct.

"It is your fault. If you hadn't pressed me to file for an indictment over a year ago, we'd have an extra thirty days to take this case to trial." He had stepped a little closer to Clyde. Weighing an extra fifty pounds and being two inches taller made Coppedge feel that he could intimidate Clyde. Clyde had talked him into filing for the indictment based on letters and telephone calls.

Tina

"I think you are scared of her. Is she a better lawyer than you?" Clyde wasn't the kind to take a lot of abuse. He couldn't comprehend what was happening.

"If I had my way, I wouldn't be prosecuting the case. I've been telling you for the longest time that there isn't enough evidence." Without something to show the state-of-mind of Tina, there was no way to prove premeditated murder. This was one of the elements of 18 U.S.C. 1114. "Letters and phone calls may not be enough to prove that without an eyewitness that she did it. This is because of the great police work that you've done."

"Okay. I'm going to get you a witness."

"Later." Coppedge turned and walked away. He knew that whatever witness that he came up with wouldn't be able to stand up under cross-examination. Though he didn't know much about Shadika Jones, he was sure she could put pressure on a witness.

Coppedge had seldom experienced defense attorneys that fought for their clients with a vengeance. Most of them tried to make a deal with him. Plus, there was also the threat that they would have to deal with him again. Most of the death penalty cases that he prosecuted were drug related and easy to prosecute because so many people were ready to testify. They were like guaranteed convictions and imminent death penalties afterwards. The federal Death Penalty Act was hard to get away from once the net was spread out. Putting drug dealers to death for murders made the district look like it was doing its job.

This cop killer case was the total opposite. Not a soul had stepped forward in a two-year period to give any information. There hadn't even been any crack callers trying to claim the reward for information. Coppedge didn't know what to think about the situation. He did know that his theory that Tina killed Atkins to avenge her boyfriend's prison sentence was a hard thing to prove with only letters and phone calls. Nothing that he had even came close to a confession. Losing his first televised trial was something his ego wasn't going to accept, especially to a female.

Tina

Chapter 5

Shadika had told the marshals that she needed to immediately see her client. Tina had been waiting for about fifteen minutes.

"What's up counselor? These people are trying to hang a sister, aren't they?" From the moment that she heard the judge say Federal Death Penalty, she had been feeling depressed.

Shadika smiled as she took a seat. "You are supposed to be scared, but we got to be tough. Believe me when I tell you, they don't have a case."

"They didn't have a case against Tyrone, but he got convicted in that same courtroom."

"He also lost his Rule 33 hearing in that courtroom." Shadika grabbed her hands. "He didn't have the most aggressive attorney that this court has ever seen. I got you sister."

"Everybody says that you are from around here." She pulled back and put her hands in front of her mouth. "You do know that your picture is hanging up in the Elk Lodge. Who are you?"

"I used to fight for the people whenever there was a problem. I'm from the civil rights era. Judge Grumpfree and I go way back." She leaned back in her chair.

"So why haven't I ever heard of you?" She had forgotten about asking her other questions.

"I left. And I'll tell you why. Black people have a tendency to be abusive towards each other. I got tired of being used and abused. It was hard enough fighting the system." A lot of memories came back to her. Her smile had dimmed a bit. "I left to make a life for myself."

"So why did you come back? You look like you are really doing well."

"I came back just to fight your case. Last Friday when I saw the news, I packed my bags and headed back. I retired just like that." As a civil attorney, Shadika was used to establishing a good rapport with her clients. To treat Tina any differently wasn't in her. Plus, she wanted Tina to have confidence in her abilities.

"I don't get it. You just saw my case on television and you decided to take it?" People in the 'hood didn't show another person love unless there was something in it. Shadika's act of kindness had Tina extremely curious. There had to be something in it for her.

"When I left, I left a lot of things just dangling. I've felt guilty about that for twenty years. When I heard about you being indicted as a cop killer, I saw a way to redeem myself. I had been thinking about it that long. I had investigated the case before you got arrested. I always knew that the case was weak."

"So that's why you pushed for a speedy trial?" A smile had come to Tina's face. It was her way of showing Shadika that she had accepted her.

"I like that in you. That is exactly correct. Usually the prosecution puts on the pressure. We are going to play this thing a little bit differently."

"Talk to me sister."

"You may not know this, but the community has a lot of love for you. I went to the Elk's the other night."

"Marcus used to tell us that you were an old friend of his. We figured you used to be his girlfriend from way back in the day."

"He's too young for me. I don't even remember that boy. What else did he tell y'all?" It was appealing to her to know that she was being honored and found attractive.

"He never said more than that."

"Let me tell you some really good news. It's going to be next to impossible for them to give you the death penalty." Shadika had taken the mental position that Tina had committed the crime and that the entire community knew it. No matter what happened, she knew none of them were going to tell. This meant that there wouldn't be a good witness. No witness meant no conviction.

"So you are trying to tell me that you got this." Tina wanted to look serious. Her enthusiasm wouldn't let her.

Shadika stood up on that. "I got that and I got you. You'll have a television by the end of the week. The money should be here tomorrow. Okay?" They hugged before she left.

Tina was thinking to herself that she had a lawyer from heaven. Her lunch tray was in her cell when she got back. The pizza wasn't that bad. When you are hungry, almost anything tastes good.

When she finished eating, she laid on her bunk and let her mind wander. She was feeling good about going to trial. There was no doubt in her mind that Shadika was going to beat the case. After that, she could go back to living a normal life. Most of all, she could visit her man. It had been over a year since she had touched him, caressed him, hugged him, and kissed him. Spending those few hours with him every month meant a lot, even though she couldn't have sex with him.

Before she knew it, she had dozed off to sleep. She was dreaming so hard that she didn't hear Joann calling her name. When Tina woke up, she had a cold dinner tray and a letter sitting on the bars.

"I was beginning to think that you had died over there. I hollered for about thirty minutes." She was smoking a Newport and popping bubble gum. The gum was part of her pay for giving blow-jobs to guards. Neither gum nor cigarettes were allowed in the jail.

"That court stuff knocked me out." It was a thick letter. She ripped it open as soon as she saw that it was from Tyrone.

"Your lawyer really did her thing. I told you that Shadika was a legend." Using the word jealous was a light way to put the way that she was feeling. She hadn't talked to her public defender in months.

"I can't talk right now. My man wrote me a letter. Later." She didn't even wait for a response. Disgust was written all over Joann's face.

Dear Wifey,

When I saw you getting arrested, I felt like I could have went through the television and strangled Clyde with my bare hands. He deserves to die just like his father did. I wish that I could make it happen.

Since the day that you told me "Vanity Kills," I've been in love with you. I feel that I'm such a lucky man to have met you and captured you. You made me see things about life that other females aren't even thinking about. From the ghetto you are, but your mind sees no limitations.

If I can't have you in my life, then I don't want to have any other female in my life. Half of the day I think about you. I'm thinking right now how good it would feel to have you sitting in my lap and making love. I can feel your vagina tightening around my tool. My dick gets hard every time I think about the incredible sex that we used to have. I don't know what you have in between your legs. All I can say is that it's the best pussy that I've ever had.

Tina

When we get up out of these situations, we are going to make love until we can't make love anymore. I'm talking about a honeymoon. Only a fool wouldn't marry you. I ain't no fool. Will you marry me?

Love,
Tyrone

P.S. Give this discovery motion and motion for a speedy trial to your lawyer.

******

Now he just made me feel like a natural woman. Pussy wet and all with that special feeling that makes me feel like I'm on top of the world.

Damn, I didn't know that one letter could have so much power. I never thought that two sheets of paper with handwriting could make me feel so good. And just think that I was already feeling good about how my lawyer was handling things. She has me feeling like I'm going to walk out of here in a few months. Clyde can kiss my you-know-what.

When I go to sleep at night, I'm thinking about Tyrone. When I wake up in the morning, I'm thinking about Tyrone. When I walk the streets, I'm thinking about Tyrone. When I eat my food, I'm thinking about Tyrone. When I play with my pussy, I'm definitely thinking about Tyrone. Ain't no other man getting up in this.

When Tyrone got locked up, he was scared that I was going to cut out on him and leave him hanging. He could have stopped coming to see me after Atkins harassed him. Thus, he wouldn't be in jail right now. So that means that my man ended up in jail because he refused to stop coming to see me. How much more love can a woman ask of a man. That took a lot of courage. What kind of woman would I be if I just left him? Plus, I love him more than I love myself. I know that sounds crazy, but that's the way I feel. I can testify that love is a drug. A good drug.

Tyrone has a dream of living our lives out together, no matter the circumstances. We had talked about getting married and me moving in with him. He said that he didn't want to make that move until he got some kind of really good job. I was looking for a good job also. We are still on our mission. So far, he hasn't done one thing to give me negative feelings about him. Even when he puts me in check, he does it in a gentlemanly manner. What can I say, I get mouthy at times. I guess it's because I was preparing myself for him to mess things up in some manner - like most black men do.

As soon as I put my hands on some paper and something to write with, I'll be writing him a long letter.

******

Shadika spent all of her time researching everything that would have any relevance in the case. She hadn't expected the cameras and the publicity for the case to be that large. It all seemed perfect for what she wanted to do. Her first move meant that she had drawn first blood. Still, she wasn't able to just sit back and relax and not be ready for Coppedge's and Clyde's next move. If they just turned over the discovery material without a hitch, she would be surprised. It was good to be home and to be putting in work.

When Shadika made it to the Elk's Lodge at five-thirty - fifteen minutes late - a table for two had been set for dinner. She expected as much.

Maurice made sure that everything was perfect for an African queen. For dinner, they had salmon dipped in hot butter and seasoned like a true Cajun would. There was macaroni and cheese with a touch of spinach on the side. The red wine and candle light made Shadika feel special.

"You've been my hero all my life, ever since I was ten years old." His mother had praised Shadika's name that much. Plus, he had always thought that she was the prettiest woman that he had ever seen. He still felt that way.

Tina

Only maturity had enabled her to keep a grip on the glass. She was just holding it to her mouth, letting things sink in. It was the most emphatic thing that she had ever heard.

"I don't think that I would have ever imagined that." She was almost flattered to the point of not knowing what to say. The statement also reminded her that he was almost eleven years younger than her.

"Just like a true heroine, you came back when we needed you the most. Thank you." Maurice had tried his best to be a hero to the community. Though he was lacking the skills to make things happen on a grand scale, he was considered a leader in the community. Many people looked to him for advice.

"You make it sound rather romantic." She meant what she said. To her, he was a gentleman with a hard edge. She took another sip of her wine.

"The look on Coppedge's face said he didn't like the move you put down. I don't think that they have a case."

A guy came up and whispered something in his ear.

Shadika used the moment as an opportunity to freshen up. Back in the day, men chased her because of her long black, wavy hair and fair complexion. Being desired as an older woman was a pleasurable thing.

When she got back to the table, she had a glowing smile on her face. "So where were we?" What a gentleman, she thought again.

"I was just told that they put out a $10,000 reward for any information about Atkins' murder. It's only on the street."

"Do you think that it could just be a rumor?" She suspected it wasn't. She still had to ask to make conversation and to see what he thought. It was his town more than hers.

"If I had to bet, I'd bet that it's for real. Clyde put out a reward before. He went around the projects with money in his hands." His tone hadn't changed.

This information meant a lot. Most of all, it meant that she had pushed the right button. "They have seventy days to find a witness and take it to trial." How she could groom him, she thought. A black male that knew how to act. Now he just has to be able to handle the business.

"It sounds like you really have this thing mapped out. I like that. I can promise that the streets aren't going to be talking. Atkins had no love in this part of town.", he assured her.

"It's a must that I always have a plan." She smiled at him seductively. She reached across the table and touched his hand. "I think that you and I make a great team."

Surprise almost caused him to go into a shell. He had never imagined her making a move on him or him making a move on her. "I think that we also make a great team. We can leave if you like." Acting any other way would have been uncivilized.

She handed him the keys to her Mercedes. "I like for my man to drive." In that simple sentence, a lot had been said. She wanted to make sure he got the message.

"That sounds good to me." She had relieved one of his pretensions. He saw her as an independent woman that may not have cared for a male leading her. "I'll take good care of you." He took her by the hand and headed for the door.

Many admired and commented on how great a couple they made as they exited the Elk's Lounge to the car.

He was surprised at the amount of energy that she exhibited. She was as ferocious in the bed as she was in the courtroom. The amount of confidence that he exhibited, surprised her. His was loving, caring, and attentive making her feel like she was living a romantic fantasy.

Chapter 6

Tyrone was on top of his business. He had been looking at everything that he could find that related to Tina's case. Some good people guided him to 18 U.S.C. 3591 (Sentences of Death) and 18 U.S.C. 1114 (Murder). He had just copied the statutes out of the Federal Criminal Code. Usually, he would have been with Steve. But Steve had been called to the Lieutenant's office. Tyrone was walking the yard and reading the statutes. Three quarters into his second lap, he noticed Steve waiting for him.

"Hey man. I thought they were going to lock you up. They made you miss chow and everything." It was now five-thirty and Steve had been in their office since two-thirty. Them keeping him past the four o'clock count was strange.

"They kept questioning me about some people that sent me some money. I had to talk my ass off to keep them from putting me in the hole or under investigation." Steve had just been approached by Clyde to testify against Tina. Steve was toying with the idea, though he acted like a tough guy when asked.

"Come on man. Let's walk." In prison, inmates did the walk and talk thing and the walk and think thing when something heavy was on their minds. At the moment, Tyrone needed to get some understanding. "I copied these statutes after dinner. Read them and tell me what you think." He handed the copies to Steve. They had walked about ten yards.

In Tyrone's short period of incarceration, he had seen many snitches tell on their so-called best friends. He was making sure that that didn't happen to him. Even if Steve could be trusted, he wasn't letting down his guards. That trip to the Lieutenant's office set off alarms.

What Steve said about the money had a slight hole in it. Steve didn't say from which inmate's family the money came from. Asking questions would only make Steve feel insulted. Tyrone felt that by being quiet, he had the upper hand and he would still be able to get good legal advice.

They had almost walked a lap when Steve finished reading what was relevant. "So what's your opinion and what's your interpretation of this?"

"I was wondering if the feds had jurisdiction of the case." When Tyrone talked, he made a lot of gestures with his hands.

"Well, it depends on where the murder took place and if he was on duty that day."

"I don't think that the projects are under their jurisdiction. It says ..." He motioned for Steve to give him back the papers. "It has to happen within the maritime or territorial jurisdiction. The projects aren't a reservation." Tyrone was always learning bits and pieces about the law. Instead of just going on his own interpretation, he would ask questions.

"That's smart of you to look at whether the feds have jurisdiction. You also have to keep in mind that Atkins could have been on duty at the time of the murder."

Tyrone was quiet for about fifty yards. "So that'll be 18 U.S.C. 1114. Protection of officers. So that means that if he wasn't on duty then the state is the one with jurisdiction."

"That's what it sounds like. I need to know something Tyrone. I'm beginning to think that you don't trust me."

Tina

"What the hell are you talking about and what does that have to do with this conversation?"

He stopped to face Tyrone. "They were halfway to the end of the yard, walking counter-clockwise. One would think that prisoners would walk in the other direction. "It has a lot to do with you asking me questions."

"What do you mean?" Tyrone looked to his left at the other inmates that were passing by.

"How do you expect me to give you the best of advice if I don't know the facts? Don't you think that you should tell me what happened?" Until that moment, Steve had only been hunting around. No advisor can give advice without knowing the facts.

From then on, Tyrone knew that he could no longer trust Steve, but he needed him. "I have no idea of what happened. What am I supposed to tell you?"

"I feel like you don't trust me. It shouldn't be that way." He started walking. His acting like his feelings were hurt wasn't an act. They had been doing time together for quite a while. There weren't many things that they hadn't talked about.

"Hey man. I'm sorry." He could tell that his man was for real about being hurt, but there was no way that he could tell what he didn't know. He had never asked Tina if she had done it, still. His gut always told him that she did it. "I don't know what happened."

"Check this out. We have to find out the facts. What do you think is the best way to find out?" He quickened his pace.

"Isn't the lawyer supposed to get that stuff?" He knew the answer to his question. It was his way of getting along with people and getting information. He had to walk faster than he wanted to also.

"You know this. Just get the discovery." They just walked without conversation.

Darrell Debrew

******

Tina had been stressing for two days. On Tuesday, she had received a letter that a $50,000 reward had been put up by Clyde for information about the murder. She wasn't worried about somebody saying that they saw her do it. She was worried that somebody would lie on her.

"Ms. Thompson, the last time we met, you didn't have that sad look on your face." Shadika had arrived at the jail a little after five o'clock.

Tina sat down and maintained her calm expression. "Haven't you heard that Clyde put out a reward for a witness?" Tina could tell that there was something different about Shadika.

"Stop stressing. We have things under control. We know exactly what Clyde is doing and we have our eyes open." Shadika felt that Tina must have some serious ties in the community to get information that fast. This made Shadika feel better about the situation.

"Since I'm not out there with you, who is this you keep talking about?"

"Just understand that there are a lot of people out there that care about you and the situation."

"So what's up with all the smiling and what-not?" Tina's mood had lightened up a little bit.

"Let's take care of business first then I'll tell you. Did you get your money and the television?"

"Yes, I got the money. The television didn't come yet. I forget my manners." She had been that preoccupied. It would happen to anyone that's facing the death penalty.

"Like I told you from the start, this is a weak case. That reward let's me know just how weak the case is."

"Are you trying to tell me not to worry about them finding a witness? At least tell me what to think." A definite answer is what a defendant usually wants. Being in suspense about getting the death penalty can be one hell of a thing.

"I can't tell you not to worry and what not to think." She wished that she could sincerely tell her that she'd be a free woman in a matter of months. "I can tell you that things look good for us because we have them on the run."

This wasn't what Tina wanted to hear. Many defendants get mad with their attorneys when they don't sound like they want. Tina had faith in Shadika and respected that she was keeping it real.

"Let's just say that they find a witness that's willing to come to court and say whatever, how are you planning on handling it?" This was the most logical thing that she could ask.

"That's a good question. Unless I'm not able, I'll know everything about the witness. That's how we do things in civil law."

"So we are going to know who the witness is beforehand?" Tina was asking the right questions.

"You have to think about how the prosecutor would think about the case if the murder happened in the projects." They both knew that the murder happened in the projects. It was just a figure of speech. "The witness would have to come from the projects and you would have to know him or her. That means that we'll be able to investigate this person." Shadika wasn't for sure what discovery was allowed under the Federal Death Penalty Act.

Tina hummed to herself. "I don't get it." She was thinking about how easy it was for Atkins to get away with lying on Tyrone.

"I know exactly what you are thinking. With an attorney like me, the witness's testimony had better be airtight. The witness's history had also better be airtight. So just relax and see what happens first. I need you to look confident in front of the jury."

"Are we going to know who the witness is before the trial? And will we be able to see their statements?" Tina planned to make this her last question.

"No, we won't exactly know. Nor will we see the statements until the direct testimony is over with." A witness list could have so many names that it wouldn't have any relevant information. It could also have names missing. Under the Jenks Act (18 U.S.C. 3500), statements were made available to the defense just before cross-examination.

"That doesn't sound that good."

"The moment the witness takes the stand, we'll start conducting an investigation on the computer to determine what is up with whomever. I have investigators that can find out many things in a matter of hours. If necessary, I'll push for a recess." In the civil arena, an attorney could take depositions – interviews – of all witnesses to determine the strength of the case. It would seem only fair that this apply in criminal cases.

"Shadika," Tina said as calm as she could. "I have to have faith in you. So tell me about this dude." It was Shadika's demeanor that let Tina trust her.

"Girl, I had such a good time last night. It's this young guy named Maurice. He runs the Elk's Lodge." What her voice didn't say, her face did.

"He must have done something really special to you. I think you turned another shade of yellow or red." Tina hadn't been prepared to be this cool with her attorney. "I know Maurice." She almost said that he ain't that young.

"Let me tell you, there ain't nothing like some good sex with an experienced man when you just get in town." She had plans on seeing him every night until she left town. Two to three months of good loving and romance would be enough to hold her for a while. At her age, she was into quality loving, something rare.

"Does he know anything about foreplay? That's

mandatory girl. I had to teach Tyrone." She enjoyed teaching him because he didn't let his pride get in the way.

"It was like he was reading my mind. What I loved the most is that he took his time and made sure that I was comfortable the entire time." She was ready to run up out of there and go find him.

"I know he held you after y'all finished making love." This was one of the things that she taught Tyrone. To Tina, there was nothing worse than a man that just fell asleep afterwards, acting like there was no value to a female other than a dumping spot.

"Yes, he did girl. Then he told me some sweet things in my ears, just like he was doing while we were making love." Shadika stood up like a fire alarm had went off. Hers had. They high-fived each other. "Bye Tina."

Tina's mind went to Tyrone. She wondered what he could be doing at the moment. Many had asked her in the past what it was that she saw in him and what made her love him so much. She just smiled. At times, she would tell people that there wasn't much more that she could ask of a man. Most didn't understand.

The ones that understood what it was like to find and have true love, congratulated her. Tina was too young to understand what it was that she was experiencing. All she knew was that any part of him made her feel good and when she didn't have any of him, she felt bad. All that mattered to her was him. To her, he was life itself.

At no time had she wanted to change that.

Chapter 7

It had taken Clyde four days to find a new face in Westlake Projects. This was also the first day that he decided to drive around the projects in an unmarked car that had tinted windows. When people saw the sheriff car, they went in the other direction. When they found out that it was him, people started heading indoors – all over the projects – when he came through the entrance. All knew what he wanted.

"Excuse me Miss," he stated with authority as he drove at her walking pace.

She didn't turn to pay attention because she didn't recognize the car. Diana just wanted to get home with her five-year-old son.

Clyde tried a few more times to get her attention before he jumped out of the car. They had just passed the spot where his father had been murdered.

She was heading into the apartment building that was two buildings over from where the murder occurred. He got out of the car and caught up with her.

"I can have you kicked out of the projects with just a few phone calls." He had almost caught up with her. He was glad that it was almost dark.

"And just how the hell are you going to do that? You don't even know my name." Diana had to say something as she turned around to face him.

Tina

Diana had lived with her mother most of her life. When it finally came time for her to move into a subsidized housing project, she was more than glad to leave. She was one of those fly red bones that loved to party and hated to work. Her beautiful figure attracted enough attention for her to be able to keep the latest fashions in her closet. She didn't feel like being tied down. Diana didn't like the drama that most females went through with most men that spent money on them. Having a boyfriend that got her pregnant and left taught her a lesson that made her protect herself.

"I'm sorry. I just needed to get your attention. I'm a police officer and I like keeping up with all the people that live around here." He showed her his badge, something police love to do.

"Would you mind if I get my son in the house before crazy things out here start to happen?" She was ready to get rid of him and get ready for the weekend.

Clyde liked her response. She didn't know him. "I know that you like money and I need some information. Just a little bit of information." She lived in the vicinity, which was perfect.

"I'm not a prostitute Mista, and you have a nice evening." She started walking into the building.

Clyde let go of his desire to run after her and bombard her with questions. At any second, somebody that knew him would see him. He'd just wait to see her another day. Since she lived in the projects, she had to have a need for money. He knew she wasn't keeping up her hair and nails with just a welfare check. He also had plenty of time.

******

"I just love the way that you take your time Maurice." They had been making love for about fifteen minutes.

65

"My hero deserves to be pleased." Marvin Gaye's "Sexual Healing" was playing in the background. They had spent every evening together since their first date.

"Oh yes, that's it. Just lean to the right and keep stroking slowly. Yes, yes, yes." She tightened her legs around his waist and dug her fingernails into his shoulder blades. "You are too good."

"I'll do anything to you that you want me to do." He kept nibbling on her ear and kissing her neck.

She closed her eyes. "That feels so good. I don't want to stop seeing you." It was the second orgasm. He managed to get her there each and every time they were together. "All my Life" by K.C. and JoJo came on.

They climaxed together. As an independent woman, she didn't have any interest in a long-term relationship with a man. Most of the men she met didn't like the idea that she had plenty of her own money. A man acting insecure turned her off quickly. She had learned to enjoy what she could out of a relationship, even if it was great sex for a few weeks. She had learned the hard way that trying to make a man be what she wanted him to be didn't work well.

Maurice was totally different. All he wanted to do – it seemed – was be with her and please her. He was just straight-up cool to be with and be around. She found herself thinking about him all day when they weren't together. She hadn't had thoughts like that about a man since she was about twenty-three. One day, she just thought as hard as she could to find something that she didn't like about Maurice.

She would have preferred for him to have a college education. She couldn't hold that against him because he was taking correspondence courses on the low. She thought to herself that he might be sensitive to a woman's needs because he was gay on the down low. She discounted that because of how the men around him respected him and listened to him.

Tina

"Maurice, I need you to tell me something." Maurice had just come back in the bedroom with a light breakfast of fruit and oatmeal. There was also a small vase with a red rose in it.

"You need to sit up first so that we can eat breakfast. You tried to kill me last night." He wanted for her to get in position before he put the tray over her legs. "If this isn't enough, I can make you something else."

"I need to know why you are treating me so good.", Shadika whispered.

"Did I do something wrong?" Maurice climbed back in the bed.

"No, that isn't it." It was one of those frustrated "no's."

"So do you want me to stop?" In a psychology book, he had learned to ask a variety of questions that he knew the answers to.

"No." If she had been thinking, she would have asked him why he asked.

"Now if I had asked a question like that, you'd think that I was slipping or tripping." He put his right arm around her and started kissing her shoulder.

"I didn't ask you if you climaxed because I know that you did." She threw an intense look at him. "I need to know why you act so differently from other men. I know you have some women."

"What is with the edgy tone? I'm not a prosecutor." He gently bit the back of her shoulder.

"Stop." It felt just good enough for her juices to start running again. She pushed his forehead to make him stop. "I need to know what is up with your women."

"That isn't something that you have to worry about. Plus, you don't live around here." In his younger days, he would have admitted that he had other females. There was no need to say something that might be taken as a negative deposit.

"Maurice, you think that you got game. What are you going to do if I decide to come back to Youngstown? What are you going to do?" Just like a lawyer, she decided to try another angle.

"Look at me." She didn't turn her head. He put his finger under her chin. "Look at me." He waited to make eye contact. "Why are you getting so serious all of a sudden? If you have something to say, say it. It's better than having an argument."

This wasn't something she was used to. Most of the time, she was in charge of a relationship, though most of them were short. Here she was with a man that seemed to know the rules by heart. She had become confused and wrapped up in her emotions.

"I don't want an argument. I would like an answer to my first question. Why are you acting ... good?" She almost used the term perfect. Maybe later she would admit that she didn't want the relationship to end.

"I changed when I went to prison. I made a decision to better myself in any manner possible. I had to start treating women better. Since you are my hero, I had to go all out for you." An older cat told him that the best way to learn about what women like is to read women's magazines and the books they write. He did that to the ultimate.

"So why do all of these people have so much respect for you?" She knew that he had to be more than the manager of the Elk's Lodge.

"Before I went to prison, I was the head gangster in charge of all of North Youngstown. If it was a crime, I did it or took part in it." He wanted to prepare her for the worst in case she searched the public records.

With her left hand, she turned the tray over and let it hit the floor. The sheets dropped from over her breast. Before he could move, she had her lips pressed up against his. She pushed him down in the pillow.

"Just relax Maurice and let me please you." With her right hand, she started caressing his tool. She quickly unwrapped the towel that he had around his waist. "I need to have you all to myself for a very long time." She was stepping up her ambitiousness. She grabbed his tool again.

"I don't have a problem with that."

"Don't say a thing." She didn't want him to make up his mind at the moment. "Just let me do you."

She started kissing him in the ear while gently scratching his balls with her fingernails. "I'm going to treat you as good as you are treating me," she whispered in his ear.

He let out a small groan. Her touch was making him relax.

As she kissed her way to his right nipple, she worked her hand up to the head of his tool. She sucked on his nipple just the way she likes hers to be done – a slight bite with long slow licks. Gently, up and down his shaft, she was still caressing. With deftness, she treated his left nipple to the same treatment.

When she was finished licking his nipples, she straddled him.

Their eyes were locked. "Maurice, I want you to know that you mean a lot to me. I mean that." It had been years since she had opened her heart to a man.

It was one of those moments that the intensity of it made words unnecessary.

Without breaking eye contact, she placed his tool inside of her. She arched her back and looked up at the ceiling. "Every time that you enter me, it feels better and better." She slid up and down a few times, just enough to stimulate him and herself. He stayed still just like she wanted him to.

She stopped to look at him. His tool was about halfway in her, which was just under half his length. "Don't move Maurice." She squeezed her vaginal muscles with all her strength. His moaning let her know that it was time to go into overdrive. "I'm going to make you a happy man." She was moving up and down just a little to keep him stimulated.

"That sounds good to me."

A devious grin came across her face. She took all of him without letting any pressure off. To get at the right angle, she leaned at him and came forward. Her position was perfect. She squeezed harder and pressed her body up against his. She started nudging back and forth.

"Oh. What are you doing Shadika? That feels so good." He threw his arms out to the side.

"I told you." She started nudging harder. She was enjoying the results from her work. "Maurice, this is how it's going to be as long as you want it to be."

"Damn Shadika. This is the best pussy I've ever had." His eyes rolled to the back of his head. Shadika kept grinding and squeezing. "Oh that feels so good." A deep tingling sensation went through his body. The intensity of his ejaculation caused him to arch his back, though he was supporting his and her weight. "Ahhh. Oooohhh."

She smiled from the extra warm feeling that she felt. She kept squeezing and grinding until he went limp. With him out for the count, she just laid on top of him and caressed his chest. It was like a moment of victory.

At her age, it wasn't going to be that often that she attracted a man like him. All the working out, eating right, and staying in shape all seemed to be worth it. To psyche herself up, she'd tell herself that she was working hard because she loved herself. In the back of her mind – just like other females – she had hopes of attracting Mr. Right.

It didn't matter that he was fifteen years younger than her. How he acted and handled himself is what mattered. Tina was first priority. He was second.

******

"Mr. Clyde Atkins, you had better have some extremely good news. We have exactly sixty days before we have to go to trial." Coppedge didn't want to have this meeting. He had come so far with the case that there was no turning back. This was the only case that he had that he dreaded dealing with.

"I came to tell you some really good news. We'll have a great witness before then." Clyde had put together a plan to make it all happen.

"Would you mind telling me who this witness is?" Coppedge sat down in his office chair.

Clyde sat by the window to watch the traffic. "I want to make sure that things are extremely tight before I bring her to you." He figured it shouldn't take more than thirty days to convince Diana and Steve.

"You may not understand what Shadika Jones is about."

Clyde turned to look at him. "She's just an experienced civil lawyer that came back to town. So what!" He was tired of hearing her name.

Coppedge smiled and let out a heavy breath through his nose. "Female lawyers like her are too vicious. She acts like she has something to prove. That means she's going to eat your witness alive."

Clyde hated it when somebody talked at him. Shaking his legs was the most that he'd do to express that. "At times I have to wonder if you're on this side or that side."

"Keep in mind who you are talking to." Coppedge stood up.

"That bitch killed my father. Can't you understand that?" He was the only one that didn't realize how obsessed he was. So far he hadn't slipped or done anything that he'd regret. He walked towards Coppedge's desk.

"Watch your tone." There was silence for a few seconds. Clyde stopped short of the desk.

"Listen Coppedge, I'm just trying to do what it takes to get this conviction. I know that she killed my father. I'm just out to get her what she deserves, the death penalty." All day long, this is what he kept in his mind. He even talked to his father's pictures about it.

"You should have found a better way of picking her up. This case wouldn't have all of this publicity. It would be easier to make things happen." He hated that everything was going to be scrutinized and there was nothing he could do about it.

"It's a cop killer case. What were you expecting?" He couldn't argue about the publicity. It had also stopped him from doing what he had planned. He had to agree with Coppedge – just to himself.

"You made it harder. We just can't break the rules like we want to. The playing field is even and we only have circumstantial evidence." He dreaded losing a case on CNN.

"I have faith in you Coppedge."

"I can't make gold from straw. A bad witness is the worst thing that we can have. We're better off not having a witness at all."

Clyde turned and walked back towards the window. "So if you feel this way, why have you been telling me to get a witness from the very beginning?"

Coppedge was at the point that he wanted to avoid Clyde and his snide remarks. "The defense received the discovery this morning. I imagine it is going to make them extremely confident. I can work a lot of theories with what we already have." As a professional, he knew that he had to keep moving forward.

"I can promise you that we are going to have two very good witnesses – maybe three." Nobody could say that he hadn't been on his job.

"These witnesses have to have their stories straight and be ready to maintain their composure on nationwide television. We'll need at least thirty days to prepare them."

"Okay. I have to make a trip to Pennsylvania."

Clyde cared for Coppedge just a little more than he cared about being in a rattlesnake pit. He knew that Coppedge felt the same way. Clyde and any other prosecutor wouldn't have

Tina

a great relationship unless Clyde was being told what he wanted to hear. Clyde and Coppedge had no choice but to deal with each other. Coppedge had been picked because he was the best and Clyde was being supported because his father was one of them. Most had given up on the case for good reason. For months, nobody could get any information out of the Westlake Projects – not even a rumor. Nobody would say a thing about the Atkins murder. That's the reason they gave up. There was also the factor that few cops liked Atkins or the way he did things. He didn't have a partner because officers hated to cover for him when complaints were filed against him.

Clyde felt like he had the situation under control. He was the one that gave Coppedge the theory for the case. He was the one that did all the traveling to collect the evidence. He was the one that stubbornly stayed on Tina's trail until he was able to run her out of town and indict her after she left. He was the only one that had enough love for Atkins to go this distance.

Chapter 8

Shadika made it to see Tina at about four o'clock. Just to be nice she brought her some pizza because Tina would miss her dinner. She hit the guard off with a few dollars.

"Rest yourself young lady. We have a few things to talk about." Shadika motioned for her to get a slice of pizza.

"So what is up with this visit? You seem to be your usual happy self." She sat and started eating. Just the smell of the pizza made her hungry.

"I got the discovery this morning. You and Tyrone have been having a hell of a romance." There was so much detail that she didn't need to ask any questions.

"You have me a little confused. What do Tyrone and I have to do with the discovery for this case?" She was thinking that Shadika was trying to tease her.

"It seems that Clyde made copies of all your letters." She pulled out a stack of papers about five inches thick. "He also has all the phone records for y'all's phone calls." She pulled another three-inch stack out of her briefcase.

"I shouldn't ask this dumb question." Shadika smiled as if she knew the question. "You read all of that stuff?" She thought about Clyde and the prosecutor and a few guards and what they would be saying.

"It's my job to read this stuff." Tina bit down on her lip at the thought of her business being out there like that. "There's a lot of privacy in the attorney-client privilege."

"Say what you have to say Shadika. That grin is a dam about to break." She started thinking that her business was about to be put out there for the entire world. She was thinking about the embarrassment.

"I just might let Maurice tie me up and do with me what he likes." Tina covered her face and shook her head. She had to laugh when Shadika started laughing.

"Tina, it's alright. You have nothing to be ashamed of. Many women would kill to have a relationship like you have. They aren't going to put out the kinky stuff in front of the jury."

Tina looked up. "Are you sure about that?" Tina was thinking that people would be talking about how far out she had gone for her man and would ridicule her.

"Relax. Let's eat some pizza." She picked up a slice and waited for her to follow. "That's it." They took a bit at the same time. "How is it?"

Tina smiled a bit. "I'm good. Thanks a lot. I also got my television. I feel bad that I can't pay you."

"Trust me, you have paid me with Maurice. He's so special to me. He hasn't shown me one sign of insecurity. I got to keep him." A strong, outspoken black female with her own money wasn't easily accepted by most black males without a few problems. Shadika had put her share of men in check. She preferred to be alone than disrespected.

"Is it that serious between the both of y'all? Ain't a female yet been able to hold him down." She was trying to tell her that Maurice had all kinds of females at him.

"I accept him as a worthy challenge. He hasn't lied to me. He hasn't tried to play me and he's in sync with me, move for move. He'd have to do a lot to turn me off." She had plans. Plans that called for something permanent. Her next move was to get in his head and know it as well as she had come to know his body.

"I see I'm not the only one that's in love. Atkins can't put him in jail." Her thoughts went to Tyrone. It was time to get a letter from him.

"Okay, let's get back to your case. He isn't as important as this case is to me." They made small talk until they finished eating. It took about three slices a piece for each of them to get full.

"So how long will it be before I'm able to get home?" She knew that there was nothing in her letters or conversations about committing a murder.

"I expect to beat this case, but we have to look at this thing in the most negative manner. We can't get caught slipping." This was her opening to say what she had to put on the table.

"How bad can it be? I'm ready to go to trial." She started sipping on her iced tea.

"You and Tyrone said and wrote some rather aggressive things that are sure to be used at the trial. Y'all openly wished him death and celebrated his death." It had been years that she had to put the naked truth to a criminal defendant. Civil clients didn't have to stress about losing their freedom or their lives – just a large amount of money or winning large amounts of money. Still, what had to be said, had to be said.

"I think it's understandable that we expressed our feelings the way that we did. Atkins is a villain." She hadn't thought about the intensity she had used in her letters.

"There is going to be a serious impression made when the jury hears some of the stuff and the theory that they have about you killing him." Shadika was thinking about how jurors that had love for the police would feel about their letters.

Tina put her tea on the table. "So all of a sudden, you think that they have a strong case?" This was the question that was meant to check enthusiasm.

"I feel that I can still beat the case because letters aren't enough to make you the one that pulled the trigger. But you don't know what else it is that they are going to do." Her biggest concern was them finding witnesses that would corroborate with the letters and calls.

"So what is there to stress about? I'm sure that you are going to be prepared for whatever they do, aren't you?" Tina like the idea of Shadika being overly cautious. She couldn't see them being able to convict her with the present evidence. She had no understanding about circumstantial evidence.

"I'm a few steps ahead of them as we speak. I have a good idea of how they may handle this. They are going to come up with some witnesses." Half the game is to be ahead of the game.

"Witnesses! If they had had witnesses, they would have arrested somebody a long time ago. Any witness that they get will be lying like we discussed the other day."

"That may happen and I plan to be prepared for that. That's what I need you to know." There was a balance for telling her client the truth and keeping her clients up. She felt that she had done well without letting Tina have false hopes.

Shadika didn't feel good about the letters and the tapes. The only thing worse that they could have done was to confess to the crime. If she were a prosecutor, she felt that she would have charged the both of them. She feared that this might happen. If there happened to be a witness, she felt that the situation would get worse.

******

Mail on a Friday for the incarcerated is the perfect way to start the weekend. Federal prisons don't pass out mail on Saturdays.

According to Tyrone's' calculations, he was supposed to have received a letter on Thursday from Tina.

It had been a long eight days for Tyrone. He hadn't gone to the weight room but once. Usually, he went at least every day – sometimes twice. On general principle, he was in the law library every time that it opened. He made it his business to know all there was to know about the Federal Death Penalty Act. He read the Federal Criminal Code. Naturally, he asked a lot of people questions about things that he couldn't fully comprehend. Most jailhouse lawyers don't mind helping others that do all that they can. They all knew that Tyrone was diligent and respectful. It was an honor to be able to advise a person fighting such a case. They were rooting for Tina and hoping that she got away with murder.

It was the first smile that Tyrone had sincerely expressed since her arrest. Seeing her handwriting on the envelope always gave him a good feeling.

I'm calling Tyrone,

Yesterday Tyrone made me feel as special as a female can feel. When I tell you that he made me feel good, I'm leaving a bit out because I don't want his head to blow out of proportion. Just joking baby. Know that Tyrone is all the man that I'll ever need. Another doesn't have a chance at taking his place. For him, I can live without sex.

Tyrone, you mean that much to me and I don't care if they give me the death penalty, just as long as you keep showing me your love until that day comes. I'm ashamed that I let myself doubt you. Our relationship has been perfect since the day you made a commitment to me. Can't nobody tell me anything wrong about you.

I have this great lawyer. Her name is Shadika Jones. I could tell when we went to court that they're scared of her. She pressed for the speedy trial before y'all sent your letters.

When she beats this case, the first thing that I'm going to do is come visit you. I can't wait to be able to put my lips on your lips, to touch my tongue with your tongue, to touch your face with my hands, to feel you hugging me and touching me.

Tina

It's time to go. Shadika is the best lawyer that I've ever met. I can tell that she wants to beat this case. Can't wait to see you.

Love,
Tina

Now, Tyrone had two good reasons to feel good: He had heard from his girl and it sounded like she was about to beat the case.

There was no doubt in his mind that he would hear from Tina. On no occasion, no matter the circumstances, she hadn't let him down, unless something happened that wasn't in her control. He didn't have a thing to complain about when it came to Tina. She was even still handling her business when she was on the run. He just laid back and enjoyed the moment.

******

I'd dare to argue that I have the best female in the world. If I could, I'd take the death penalty so that she could live. I'd be some low-level cut if I did not feel that way. There's no doubt in my mind that she'd do anything for me. I've tested her and it's a special thing.

When a man loves a woman, it's a serious thing. At times, I wonder if she put a root on me or something. Somehow, she has me hooked for life.

Now she seems to think that she is going to beat this case because she has an aggressive lawyer. I'm hoping this lawyer doesn't sell her out like so many other lawyers have done their clients. I'm talking about paying clients. I hate to doubt this Shadika Jones, but I have to until I know for sure she's sincere.

I'm going to have to find out how Shadika got on the case before the preliminary hearing. Everybody that I've talked to also thinks that she made a suspicious appearance. When I write Tina, I'll ask.

Let me tell you how I'm looking at this thing. The best thing that happened is the publicity. That makes it harder for the prosecutor to be dirty. That means a lot. I've been wracking my brain to come up with what Clyde and the prosecutor might do. As far as I can see, they don't have anymore evidence than they had when they were harassing Westlake Projects. I was scared as hell then.

It's my dealing with the federal court that makes me so cynical. You'd probably feel the same way if you have been convicted as an innocent man. Whether Tina did or didn't do the murder, I know there's a chance that she might get convicted. They aren't just going to let her go. They aren't going to take her to trial and make fools of themselves – so there has to be some dirt.

******

I need to know what Maurice wants out of life. Shadika had invited him to an elegant dinner at one of the finest restaurants in town. Part of dinner was a test.

Outside of talking about Tina's case, this was the most serious thing that she had asked him. "I just want to keep doing things for my people and keep as many out of prison as possible." She didn't know that he had seen, done, and had it all.

"That's it." This is the first time that what he said wasn't sensitive to the situation, though she appreciated his response. So far, he was handling himself well in a classy restaurant.

"I thought about having a serious relationship. I've also thought about getting married again." His first wife couldn't stand having an incarcerated husband. "Why do you want to get all serious then go back to California?" He had to wonder if she was playing with his feelings.

"What if I chose to stay?" She gave him an intense look as she sipped her white wine.

Tina

He took a sip of his wine to waste a few seconds. "I was just enjoying my hero while she's here, without making any plans. In an honest manner, I can't answer that question yet."

"When you say that you can't answer that question yet, does it mean that a long-term relationship isn't a possibility between us?" She felt that they were on the right track. Working for what she wanted was a good thing. It made her feel like she really had something.

"For my hero, there's always a possibility, but I want you to concentrate on Tina. We're free. She isn't." Marcus had learned the art of dealing with people a long time ago. He truthfully needed time to think about what she had asked. Playing with her feelings was the last thing that he would do.

She read into the answer that she could get what she wanted. "I have something for you to let you know how special you are to me." Out of her purse, she pulled a small rectangular box.

With a slight grin on his face, he said, "You didn't really buy me something, did you?" He was thinking to himself that she was aggressive all the way around. It didn't bother him. In fact, it was a turn-on.

"Open it. Let me know if you like it or not."

It was a thick bracelet made of white gold and diamonds. The diamonds said Maurice. "Yes, I definitely love it." He appropriately walked around the table to her, just to give her a kiss. "Let's get out of here. We need to get our dance on."

She stood up. "Put it on. I want to see how it looks on you." He did.

"I love this piece Shadika."

She kissed him on the lips as she was putting her arms around him. "I want you all to myself in a permanent relationship." She had forgotten about her other questions.

"I understand." He kissed her to make the moment perfect. Before she realized it, he had paid for the dinner by dropping three fifties on the table. It was too late for her to contest the situation. Plus, she liked the way that he did it so smoothly.

******

It was another beautiful night – almost too beautiful for her. As usual, their love making was superb. This time they were at a hotel room she had reserved. Just to change things up, she brought along a few toys and lingerie.

As she lay in his arms, she watched the sunrise and ran the last few hours through her mind. She was trying to figure out if she had made the right move. She hadn't minded him bringing Tina's case up and making it a priority. She wondered what he would have done if Tina's case hadn't existed.

The relationship had become extremely serious for her. More serious than she had anticipated. She had begun to see the situation as something she couldn't fail at. As an independent woman, at her age, it felt strange to want a man in a certain way so bad.

She wanted to wake him up and drill him with questions to get at his true feelings and intentions. Was he really susceptible to having a long-term relationship? Was he willing to remain the kind of man that he was now? Was he just humoring her to get her to do her best on Tina's case? Would he all of a sudden change when the trial was over? Did he really mean any of the things that he had said, or were they just words?

Her emotions had taken over her usual way of rational thinking. There was no way of figuring out what was on a person's mind. There was no guaranteed way of calculating if a relationship would or wouldn't work. What was making her happy was making her anxious. She had no choice but to wait for him to express his feelings and make a decision. She had already decided that she didn't mind changing states for him.

Tina

Thoughts of him rejecting her were on the top of her head. It was a situation that she didn't have full control of. It was too late to turn around. She bit down on her lip and closed her eyes to say a small, silent prayer. We know what she prayed for.

"Shadika, look at me. I know that you aren't asleep." Maurice had been woke for about fifteen minutes. It took a while for him to get his thoughts together and figure out what he planned to say.

"Tell me what's on your mind." She still had her head on his chest.

"Do you think you could look at a brother?"

"I'm listening to you." She was thinking that he might be able to read her mind by seeing the expression on her face.

To be sensitive, he started rubbing her back. "I have a good feeling about who Clyde is going to get as a witness."

This made her eyes open wide. "How could you be able to do that?" How he said it made her take him seriously.

He started pulling himself up so he could get her full attention.

She grabbed the sheet to keep herself covered. She looked up at him.

"My people have been keeping track of all the people that have talked to Clyde."

"What kind of people are you talking about?" She knew that he was serious, but she wasn't getting the full picture.

"I know everybody and people that know the people that I don't know." This was the benefit of being an ex-gangster and community leader.

She looked up at the ceiling to think about what he had said. It made a little sense. "You aren't about to tell me that you are going to do something illegal?"

"No." He would if he felt that was the only way.

"So what are you talking about?" She sat up in the bed. "I need to know what's on your mind."

"I want you to know who this witness is before it's time to go to trial so that you'll be fully prepared. You don't mind that, do you?" He didn't like the expression that she had on her face.

"Of course I don't mind that, but is that all you have on your mind?" She thought back to how he put the trial ahead of their relationship.

"Why are you tripping? I'm only trying to help." He got up off the bed and headed into the bathroom.

"Please don't walk away from me while I'm talking to you."

He put on his pants to get comfortable. "All lawyers and paralegals have investigators. What's wrong with me doing some investigating?" To be polite, he came back to the bed and sat down on the side of the bed.

"Why are you taking such a deep interest in this trial? Tina isn't one of your relatives or something." She had wanted to wait to ask this question.

"She's part of the community that I care about and love. Also, I don't think she did it." What he really felt he couldn't tell her.

"I don't care about *that*." This just blurted out. "I want to know why you put this case ahead of our relationship. Don't you see that I love you?" It was part of her persona to lay it on the line when things got heated.

"Maybe this is moving too fast and too far to soon." He stood up and started putting on the rest of his clothes. "I want to make a decision that I plan to stick by. At the moment, my community is on trial with Tina." He turned around. "I'm sorry."

She wanted to be upset with him. Back in the day, she had put her missions and her career ahead of her relationships. She had told many men that she was a career girl. Respecting what he said was mandatory, though her womanhood was insulted. Though she was gorgeous for her age, she had to wonder if he'd be acting the same way if she was twenty-four.

"I need to know something else." It took a few seconds to figure out what direction to go in.

"Ask." He was thinking that she just might push his hand too far and draw a divide between them. Getting off his mission wasn't going to happen. To complete his mission, he'd lie to her and use her, though that isn't what he wanted to do.

"How do you feel about getting a college education? I need to know." She decided to get it all over with. All that prolonging with her feelings wasn't about to happen. She had decided that her heart would either be opened or closed.

"If you want me to finish getting a degree, I feel that I could do that for you. But I already have a job and I love it." Naturally, he had to put a limit on how far he would go. Getting a degree wouldn't take that long; he already had plenty of college credits.

She pulled herself up to the top of the bed. "I'm going to tell you what I want." She stopped to examine his demeanor.

Damn, she's beautiful when she's serious. She was the first female that he had a crush on. He pulled up a chair and crossed his legs to get comfortable. "Go ahead."

She looked up at the ceiling and tightened her arms around herself. "I want to be your wife and we can live wherever you want. I just want you to keep treating me the way that you have been and become a college graduate. And, if you have to cheat on me, do it in a manner that I'll never know. Do you understand?" She let out a long, slow breath and prayed a silent prayer that she hadn't been too forward or too weak at the end. In all, she knew she was saying she just didn't want to be lonely.

He just knew that she was about to go all out. It was the deepest thing that a female had ever said to him. He didn't know what to think, feel, or exactly say.

"So what am I supposed to say to all of that? We just started this relationship. It hasn't been thirty days."

"Come here.", she whispered. As long as he didn't say no, there was a chance. He moved to the side of the bed and sat down. "I know that I want you and what I want from you. Either I can or can't get it." She crawled from under the sheet and got in his lap. "When the trial is over, no matter the decision, I need an answer." She felt that she might have pushed too hard. He agreed to tell her then.

She didn't want to be in limbo no longer than necessary. She had done what most beautiful and intelligent women would have never done – laid it all on the line to get her man. Though she was still scared that she might not win him over, she felt better because they had set out a time frame and the parameter for their relationship. What she had done was propose a marriage to him. In the meantime, she'd enjoy him and keep trying to win him over.

On the way to his house, they discussed how to figure out if anybody in Westlake would become a witness and how to get all needed information on that witness, if necessary. Maurice had plans in effect that he didn't tell her about.

Chapter 9

"Hey baby, what took you so long to call?" Diana answered the phone in her usual sexy tone.

"Diana, I need your assistance. I'm willing to pay you very well. I'm sure you are interested." Clyde had gone through Social Services to acquire her information.

"Who the hell is this? What is this, a joke?"

"Calm down, I'm not a stalker; I'm a cop that needs a bit of assistance."

"Listen here, Mr. Whatever your name is, I'm getting ready to hang –"

"There's ten thousand in this for you. I can give it to you in cash." Her silence told him that he had hit the spot.

She looked at the phone. That's a lot of money, she thought. Shopping came to her mind. That could be a lot of shopping for a lot of things.

"So what makes me think that you are serious? Why didn't you just knock on my door? You ain't scared of the projects, are you?" She put that out there to see if he was for real.

"We can't be seen together. That's all that I can tell you." Clyde didn't want the other residents of Westlake to influence her.

"You prove to me that you are serious and I might meet you in a public place." She wasn't going to let her guard down until she felt totally safe.

Clyde had to think first. "If I send you $200 in the mail, will you meet me somewhere?" A little bit of money should convince her, he thought.

"That sounds ... why can't you send $500? Let me know that you are really serious." She had enough experience to know not to accept the first offer.

"Listen to me girl. If you think that you are going to rob me, you'll regret it. I mean that." It was a matter of principle to present a threat when the opportunity came up. The sooner the better!

"The five hundred means that I just agree to meet with you and that's it. It has to be a public place." She could have a real good time with the $500.

"I'll meet you at the mall by the phone booths on the second level. It's going to ring. You get that?"

"I got that. What time? I'll have to get a ride."

"You'll get the money on Thursday. I'll put it in the mail tomorrow. If you get it earlier, the meeting is still on Thursday at eight o'clock in the evening."

"Make it at six o'clock." She felt better if she stated the time.

"No problem, bye." Clyde hung up.

Clyde was satisfied. He could see it being all just a matter of money with her, just like most confidential informants.

He was already envisioning her on the stand, saying exactly what he wanted her to say and making it sound convincing. Her demeanor was just perfect for a witness, he thought.

He reached in his desk's bottom drawer and pulled out one of his father's pictures.

"Dad. You don't have to worry about a thing. I have Tina in the bag. She'll be joining you in hell. I guess that when she gets there that you are going to have the chance to kill her again. I finally found a witness. It's a money-hungry, black bitch that's willing to turn on her people for just a few dollars. You used to tell me that most black people have a weakness for material things. So just be patient. I'm not going to rest until Tina is put to rest. I don't care if she wasn't the one that pulled the trigger."

******

"You have to be playing. You said that the discovery is nothing but letters, police reports, and BOP telephone calls. You have to be playing." Steve had come from the pool room on the nine-thirty recall.

"I read through all of it since about seven-thirty. My Tina is about to be set free." Tyrone leaned back on his pillow and laid down. Their two Mexican cellmates came in.

"That's a good reason to be excited. What they might do is bring out some surprise evidence – then say that they just discovered it. We can't get excited and slip." Steve knew that there had to be more to it than that.

"I've been telling you that they just want to blame this thing on Tina." Tyrone had enjoyed reading the police report. Being there when the body had been found would have been the only way to make it better.

"Listen here, playboy. Have you ever heard of a circumstantial evidence case? Have you forgot about witnesses showing up on surprise?" Steve had figured their phones calls and letters referred to Atkins' death and other things of that nature.

"Damn Steve. You can't let a dude be happy. You got to always rain on my parade." As usual, he'd thank him for making him see the light. Seldom had Steve been wrong. It was just at times that Steve seemed to be a bit over cautious.

"We're talking about the death penalty. What makes you think that the feds are going to go out like that?" He had seen so many cats go into a deep depression after they didn't get the results – freedom – that they had expected – more like they had hoped for.

"Tina's lawyer, Shadika Jones, said that she doesn't think that they have any witnesses yet. Read this letter." Tyrone was hoping that this changed his point of view.

Steve read the seven lines of the letter quickly. "I see what you mean." Steve smiled. "We have to remember that they have sixty days to get it together. I know that Clyde wants to win more than he wants to live." To Steve, the ante had just gone up.

"I guess you are right. In that time frame, they could find some witnesses that'll say anything." He understood why it wasn't a good time to be excited. "We are really going to have to be on point." He started rubbing his big chin.

It was one of the times that a person hates being locked up more than usual because he wants to be able to do something for someone. If Tyrone was in the street, he'd make sure that he'd be on top of witnesses and doing what he had to do. If it had been in his area, he could have sent some people to keep him posted on what was happening. It's a hurting feeling not being able to help like you want to.

All that he could do was study the law and make suggestions to Shadika. So far he liked the way that Shadika was handling things.

******

I think that somebody could write a book based on the letters that Tina and I have written each other. The phone calls would be the icing on the cake.

Shadika stated in her letter that we acted rather aggressively about a few things. I understand exactly what she meant by that. We wished a lot of death on Atkins – something that a lot of people do.

Tina

Nobody can convince me that a bunch of words is enough to convict somebody of murder. That's why I'm rather happy with what has happened so far. I wish that trial would happen tomorrow.

My man Steve be making some really good points at times. Though what he says at times scares me to death, it all be logical and relevant. Them feds have to do something dirty to put my baby to sleep. I have a good feeling that she's going to walk out of the courtroom a free woman.

Since the other day, my man has been acting really distant. I know this guy like I know myself. In prison, you just don't see a person like you live with them. I'm talking about seeing a person no less than fourteen hours a day. With all that time spent together, you really get to know a person.

When I say that he's been acting strange, I mean that. *Trust no one fully* is a real thing.

******

"Mr. Clyde, or whatever your name is, you're making me look bad by having me called to the Lieutenant's office. Maybe I should call you." It was six o'clock the next morning. Steve had barely woke up.

"The last time that I saw you, you told me to go to hell. So what makes me suspect that you are going to call me? I need you Steve. I need you bad." Clyde intended to make as many appearances in the prison as necessary. It's easier to break a person down in person than it is over the phone.

"That's the best friend that I've ever had and you want me to testify against him?" He went closer to the desk – just in front of Clyde's feet, which were thrown up on the desk. Having a sixty-five-year sentence makes a person rather bold. "What you really want is for me to lie on him. What kind of shit is that?" The Lieutenant was loving it. Four out of five inmates that he'd seen approached like this, rolled over. He knew that Steve was tough, so he was interested in what he would do.

"When you think about it, you'll understand that it's the American way. When you left the streets you weren't able to purchase beer. When you get out, you won't be able to carry a case of beer. I'll still be on the streets." Clyde knew that Steve had to be thinking about all the things that he hadn't done in his life.

"May I leave Lieutenant? I'm tired of talking to this cop."

"No," the Lieutenant answered. "If you walk out of the door, you'll be going to the hole for disobeying a direct order." They all worked together.

"Steve, don't be stupid." Clyde saw a crack. "He's just another black dude that doesn't have a thing and can't help you with nothing but getting high." Steve looked at him like he was a little madder. "Yes, we know that he feeds you weed to get your assistance."

"Now you want to lie on me and him? Ain't that a bitch." Steve threw the Lieutenant a nasty look.

Clyde stood up. "I know everything about you and him. I know that he went broke and you have always been broke. I can make all things change for you."

"You need to change your mouthwash." Steven stepped back. "I don't have anything else to say."

"Lieutenant, would you do me a favor?" Clyde turned around. "Take this man's urine and process it today. Might as well give him a street charge for Simple Possession of a Controlled Substance." Clyde turned back around to see Steve's expression.

"What are you talking about?" Steve laughed like it had to be a joke.

"Since you want to be a tough guy, we are going to play hardball. See if you can beat this case." Clyde walked out and headed towards the exit.

Tina

What Clyde had just pulled was a one-two punch. Even if Clyde didn't convince Steve to turn into a witness, Tyrone would no longer be able to get his assistance. That also meant less assistance for Tina. If Tyrone also had a dirty urine, that would also be nice.

"I have to take you to the hospital to give a sample. I hope that you don't have dirty urine." The Lieutenant was trying to tell him how bad things were about to get for him.

"How fast are the results for this going to take?"

"You are smart. It's going to be in a few hours. It's an express thing. You'll be in the hole before the evening meal." Usually, it took four to six weeks for results to come back.

"Let's go," Steve said, trying to be a tough guy.

Steve had to make a few decisions. Like most, there was a part of him that wanted to testify so he could have his freedom. Only the hardest of men dismiss the thought. He had been entertaining the idea since the first meeting. Every time that he saw a magazine article with a half-naked woman, he thought about doing it. Thinking about all those years without having sex always came to his mind. He certainly had not ruled the thing out.

Steve hadn't been brought up around criminals that always told underlings to keep their mouths shut. In his case, there was no one to tell on. Naturally, he had to think about it.

Tyrone's friendship had a value to it. Their closeness automatically caused him to say no off the top, though he didn't mean it one hundred percent – ninety percent was more like it.

Steve started thinking differently because he was about to be separated from Tyrone. In the next few hours, he'd have to decide if he should or shouldn't tell Tyrone what was happening.

While Steve was eating his breakfast, he thought about whether Tyrone was worth all the drama that they were going to take him through. If they charged him, the extra time wouldn't mean that much. Having to spend all that time in a County Jail would be a hardship. Six months in a county jail can seem like six years.

In the County Jail, there wouldn't be any going outside every day. Instead of being able to walk around a large compound, a tier, about the size of a porch, would be as far as an inmate could walk. That is, if confinement wasn't limited to a cell – an eight by fourteen – all day. Instead of being able to take a shower at almost any time, showers would be given three days a week. Instead of being able to go to the law library almost every day, there would be none. If they were allowed to go to the law library, it would be for a small amount of time – most likely only one day a week. Instead of being able to cook a meal with food that came from the commissary or stolen from the kitchen, other than County Jail meals that are terrible, there were candy bars sold on a weekly basis. Instead of being able to change clothes on a daily basis and wear sweat clothes, there is one jumpsuit issued and it's exchanged once – sometimes twice – a week. Instead of being able to wear sneakers or boots, a pair of – most likely orange – shoes would be issued.

Life in a county jail is drastically much worse than life in a federal prison. It will make an individual beg to be back on a federal compound.

As bad as that is, there's something that's much worse. Diesel therapy is dreaded by those that have heard about it. In a three-week time span, an inmate can end up in ten different holdovers and compounds. An inmate's mail won't have a chance to catch up with him. Every time that he lands in a new spot, his designation would change so that he never stops moving. When you don't stop moving, you don't get a chance to use the phone. Your people may not know where you are for months.

Tina

Steve pondered these things all day until they called him to the Lieutenant's office at three-thirty in the afternoon. They took him straight to the hole and wrote him a shot for having dirty urine. Tyrone's came back clean.

Steve had some serious thinking and decision making to do.

******

Tyrone spent most of the day trying to answer a legal question: Whether the prosecutor was required to give the defense a witness list, and if they had to, would they be able to exclude any names?

This was one of those legal questions that took some lengthy and tedious legal research. The average jailhouse lawyer wouldn't be able to answer the question because it wasn't an issue that usually came up for getting post-convictions relief. After a direct appeal, it was hard to get relief on minor issues. This meant that Tyrone had to search through several books to see if he could get some kind of lead. Most of the people that he talked to said that the issue never comes up.

Off the top, he read all of Rule 16 (Discovery) under the Federal Rules of Criminal Procedure to see if it said anything about a witness list. Rule 16 laid out the rules for the prosecution and the defense to disclose material to the other side. He didn't even see the word witness list. Out of curiosity, he looked up Rule 15 because it dealt with Depositions. Deposing a witness would have a beautiful thing, but it was for witnesses that couldn't attend the trial. Before he closed the Rules of Criminal Procedure, he decided to see if the Federal Death Penalty Act said anything about disclosing the identities of the witnesses. No such luck.

Tyrone turned around to put the Criminal Code up and get the last three editions of the Criminal Law Reporter. Steve had taught him how to use these to do legal research. There were twelve volumes available. Each had an index. In the indices, he looked up Discovery, Federal Death Penalty, Witnesses, and Trials. It took about two hours to go through all the editions and read the leads that he had found. The leads were the kind that might lead to something big. When he was finished, it was time to go back to the unit and wait for lunch to be called.

Tyrone figured that Steve had stayed on the yard to work out when he didn't see him come back to the cube. Not seeing him in the chow hall didn't mean much.

When the law library opened back up at twelve-thirty, Tyrone was the third to walk through the door. Instead of grabbing the Criminal Code, he grabbed the Annotated for Rule 16. He went straight to the word "witnesses." Progress had been made. There was a part that stated when disclosure was required. The first paragraph said that a witness list is to be provided in capital cases. Murder came under capital offenses.

Tyrone wrote down the cites for the cases. There were only four and all of them were old. With the quickness, he grabbed all of them off the shelves. In none of the cases could he find what he was looking for and none of the cases were murder cases. The language in all the cases was too vague. Their citing Rule 16 made it a little more confusing. Tyrone was hoping to find a reference source that determined what could and couldn't be done.

He went back to the Annotated to find some more up-to-date cases. He turned to the pocket part, which is what he should have done when he wrote down the cites for the other cases. Most pocket parts aren't that thick. Some only have four to ten pages. This one had about seven pages. Tyrone pulled the four cases that were listed.

The last case put him where he wanted to be: *United States v. Karake*, 281 F.Supp.2d 302, was perfect. It was a murder case with lots of supposed witnesses. The case referred him to Rule 16(a) (1) (E). There was nothing there that stated anything about a witnesses list. Still, it had been interpreted to mean that. That's what mattered. Tyrone quickly copied the case. He made two copies.

Though he had found exactly what he had been looking for, he wanted to be thorough by looking at one more resource. It was time to look through the American Jurisprudence books. He pulled the two books that contained the heading Criminal Law.

American Jurisprudence takes a subject and breaks it down into several subsections – then into more subsections. Many hate reading these books because it has so many details. Hard to read and hard to understand is one way to put it.

Tyrone picked about seven subsections to look under. On the third one, he found a jewel. It was 18 U.S.C. 342. It required the government to disclose the identity of the witnesses three days before the trial.

Now it was time to Shepardize. Shephardizing is the way to find out where a case, statute, or rule is cited in other cases. There were plenty of sites to look at,Tyrone looked at about fifty. When the law library closed at three-thirty, he settled on *United States v. Lee*, 374 F.3d 637 to make his point to Shadika.

Lee was a federal death penalty case that required the government to turn over a witness list before the trial began. Tyrone made copies before the library closed.

When Tyrone got to his bunk, he laid it down. Within seconds, he was fast asleep. All that reading and researching had taken a toll on him.

His Mexican bunkies woke him up about forty-five minutes later to stand up for the four o'clock count. When he came to, he noticed that Steve's bed had been stripped. Next he noticed that the lock had been taken off his locker. When he pulled the locker open, he found a lot of empty space.

He looked at the cats across the hall to see if they knew anything. They all shrugged their shoulders.

Tyrone figured that it would just be a matter of asking the right questions of the right staff member to find out what had happened to Steve for him to be in the hole. That was the only place he figured that he could be. At most, Tyrone figured that Steve would be let out of the hole in a few days, like most were.

All that evening, Tyrone tried to find out what had happened to Steve. A few people had seen him go into the Lieutenant's office at about three-thirty, after his name had been called over the P.A. system. It was odd for a person to go to the hole without anyone knowing why.

Tyrone finally decided to make his next move without consulting with Steve. A letter had to be sent to Shadika immediately. On the seven-thirty move, Tyrone headed to the law library, with typing ribbon and all, to get a letter done. He found himself a typist and handled his business. It was time to relax until he figured out something else that he could do.

******

"Mr. Steve Harrison, would you please tell me how you plead?" It had barely been twenty-four hours since Steve had spoken with Clyde. Right after they took Steve to the hole, he was arrested for Simple Possession of a Controlled Substance in violation of 21 U.S.C. 844.

"I plead not guilty." As far as he knew, no one that had caught dirty urine had been given an outside charge, especially so quickly. He was having his first appearance at the United States District Court located in Western Pennsylvania.

So far, he had not seen any other prisoners. He had been placed in an isolation cell the night before and transported to the courthouse by himself. The marshals kept asking him what he had done. They had been ordered that he wasn't to have any contact with any other prisoners. When the marshals heard what he was charged with, they knew that he had some important information. Just as soon as they finished with him, they took him back to isolation.

There was nobody to talk to. There was nothing to read and nothing to do, but eat and sleep. The brightly lit room would be that way day and night. The small amount of recreation that he got would be by himself. Ingredients to drive man crazy.

On a cop killer case, all the authorities cooperate.

Chapter 10

Clyde liked that Diana got in place early. It was okay that she had brought somebody with her to watch her back.

From a store that he couldn't be seen, he called the first phone booth.

Diana jumped when she heard the phone ring. The guy that was with her got curious. He was being paid just to hang out. "Hello, this is Diana."

"You pretty good people Diana. You are right on time. I like that." There was little time for him to feel her out like he desired to do.

"Okay. What is it that you need? My time is valuable. What is it that you really want?" She was looking around to see if she could see someone looking at her.

"I'm that white guy that was talking to you the other day. I'm sure you remember."

"You're that cop that's been looking for a witness." She knew what he was going to ask her to do. It was one of the biggest subjects in Westlake.

"Yes, I am." He liked that he didn't have to explain a bunch of details to her. "This is going to be some really easy money for you."

"We have a problem. I didn't see that happen. How am I supposed to be a witness?" She didn't mind his offer because she had made $500.

Tina

"That isn't a problem. We'll take care of that. Many people tell lies to make money. This'll be the most money that you ever made telling lies."

She smirked and let out a small breath. "I don't think that you have this entirely worked out. I can't help you." Diana hadn't hung up the phone because the pay was so good just for her to talk to him.

"It's really simple. I'll pay you and you say what I want you to say." He figured that he was almost there.

"Listen to me good, Clyde. I understand that you want to get revenge for your father's death, but I'm not going to let me and my family get murdered for any amount of money." She sucked her teeth to let him know that she was extremely serious.

"Okay, you have a point." Arguing with her hadn't entered his mind, not that he really cared. But he couldn't argue with what she had said. "Let's say that I can make it so that you and your entire family are protected."

"Mr. Clyde. It is Clyde?" These were words to buy time. She just couldn't dismiss the money without hearing his solution. "I can't imagine you coming up with a solution."

"Let's make an agreement." He was still thinking.

"Another deal. I love my mother and my child. I don't think that we can make a deal. Maybe you should try somebody else."

"All I need to know is are you willing to relocate? I can make it happen." Clyde felt a little foolish because he hadn't thought of this before. Selfishness had caused him to disregard her life.

"I'll have to think about this." She was ready to get ghost. She knew that if people in the projects found out that she was talking to him that they'd do something to her.

"In a few days, you'll get another call from me. I'll make sure that all of you are safe." He hung up the phone.

She cursed him out for hanging up on her. There wasn't a doubt in her mind that she'd be getting a call.

Two potential witnesses. One as the star witness. The other would be back up. With about sixty days to go, Clyde had his work cut out. Diana was the most important because she'd be the eyewitness. Whatever she wanted, he planned to give her. He hated that he'd have to turn to Coppedge to make it all happen. They'd have to have the relocation approved by the higher-ups in Washington, D.C. Then they'd need enough time to prepare her for the stand. One slip and the entire case would get slammed.

Steve would be easy to prep because he had experience with the law. It would be a matter of making him suffer to make him change his mind. Clyde expected isolation to take its toll in the next five days.

******

Coppedge stopped short when he saw Clyde sitting behind his secretary's desk. Usually at seven o'clock in the morning, he was the only one in the office – one of the reasons that he was so good. He looked at his watch to check the date. Clyde was sitting there grinning.

"We have sixty days to go before the trial. I hope you have something really good to tell me." If he didn't have anything good to say, Coppedge planned to kick him out of his office.

"I'm here to tell you that we have two potential witnesses. Things look really good."

They stared at each other. Coppedge was doing it to determine if Clyde was that fortunate and serious. Clyde was gloating because of the way that Coppedge had been acting.

"Let's see what you have Clyde. You need to stay from behind my secretary's desk. You got that?" It was way too late in the game to tell Clyde to kiss off.

Tina

Clyde stood up. With a smile, he said, "Lead the way." It was rare that he was in a good mood.

For the past three days, Coppedge had been figuring out what expert witnesses he planned to have testify. "I hope that you have done some good work and picked some good people." Coppedge sat behind his desk.

Clyde sat in the chair in front of Coppedge's desk and crossed his legs. "Tyrone has a buddy named Steve that's susceptible to testifying. We just charged him with Simple Possession of a Controlled Substance."

Coppedge raised his eyebrows then squinted his eyes. "I know about Tyrone. Who is Steve?"

Clyde shook his fist in the air and hit his forehead with his knuckles. "I'm moving a bit fast. Steve used to sleep over Tyrone in prison. He's the one that did the paperwork that got Tyrone back in court. In prison, they were like the best of friends." Clyde had been talking slow to make sure he got the details right.

"Simple Possession doesn't carry a lot of time. What makes you think that Steve is going to testify against his best friend?" Most of the jailhouse lawyers that he knew of hated the government and wouldn't testify to save their lives.

"The most important part is that he has sixty-five years to do and no means to get himself out. We are going to start diesel therapy next week." He was sure that he had said what needed to be said.

"Are you sure that he'll go along with the program?"

"I can tell by his body language and his voice that he wasn't totally against the idea. It's just a matter of isolation and thinking time to make him get in tune." Clyde slouched down in his chair to get comfortable.

"That sounds like a work in progress. What are you expecting him to say since he isn't an eyewitness?" Coppedge had to ask.

"He heard Tyrone say that he knew that Tina did it. And a few other things on those lines. We could also get a few snitches from FCI Loretto to say that they were really close."

"I like that. It might be better to use a prison guard to establish their relationship." He liked the rest of the plan and felt that it went well with the letters and phone calls.

"That'll be much easier and the guard can make a few extra dollars for his time." This was the first time that they agreed on something. "Tell me about the other witness." He was having doubts about what was coming next.

"We have somebody that we can use to make an eyewitness out of." Clyde paused to make a deliberate effort to sell Coppedge on this. Coppedge remained silent. "She's willing to do it for the reward money. With her, I believe we'll have this thing guaranteed." Acting humble was a new thing for him.

"What is the catch?" Coppedge prepared himself to be disappointed.

"Well, she wants protection for herself, her son, and her mother. That'll seal the deal." He just knew that Coppedge was going to say that they should have discussed that earlier.

"Are you sure that that is it?" Coppedge was satisfied that he was putting in the footwork.

"I'm willing to bet my life on it." What a relief. Most of the time, Coppedge screamed on him for not fully handling all of his business, just as he had done to all officers.

"Do you think that the people in Westlake would do something to her if she testified?" He was just talking to give himself some time to think.

Clyde got up and walked over to the window. "I think that we both know the answer to that. They love Tina because she killed a cop." He should have said killed a dirty cop.

"That isn't going to be that easy. She's got to be able to do the job. This means that I'm going to have to meet her. When can that be arranged?" So far, Coppedge had been calm the entire time. This was a surprise to him.

Clyde kept looking out the window. The city was slowly coming to life. "It seems that you don't trust me. I'm telling you that I have a good witness."

"She has to be relocated. That means that she has to be interviewed. We can't have her getting killed or kidnapped if you know what I mean." He was thinking that this subject should have come up earlier.

Clyde looked at him. "What are you talking about? She's just going to testify and move to another part of Ohio or maybe Pennsylvania."

"It isn't that simple."

"Would you please explain that to me?" Clyde was wondering why he was making this thing so complicated.

"We just can't move that girl across town. We have to move her out of the state and make sure that she doesn't come back." That is the way it's supposed to go, but we all know that often they get what they want and the rest doesn't matter.

"So what do we have to do?" Clyde walked towards the chair. He stopped right next to it.

"An application has to be put in. I'll have to pull some serious strings so that I'll get it rushed through. I need to meet her like yesterday."

Clyde shook his head and headed towards the door. As a team, they were coming together. Words weren't needed to express this. Clyde could see it all going down. Coppedge was skeptical about the female. He didn't have a good reason to feel good about her. He was patient though and willing to meet her.

******

Shadika had been busy all week studying the Federal Death Penalty Act to make sure that her first hunch was correct. If she wasn't able to win the case, she – at least – wanted to be able to keep Tina from getting executed.

Shadika wasn't going to let her time away from practicing criminal law be a weakness. On a daily basis, she practiced making her courtroom presentations. Most civil cases didn't go to trial. The biggest thing that happened was discovery – the exact opposite of a criminal case.

She also had to bone up on criminal procedure and the Rules of Evidence. The rules had slightly changed in the past two decades, but most things were pretty much the same. When she was not researching, studying, and practicing her presentation, she was with Maurice. She liked the idea that he volunteered to test her and study with her.

When she got a letter from Tyrone, she had to drop in on Tina. "You look pretty good, young lady, considering the circumstances. I have to say that you are taking this well." Shadika was shocked that Tina came in the room with a smile on her face.

"Tyrone mailed me the letter that he mailed you. How couldn't I be happy with a man like him in my life? You look pretty happy yourself." Tina had been getting about three letters a week from Tyrone.

Shadika's mind went to Maurice, wondering what it would be like to get a letter from him. "I can feel you girl, but we have business to talk about."

"So that means that you are going to use what he suggested?" Tina was extremely proud of Tyrone for doing all that work on his own and just for her.

"I'm putting in a motion today to see if we can get the witness list as soon as possible." Researching discovery for criminal cases was the next thing on her agenda. Tyrone had saved her lots of time and energy. This was what lawyers hired paralegals for.

"So how long will it be before we are going to get a response?" Trina inquired.

Tina

"Since this case is so public, I imagine that it's going to be next week. I'm expecting to have Judge Grumpfree have a hearing. That's one of the things I asked for." The sooner that she put her hand on a witness list, the sooner she could decide what she planned to do to beat the case. She had something slick in mind.

"Do you still think that they don't have any witnesses?" Tyrone had written to her about the case not going to trial if they didn't have any witnesses.

"I do have the feeling that they are still working on that. We are about to find out." Shadika really wanted to say that she was sure that they wouldn't be able to find one, but that might have excited her too much.

"What is going to happen? Tell me what's happening with you and Maurice." There wasn't anything else for her to ask about the case.

"I told him that I want to be his wife." A bright smile came across her face.

"You asked a man to marry you?" The act was a taboo thing for most females and a sign of weakness.

"When I see what I want, I go get it. Why take the chance of not getting what you want?" She had also done it to see how strong he was on the inside.

"I'm not sure that I'd do that. So what did he say and do?" She wanted to be up on all the details.

"He just listened and we decided that he'd make a decision after a certain amount of time." She didn't want Tina to think that she was about to rush through the trial.

"So what do you think that he's going to do? Where are y'all going to live? I wish that I had been there." She could see a female like her being able to keep his attention.

Shadika shook her head to make her hair go back a bit. "He seems to be preoccupied with other things." She was using a metaphor to keep from mentioning the trial. His interest in the trial had her also thinking that he was being so good to her because she was the lawyer. "I can't read how he feels about it, but he didn't try to run from the proposition."

"Let me tell you that he has had a thing for you all his life."

"What are you talking about? I can't see all of that." She felt that she hadn't broken the surface with him to get at his true emotions. He always seemed to do things to throw her off. She still liked the unpredictability.

"The way that he used to look at your portrait when asked about it said a lot. I mean he has a thing for you." They used to tease him about Shadika never coming back to town.

"Well, he's really good at hiding his emotions then." She started debating if she should bring this up to him.

"Think about this. Do you think that he was celibate until you got back in town? He has females at him. He has the reputation of an old gangster." She had the feeling that they'd be getting married.

"Oh yeah. He seems to have a lot of influence around here. So there must be something to what you are saying. I'll just respect his space and give him time to make a decision." She wished that she could be as excited as Tina was.

"Tell me the truth. Are you scared of the competition?" Tina read into Shadika's last response.

"If you were my age, how would you feel?" They started laughing at the same time. It was as if Shadika had cracked a joke that they had been waiting to hear.

"Shadika," Tina said when she almost had her breath back. "You don't look like you are in your forties. I thought you were about thirty-five. And you got a booming figure."

"Thank you girl. I've been taking care of me since I was in my early twenties. My mother put me up on game when I was a teenager. But it don't mean a thing if he wants to stray." She had already accepted this possibility and had taken a concession.

Tina

"After Tyrone and I got serious I don't think that he's dealt with any other females. He always made sure that I knew where he was at. We never had any problems like that." She was thinking about the lines she'd drop on him when she got back to her cell.

"Let me tell you a secret. I didn't have to deal with the issue that much. As soon as a man started slipping, I kicked him to the curb and kept it moving." She flicked her hand and wrist in that manner that means good riddance in the most serious way.

"You know what? I don't think that you have to worry about the other females. I don't think that he has enough for you and them. Girl, you've been trying to kill the man." Tina knew that they were having more than just a love affair. All the time that they spent together meant something.

Shadika pointed her finger at Tina. "That is for sure and you had better say it. He doesn't have much left when I get finished with him. I'm just a greedy old lady." They had to high-five each other.

As usual, they had a good time talking about their men and related matters. Shadika left fifteen minutes later when she felt she had made Maurice wait long enough. She was testing him in every manner that she could think of.

"So what does my lady want to do this weekend?" For the past few days, he'd been working so hard with her that he was exhausted and ready for a good time.

"I need to ask you a question first."

"Oh boy. Another one of those supposed this-or-that exams." She turned her head so he wouldn't see her blushing. "You must want to know the length of my toes. I'd hate for you to cross-examine me." He cranked up the Mercedes and headed out.

"That isn't fair Maurice. You knew me for a lifetime before I met you. I'm supposed to ask you lots of questions.

You ain't scared, are you?" She had laughed all the way through her defense.

"Maybe I should drive by the hospital where I was born so that you can make an inspection. Would you like that?" If pressed, he'd tell her that he had much respect for inquisitiveness.

"We can't be serious this weekend?" She was doing most of the laughing.

"I'm serious now." He pressed his lips together to stop smiling. It didn't work that well.

She had to look out the window for two minutes to get serious. "Okay." She turned her head. "I need to know about the females in your life." Before the words had finished coming out of her mouth, she was feeling foolish.

He looked at her to check her facial expression. For days, he had been wondering if and when she'd ask this question. He took a few minutes to formulate an answer that would be perfect.

"I haven't been with another female since I've been with you. Now will my lady tell me what she wants to do this weekend?" Saying something about another female would have been the wrong thing. She would have been forever asking questions about this girl and that girl about his feelings. He phrased his answer to let her know that she was on top while being truthful.

She was relieved that had come up with a simple answer that semi-appeased her ego. In her heart, she didn't want any information that would make her distrust him.

"I want to go to New York right now. I want to see a play. I want to have a romantic dinner. I want to ride in a horse drawn carriage. I want to take a long stroll in Central Park. And I want to make love to you all weekend." She rattled it all off like she had a plan before she had gotten in the car.

Tina

"Don't you think that's a bit much? We haven't even packed any clothes."

She grabbed her purse and pulled out a platinum American Express Card. "We can go shopping for clothes tomorrow. Let me find out you are scared."

He laughed as he looked at her. "Let me have that." He snatched it out of her hand. "We have to fill up on gas."

******

"Girl, you smiling like you just had sex with your man."

Tina thought about saying something about her being jealous. "I'll say this much. You are reading my mind. That was my lawyer. She's putting in a motion to find out who the witnesses are going to be, if there are going to be any witnesses. Can you feel that?" Tina had started to feel sorry for her because it seemed like no one cared about her.

The subject meant a little to her. "Do you think the feds are going to do that? Let y'all know who the witnesses are going to be?"

"My man did some research to make it happen. He ain't about to let these people send his wife to the gas chamber." Every time she said something about Tyrone, a certain look came in Joann's eyes.

"If they don't have any witnesses, you don't have a thing to worry about. Ain't nobody in Westlake going to get caught working as a rat. That's just the way it is." That had been the word on the streets for months. Joann figured Tina was going to beat the case with ease.

"That's how I see it. So that means you are wishing me good luck." Joann had said one of the things that was on her mind.

"It would be nice." She fired up a Newport. "I can definitely see you going home. I'll be watching the entire thing on television." Tina said, backing away from the cell bars.

Darrell Debrew

"I have to write a letter. We'll kick it after dinner tonight. I'll tell you what Shadika is up to."

******

I hate to be mean, but that girl across the hall is pure poison. That's the vibe that I get from her when we talk about certain things. Forget the crackhead heifer.

Do I have to tell you that I'm proud of my man? When I read in his letter what he had found in the law books, I was skeptical. This was the first time that he did something without Steve's assistance. Now that Shadika has moved out on what he found, I'm feeling extremely good about him.

What I'm talking about is that he just has a G.E.D. and a few college courses and is able to help me fight my case. I knew that he had great potential in him the entire time. I knew that it would just be a matter of time. If I can push him to make more progress like that, there's no telling what he might end up being. Might as well prime his head up for being a lawyer. A convicted felon can still be that.

I can see that Shadika is going to get me home. No matter what witness they get, that witness is going to be lying. Since Shadika is going to know who the witness is going to be beforehand, she'll be ready to make him or her look bad on the stand. The case should be shut down from there. Now, if I take the stand, I feel like the jury will feel that I'm not trying to hide anything.

Of course, I'm making plans to see my man in a few months. Speaking of my man, it's time for me to write him a letter.

Chapter 11

Clyde stood at the cell door for about ten seconds before he decided to bang on the door. "Wake up Steve. It's your savior." Clyde had been pulling strings on every level since he'd started the case.

Steve had been sleeping for about three hours since they had served brunch. He was still hungry. What was killing him was the boredom. They wouldn't even give him a magazine to read.

Clyde banged on the door again. "Wake up Steve. It's your savior. I can get you out of this. All it takes is a phone call." If he didn't turn him into a rat, he planned to enjoy trying.

Steve was in a fetal position. Without the blanket over him, it would have been discernable that he had his hands in between his thighs to keep as warm as possible.

His system had gone into a relaxed zone. Knowing that there was nothing to do and nowhere to go, he had partially shut down. Slowly, he opened his eyes. He had been sleeping so hard that it took a while for his eyes to focus on the figure at the door.

"Get up Steve. It's the middle of the day. You're supposed to be up and trying to file some kind of motion." This was a technique to get what the target had on his mind.

Steve had already sat up on the side of the bed. In a few more seconds, he'd have his composure together. His appearance resembled that of a person that had been sleeping for days.

"Steve, you don't have to do this to yourself. It's real simple. Just help me and I'll help you." Clyde was looking around the cell to make sure there was nothing there to read, not even a bible.

Steve stood and stretched. It was taking longer than he liked for his blood to start pumping. It was the affects of the controlled environment. After he took a few deep breaths, he walked over to the door.

"You look terrible Steve. Why are you treating yourself this way?" Clyde's smirk was meant to hurt Steve's feelings and agitate him.

"So you're a dirty cop, just like your father. I was thinking about helping you. But since you're trying to be nasty, see if you can do it without me. I saw the discovery." It's funny how a state of mind can change with the change of location. Steve now felt that he and Clyde were battling; the same way he felt when he thought about all the time he'd been given for just guns.

As nasty as that statement was, Clyde had heard something in there that pleased him. Because of the circumstances, he couldn't stand somebody saying something about his father. "It won't be that long before you change your mind. With or without you, Tina is going down."

Steve turned around and walked to the other end of the cell. He turned around and said, "Clyde, you must be out of your mind if you think that you can get a conviction with a bunch of letters." He had slowly walked back to the middle of the cell.

"What are you going to do when the entire thing happens without you? I can get you to the house. Think about it." Clyde walked away.

Tina

"Hey. Don't you walk away from me. I'm talking to you." He banged and kicked on the door a few times. "You had better keep it moving."

Steve was caught up in his emotions and his confusion. For a little while, he'd think about Tyrone and the love he had for him. With those thoughts, he'd think about how much he hated the system and cops, especially dirty cops. For a while, he'd think about how nice it would be to have freedom and all the things that went with it, especially the women. Along with that, he'd think about his honor and his self-respect and what he stood for as a man.

Being isolated wasn't helping him. Not seeing Tyrone was already causing him to lean towards Clyde's way. Also, there was no one to give him moral support to emphasize to him what he believed in. There wasn't much he could do to build his moral strength up.

When he was screaming at Clyde, it was out of anger because of the situation. He recognized that it had all been orchestrated because he was the best friend to the wrong person. He was mad at Tyrone also, though it was illogical.

By the time he would file a petition to the court, the entire situation would be over with. If he wrote his family, the letter might not get there. If it did, he'd just shoot her some bullshit about why he was in isolation.

Feeling like a mouse in a mouse trap was hurting his pride. As a man, he wanted to be able to throw a punch that had at least a slight chance of being effective. For him to give in at the moment, he'd feel like the weakest individual in the universe.

******

Clyde had the resolve to let the weekend play out before he made his next move. He decided it was time to give Steve diesel therapy and re-approach Diana.

Clyde had put a lot of thought into what to do about Steve. He was surprised to see Steve act so belligerent. Clyde had come to terms as how to interpret it. He could only conclude that the pressure was getting to him. No matter what he thought, he planned to go full steam ahead.

Diana was the one that he needed the most. "This is Clyde. I've been trying to catch up with you all weekend."

"I've been right here." They both told lies. She was expecting him to ask for sexual favors for the $500. Right on the tip of her tongue was "hell no."

"What you want can be provided, but it's going to be rather complicated." He picked up his father's picture.

"I thought that you'd give up on that. What do you mean that it's going to be rather complicated?" She had done a bit of thinking on her own.

"We can protect you and your family, but we have to be sure that you can do the job. If you can't, we can't use you." To make himself be patient, he was tapping against the desk.

"When you say that you have to be sure that I can do the job, what do you mean?" Diana saw herself making the biggest and slickest lick of her life.

"Being a star witness isn't going to be as simple as you think. It may not be something that you can handle." He was wishing that training her would be easy. So far, he felt she could handle it.

"I told you from the other day that I can handle it. Why are you still dwelling on that?" She had prepared herself to say whatever needed to be said. It would be like she was fulfilling her dream of being an actress.

"Just be cool. I'm going to set up a meeting so that you can meet the prosecutor. He has to approve everything."

"Before we meet with this guy, I need to get something straight. Are you listening?" She had listened enough.

"Okay. I'm listening." He was thinking that she needed to sound that authoritative on the stand.

Tina

"After you relocate me and my family, we are going to need at least $100,000. Ten thousand isn't anything when you have to relocate and start all over." Her mother had put her up to this. Diana had just been thinking about getting some money and going shopping and partying.

"I'm going to have to discuss that with the prosecutor. He's the one that has to get the money." To get the $100,000, he'd mortgage his family home.

"Well, you need to hurry up before I change my mind." She understood how bad they needed her. The trial had to start in fifty-eight days.

"I'll tell you in a few days." He hung up before she could say another thing.

It wasn't about to be nearly as easy as he had thought. With the ante higher, he was scared of how Coppedge was going to feel about what she wanted. There was also still the issue of if she could handle the task and surpass Coppedge's test. The only thing that he knew for sure was that he had to get with Coppedge first thing in the morning.

******

It was about five p.m. when Maurice and Shadika crossed the Ohio state line. Their weekend had been non-stop. If Maurice had tallied what they had spent, he'd have realized that she had just blew about forty thousand dollars. Most of that was spent shopping. They had gone to stores that didn't have price tags on the clothes. She told him not to think about it. They had done everything first class, from the limo to the Cristal.

"Wake up Shadika. I have something to tell you." She was supposed to be driving.

She opened her eyes to see where they were at. "I thought that you were going to tell me that we were home." She was that exhausted.

"No. Get it together. We have something to talk about. It's real serious." He knew that his timing wasn't the best.

She pulled the seat up and started looking at him.

"Are you ready for this?"

She rubbed her face with both hands. "I think that I'm ready for this." She presumed that he was about to make that decision. That would be the perfect way to end their romantic weekend.

He looked at her. "I guess you are ready. I think that we know who the potential witness is." He put his eyes back on the road.

She repeated to herself what he had said. She did it twice to make sure that she was correct. "How is it that you could know something of that nature?" She sat straight up in the seat.

"It's simple. We've been keeping track of all the people Clyde has approached in the projects. There's one person that no one is sure of." He had waited to get into this because of her previous reaction. Now it was about to be crunch time.

"So tell me what do you have in mind?" As a professional, ethics came to mind.

"It's real simple." He had his eyes glued to the road. "No witness, no conviction. It's as simple as mathematics."

She wanted to tell him to look at her. "Do you understand what Witness Tampering and Obstruction of Justice can get a person in the feds?" She didn't know the amount of time at the moment.

"I wasn't thinking of anything of that nature." He lied. "You could just talk to her or investigate her to have an advantage. The sooner the better."

"Are you sure that that is what you are thinking?" She turned sideways in her seat.

"If I wasn't thinking that, why would I have said it?" He looked at her to make her feel bad for asking.

Tina

"So, how did you go about figuring out this conclusion of yours, Mr. Maurice?" She didn't mind switching up. It was just her style.

"We've been keeping a tap on the entire project for the longest time. Atkins deserved to die. And nobody should pay the price for his death." Maurice was using his street instincts to tell him what to say. Since Atkins' death, many in the projects had come together so that another Atkins would never happen. Maurice was the one that lead the group. They all respected him and agreed that Westlake had to be united for the cause.

She had to think about this for a few seconds. The unity that they exhibited was strange and scary to her. What he said confirmed what she had already been sensing. It was a blessing in a way to see that in an African-American project. Still, part of her had to wonder if she was being used by him and the community and whether he'd be acting the same if she wasn't the defense attorney.

"Okay Maurice. Please tell me who this person is." This was one of the first times that it had been hard for her to keep her priorities straight.

"Why do you have to be so nasty about it? I'm only trying to help."

She took a deep breath to make sure she changed her tone. "I don't want to get disbarred and lose this case because you and your people decide to harass the witnesses. Those people have eyes and ears." This was the other negative factor she had on her mind.

"Perhaps we could find a medium place that gets the job done and please all parties." As a natural born leader, he remained calm and took charge of the situation by being logical.

"Okay." She slouched back down in the chair. "I just need her name and address. I think you said that she lives in

Westlake, right?" She closed her eyes after looking at him to sense his emotional state.

"Her name is Diana. She lives about two buildings over from where the murder took place. I'll have her address for you in no time." Maurice still had his mind on doing what he may need to do. He would just have to be slicker about it.

"That's all I need. Remember to let me take care of the rest."

If necessary, she would admit that having a name and address would be of great assistance. In a matter of days – maybe hours – she would know plenty about Diana. This scared her.

******

All of Tuesday had been rough for Tyrone. All day he'd been reading law books, trying to find something significant about the Federal Death Penalty Act that would be of assistance. All of that reading had exhausted him and put him to sleep just before the four o'clock count.

Steve disappearing didn't help the situation at all. Tyrone had to get used to a cell mate that was the exact opposite of Steve – talked all the time, mostly about nothing and wouldn't clean up. Tyrone couldn't talk with other jailhouse lawyers like he could with Steve. Not having Steve around had dampened his enthusiasm. This was the time that he needed him the most. Most depressing was that he'd heard that Steve had been taken out of the institution.

Instead of going back to the law library, Tyrone decided to watch a little television after he came from the chow hall. Tyrone realized how preoccupied he had been when he saw the mail list taped to the officer's window. Usually, he checked the mail list just after the count cleared. Seeing "2X" by his name meant that he had to have a letter from Tina. Sure enough, there it was. He stepped just outside of the officer's office.

Tina

I had to call Tyrone,

I know that my man Tyrone loves me because he did something that I hadn't expected of him. You see, he pulled off a major move from a prison cell that just might set me free. There's nothing that anybody could tell me to make me not believe that my man loves me.

Tyrone, it's plain and simple. I love you and I'd do anything for you. If you asked me to do it, I wouldn't question it. My mind, body, and spirit belong to you and you can do with them what you like. All you have to say is the word.

I envision you and me beating these cases and having several children. What you just did let me know the potential of that brain. Just imagine what you can do with a college education. Yes, that's right. We still have to get our college educations. We'll be going to school together. I know you haven't forgotten.

Oh yeah, there's something that I can never forget. The first time that we made love, not the first time that we had sex. When I saw how you treated your son and your mother is when I decided to open my heart up for you. I put my all into it. You were right there for me. We made love for about two hours straight. I'll never forget those orgasms. That was the night that you and I became "WE."

I love you Tyrone.

A letter from her couldn't have come at a better time. In the few minutes that it took him to read the letter two times, his entire persona changed. He headed towards his cube wondering what he should write her back. A smile was glued to his face as he reminisced about that special night. It had been one of those nights that are never forgotten. He thought to himself what more could he ask of a woman.

When he sat on his bed, he realized that he hadn't opened his second piece of mail. It was a 9x12 envelope from the Sixth Circuit Court of Appeals. By the size of the envelope, it had to be an opinion that was at least twenty pages long. Tyrone set the envelope beside him on the bed and contemplated whether he should open it or not.

Being in prison makes a person appreciate those moments of feeling good, like Tyrone was experiencing. It's a natural high that no one wants to risk losing while it's happening. Tyrone was feeling that good at the moment.

The envelope held in its balance whether he'd be a free man or have to do another seven years. There's very little that can make a person feel good about losing the battle for his freedom. So far, the courts hadn't shown him any kind of love. He was dreading having to deal with his case and Tina's trial at the same time. Plus, the next step, if he got denied, would be the Supreme Court of the United States. Getting a case accepted there was a one in a million shot. A person has a better chance of hitting the lottery.

No matter what, he knew he had to deal with it. If he opened it up then or later, the results would be the same. As hard as it was, he picked up the envelope.

To steady himself, he put his pillow behind him and sat back. He wanted to get it over with. If he didn't, he knew that he'd be thinking about it until he did.

With his eyes closed, he took the document out of the envelope. Before he had opened his eyes, he said a silent prayer. At the bottom of the first paragraph is where he set his eyes. He couldn't believe that he had a published opinion from the Sixth Circuit Court of Appeals that said, "Reversed."

He jumped up off the bed and screamed, "Yeah." He was up in the air the second time he yelled and was punching the air with his fist as far as he could reach.

A reversal meant that the lower court would have to give him a new trial. Now he'd be able to use all of Larry Atkins bad deeds against him. It was like a guarantee that he'd win his trial.

He could see him and his girl being free.

Chapter 12

It was late Wednesday afternoon before Clyde was able to meet with Coppedge. Coppedge had been busy with a trial for two and a half days.

"What does a man have to do to get with you?" Clyde had been waiting for half an hour.

"I hope that you have some good news." Coppedge had just finished with a trial that he wasn't sure about winning.

Clyde followed him into his office. "I can tell you for sure that she's going to be a really good witness." Clyde was thinking to himself that fifty-six days may not be enough time. Most of this paranoia came from not being able to meet with Coppedge for two days.

Coppedge was tired and sunk down in his chair like he was punch drunk. "I imagine you are going to make me guess the rest." He looked towards the window where Clyde was.

Clyde headed towards the chair. "The girl wants $100,000 and to be relocated." He stepped behind the chair and put his hands on the back to support himself.

"Now, I don't care how good a witness she is, she can't get $100,000. I don't even make that much in a year." It wasn't his choice as to how much a witness would get. It was his job to get her as cheap as possible.

"You seem to forget that this is the only witness that we have." He was confident that he could talk Coppedge into doing something reasonable. The object was to talk her down and to talk him up and, if needed, he'd put up the rest.

"I thought that you told me that you had two potential witnesses. What happened to the other one?" Coppedge himself had been working on a potential witness.

"This is the potential eyewitness. The kind of witness you've been saying that we need." It was a miracle that Clyde could be this calm.

"I remember what I said. Before we talk about money, I need to meet her and to test her. When can that happen?" Coppedge was in a rush to get a witness if he was going to be able to get one..

"We are going to have to meet her outside of the city limits. If she comes in this building, there's a chance that word will get back to Westlake Projects."

"See if you can set it up for Friday at a hotel in Pennsylvania."

"I'm out." That was as simple as he wanted it to be.

Coppedge immediately went about writing a sequence of events that would serve as a script for her. After he finished writing it, he'd have one of his assistants help him critique it. The object was to get it air tight for cross-examination. There was no time to be tired.

While that process was taking place, he would be processing an emergency application to put her in the Witness Protection Program. The money issue would be handled later.

******

The first thing happening for Judge Grumpfree's courtroom was a hearing for Tina's case. Just in time for the hearing, Tina was brought in.

"I didn't think that they were going to get you here. What happened?" Shadika had been calling all morning so that Tina would be there early so that they could talk. Shadika wanted her to know what to expect.

"I don't know. They didn't tell me ahead of time that I'd be here. What's happening?" She stood when the bailiff ordered everyone to.

Before Judge Grumpfree was able to come out, Shadika whispered, "Your man was granted a new trial. The Sixth Circuit Court of Appeals reversed his case."

Tina let out an "oooh" that she wasn't able to contain from being heard by the rest of the court. She had all of Judge Grumpfree's attention. "Oops. I'm sorry," she said in a low tone before she could seal her lips.

Coppedge had been taken by surprise with this hearing. He had become aware of the witness discovery petition on Thursday and didn't think that a hearing would be granted so soon. Clyde was standing beside him and was a little tense about the situation.

"Good morning ladies and gentlemen. I think that we're here to decide a discovery matter. I believe the defense filed this petition." This was the first time that a petition of this kind had been filed in her court.

"Your Honor, it's extremely important that the defense have a witness list and the contact information for all of them. This information should have been provided under Rule 16 (a) (1) (E). The defense needs this information in order to prepare its defense."

Judge Grumpfree looked towards Coppedge. "Does the prosecution have anything to say?"

"Yes we do," Coppedge said proudly. "It's a bit premature to be asking for a witness list and doesn't have the proper authority for the matter." Coppedge was feeling pretty hot because he had won another trial and he had a slight surprise up his sleeve if his hunch went correctly. What he had just said was a low blow meant to agitate Shadika.

"Very interesting. I'm sure the defense has something else to say." This was the kind of action that made Judge Grumpfree excited about sitting on the bench.

"Yes, I do have a case. It's called *United States v. Karaka*, 281 F.Supp.2d 302. This is a court case that concerns the murders of several individuals. A witness list was ordered to be turned over immediately, not three days before the trial." She sent a copy of the case up to a judge by the bailiff and handed a copy to Coppedge.

Coppedge took a few seconds to read two pertinent paragraphs. He knew exactly what he was looking for.

"Mr. Coppedge, what do you have to say about this?"

"It seems to me that Ms. Jones is a little premature with her request. Under Title 18 U.S.C. 3432, she was only entitled to get the witness list three days before the trial. That's when we were planning to do that." Coppedge liked that he was able to have the ups on Shadika.

Judge Grumpfree looked at Shadika. "I would think that y'all discussed this matter before this matter was scheduled." All judges hate it when their time is wasted.

"If Mr. Coppedge would have returned some of my calls or letters, I would have been well aware of that." She looked at him with her eyes slightly squinted.

"Is that true Mr. Coppedge? I certainly hope not." She took her glasses off and placed them on her desk.

"I'm sure that one of my assistants got back with her while I was in trial. I'll check as soon as this hearing is over with." Coppedge knew that he had made a mistake. He was sure not to make the second mistake of admitting to it.

"Mr. Coppedge, you need to make sure that you get that list to her this afternoon." She had on one of those glares that looked like she was ready to kill in an instant.

Now he had to make sure that he didn't make a third mistake. "We don't have any witnesses at the moment so that can't be provided." Judge Grumpfree was tapping her fingers against her desk. "What I mean is that I'm not able to provide you with the kind of witnesses that she's talking about. All we have so far are police officers and expert witnesses. I don't think that's what she's after." Coppedge looked at Shadika in an attempt to clean the situation up.

Judge Grumpfree looked at Shadika also.

"Your Honor, I'd like to have all of them. I can't see how any of them aren't significant." Shadika had to say it that way. Most of the cases that she had cited dealt with eyewitnesses though.

Judge Grumpfree was definitely going to put a mental note by Mr. Coppedge's name. "By the end of the business day, you need to make sure that Ms. Shadika Jones has a witness list and as soon as you get new witnesses that she is kept apprised of them." She hit her gavel.

A judge may use her discretion to disregard a statute. That's the privilege of having power. The only source to turn to when a judge makes a decision that disregards the law is the Court of Appeals. That's to another set of judges.

If Coppedge took this route, he'd take the chance of making her that much madder at him. That he didn't want, taking the chance that she'd always rule in Shadika's favor. That could be the cause of an ultimate loss.

Much of a trial isn't dependent on what the evidence says, especially in a circumstantial evidence case – what the case may end up being. A jury has to also accept the presenter of the case. If the court shows dislikes of one of the presenters, the jury senses it, and may cause doubt in their minds. Even worse, the presenter may lose confidence and it will be communicated to the jury. What was already a tough case had just gotten tougher.

******

"That was really good Coppedge. The judge is pissed at you for trying to be smart. " Clyde waited until he closed the door to his office before he made his comment.

Coppedge had taken a bottle of bourbon out of his bottom desk drawer, along with two glasses. He looked up at Clyde and slid him one of the glasses to the end of his desk. Clyde walked to the desk and sat. Coppedge poured him a drink – then he poured himself one. It was a needed relief for the both of them.

"That witness of yours has to be really good. I had no choice but to admit that we didn't have an eyewitness. That's going to boost Shadika's confidence level to the ceiling." He continued pouring.

"I have the feeling that you are letting Shadika get to you. The witness is going to be able to handle it. I can tell." Clyde figured that Coppedge would be more willing to pay her now.

"It isn't just Shadika. Tyrone's case just got reversed by the Sixth Circuit Court of Appeals. That makes the case that much more complicated. That gives them more confidence." Coppedge planned to make sure that he was never placed in this position again.

Clyde had heard this several times in the past few days. "You could have sent me a message to let me know." He finished his drink. Coppedge finished his and refreshed both of their glasses.

"What does it matter? What are you going to do? You had better worry about Tina getting convicted."

"You are supposed to charge him with the murder also. He definitely has a motive." He made it sound like there couldn't be a more logical response.

"That sounds like the thing to do." Coppedge drank half of his drink. "That's exactly what I'm going to do. I wonder how Shadika is going to feel about this." The battle had now become personal.

"I want to pick him up from the prison. We have fifty-three more days."

Tina

Clyde was feeling like it would be better to try the both of them together. He hadn't pressed the issue before because of how hard it was to get Tina indicted, charged, arrested, and captured. This made him feel that what Coppedge had done was a blessing. They had been so preoccupied with getting a witness against Tina that charging him had slipped their minds. That's how weak the case against Tina was. As incredible as it seemed, Clyde thought to himself that he might get one of them to tell on the other.

******

"What took you so long to get in here girl?" Tina was still at the courthouse.

"It's only been ten minutes. What is the rush Ms. Tina Thompson?" Shadika sat down. "If you smile any harder, your cheeks are going to blow up like balloons." Shadika was glad that her client was pleased with what was happening.

"You look pretty happy yourself. You really put it on Coppedge. The judge put it on him also. And, he doesn't have any witnesses."

"I wanted to tell you before we went to the hearing that Tyrone is going to get a new trial." She was debating if she should tell her that Tyrone was probably going to get charged with the murder case.

"With all the evidence from Atkins' criminal case, I'm sure that they aren't going to want to try him again. Atkins' credibility is going to be shot. My man is about to be set free. Talk to me Shadika." She shook Shadika because she had been dominating the conversation.

"I must admit that you have it all figured out. We just have to get you home, you and Tyrone." She couldn't let herself rain on Tina's parade.

"You got that right. I have some good stuff in mind. I'm going to blow his mind. Ooh girl. Can you feel me?" They high-fived each other.

"Do y'all really love each other like that? You act like he's the greatest man that has ever been in existence." She had seen pictures and didn't get the impression that he was some great lover.

"All I can say is that he makes me that happy and I make him happy. He and I have to get married. That's all that there is to that. Tell me about you and Maurice. I heard that y'all are together." When a defendant is on trial, that's how much enthusiasm comes through when freedom is in view.

"We are together. You can't believe how much he cares about your case. He seems obsessed that you win this case." Her smile waned a little bit.

"He's always been that way since he got out of prison. He does all that he can to help out in the community. We have a lot of respect for him. Can't you see that you are his role model? He can't do a demonstration like you can. That's why he looks up to you. Though he can't do what you do, he gets results the way that he knows how." She had been hoping that Shadika would come to understand him on her own.

"What does that have to do with our relationship?"

"You don't understand a damn thing about men. I bet he wants to do something that you don't approve of."

"What makes you ask that?" She was for sure that she didn't know about what he might do that she didn't approve of.

"That man is a gangster and a gangster is going to be a gangster. If you don't accept the fact that he is what he is – then how do you expect for him to act?" As a friend, she wanted to see them as a permanent couple.

Shadika had to think about this for a minute. "That's pretty deep. I hadn't thought about it that way."

It was time for the marshals to transport Tina back across town. "You had better think about that. Don't lose your chance."

Tina

Shadika didn't have the desire – as many women do – to have a bad boy in her life. Shadika had grown up with plenty of them. Shadika did like the idea that Maurice was respected in the community and was a natural leader. It was the idea that he might do something illegal to make something good happen that bothered her. She could be affected by this in two ways: He could end up going to jail. And, she could end up going with him. She wasn't particularly keen about either of these results.

On her drive back to her hotel, she put some serious thought into what Tina had told her. It was as if she was the one that had to make a decision of accepting him and staying or leaving. Getting him to change was a waste of energy for her to think about.

She avoided him that evening so she could think.

******

A week of isolation can do a lot to a man. Steve was badly in need of a shave, a good bath, and a haircut. Other than that, he was holding up pretty well. He had been placed in an interview room.

Clyde made him wait for a half hour. Making Steve anxious was the purpose.

"My man Steve, you look terrible." Clyde was dressed nicely to make Steve slightly jealous. Steve didn't respond. "Like I told you before, you don't have to go through this." Steve had on a cold stare that was near emotionless.

"Tyrone is about to get charged with the murder also." Steve leaned back in his chair. "I'm dead serious. I should have thought to charge him before. I guess it slipped my mind." Eye contact hadn't been broken. "They are going to get the death penalty. You get the chance to go home. You get the chance to see all the pretty girls. I know that you want to get some pussy. You don't have to do yourself this way."

Clyde hadn't ever experienced a person being that quiet on him. This was the part of the police work that he usually left for the detectives. Clyde was trying to figure out what was the motivation that would open him up?

Clyde couldn't think of anything else to say. So he just sat there with Steve for over fifteen minutes and shared stares. It was the same person he had approached a few weeks ago, yet totally different.

"By the end of the day, I could have you in a nice set of clothes and clean shaven." He wasn't thinking that Steve hadn't shaved on purpose. "In less than ninety days, you can be a free man. I know that you aren't going to give up your freedom for a black guy that doesn't care about you." Somehow out of deep thought, words seem to come out of nowhere. "He'd probably tell on you quicker than you could call your mother. If he's really your friend, he'd tell you to tell on him so that you can get yourself free. Wouldn't you do that for a real friend? No matter how you look at it, you need to look out for yourself." Clyde felt like that was his best stab at it.

"Stop wasting your time. I'm not going to testify against Tyrone. Tyrone *or* Tina. I'm not going to do it." After a lot of deep thought, a man can find that all he really has is himself and there is nothing that he can do to avoid dealing with himself. Peace of mind can have that much value.

"You are not going to do what? Are you crazy?" Steve's statement had caught him off guard.

"No matter what you do, I'm not going to turn against my friend. That may be something that you can't understand."

Clyde got out of his seat and gave a stare that could kill. The abruptness of him getting up caused the chair to rattle against the floor, making that much more noise.

All of the instant commotion rattled Steve a little bit. He sat up in his chair a little straighter. There was the chance that Clyde would jump on him.

Tina

Clyde was feeling like he had been played and disappointed at the same time. "Has your ass went crazy? You haven't even been in here for a month. You might as well be a senior citizen that has one foot in the grave."

Steve had gone back into his silent mode. Steve had decided that he couldn't testify against Tyrone. Plus, if he testified, he'd have to lie on Tyrone by saying that Tyrone admitted to the crime.

Clyde sat back down. It wasn't one of those situations that he could bluff like he didn't care. Every bit of testimony and evidence would matter. Though Steve wouldn't be on the stand but thirty minutes at the most, he could be that feather that makes the scale tip.

"Listen to me good Steve." This sentence was added for theoretical purposed. "They are getting ready to ship you all over the country until you break. In a month's time, it's going to be too late for you to help yourself. Absolutely no one is going to know where you are. If I really pressed the issue, I can have you murdered." Clyde took note that Steve's expression hadn't changed. Ordinarily, a person would be shook up a bit. "For sure, in time you are going to start to go insane. When those signs start to surface, you'll be put on medication. I can promise that your life shall never be the same."

Visual thoughts were going through Steve's mind. He knew that it was possible for a therapist to keep a patient on medication. He had also heard about prisoners *acting* crazy – then ending up *being* crazy after the doctors had finished with them. There wasn't much doubt in his mind that they'd do that to him because of a cop killer case.

"That's right. This is something that you'd better give some very serious thought to." As a cop, he had been trained to look at a suspect's pupils to determine a change in thought patterns. This told him that Steve had gone into deep thought. "Go back into society and start all over again like none of this ever happened. You got a good brain. You could still be a lawyer if you liked. It'll be better than rotting to death. What are you going to do?" The last part was an appeal to his ego.

Steve's brain had warmed up to the point that he'd started sweating. On his forehead, he could feel a noticeably cooler sensation. There was some fear mixed up with the cause of his perspiration.

To keep the sweat from gathering, he placed his forehead into his hands and ran his fingers through his hair. Staring into Clyde's eyes had become tough. His focus had started to drift. Vivid images of himself being kept in a padded room and wearing a straight jacket wouldn't leave his mind. It was so real that his breathing had become shallow.

His mental barrier had been broken to the point that he wasn't able to fake it. His head was down and he was trying to change his thought patterns. It wasn't working. He started imagining a nurse shooting something in his arm. Whether his eyes were opened or closed, he kept having different visions.

"I can't help you. Get the fuck out," Steve hollered as loud and arrogantly as he could. He had to take some kind of action to stay strong.

An evil smirk came to Clyde's face. What had just happened provided him with the resolve to not laugh at him. It pleased him to see Steve change his entire demeanor.

"What do you mean that you can't help me?" This is where the Socratic method of asking question after question is appropriate.

"It's a matter of principle. Do what you have to do. I'm not going to lie or testify against my friends. Atkins deserved to die. I hope that she did it and gets away with it." It was a matter of a man being pushed too far - really out of his cocoon.

Tina

"In the morning, we are going to the next level. We're about to see what kind of principles you have." Clyde had mistakenly jumped in the challenging mode. He left out with the demeanor that he was life itself for Steve.

Steve had been taken to the point where it feels better to argue about the subject instead of dealing with silence or an agreement. That way he would have felt like he was exerting his power. His power to say "no."

The situation had come to the point that Steve was dealing with a living horror. After a few minutes of being left alone, he started trembling and crying. Fear that he wouldn't be able to deal with the situation was taking him through the most serious changes. The situation had turned into a battle between him and Clyde and him and the system. Pride and his manhood were what he planned to stand on and keep. He didn't know if he could take it. But he planned to take all that he could until it killed him or drove him crazy.

He planned to file a lawsuit and for a speedy trial when he got back to his cell.

******

When Clyde saw Diana get out of her car and walk to the appropriate phone booth, he smiled. His star witness had arrived and was on time. He also took note that she was with the same guy. He didn't notice the car that drove up after them about two minutes later. The second car made a pass first to see if Diana got out of the car.

Clyde felt that he was safe from the camaraderie of Westlake Projects. Instead of calling the phone booth, he walked over to her and escorted her to the hotel entrance.

"I'm pleased to meet you Diana. My name is Mr. Coppedge." He was checking out every detail about her. The walk and facial expressions spoke the kind of confidence that made for a good witness.

"It's nice to meet you also. Can we get this over with?" She wasn't feeling that comfortable being alone with two white men. If they started drooling, she planned to start screaming. She shook his hand and smiled.

"Have a seat Ms.--" He had been working that much and that hard.

"It's Ms. Smiley." She pointed to a chair. "May I have a seat?"

"Sure, please sit down. We have a lot of work to do." She sat in the chair next to the desk. Coppedge sat on the bed, which was about two feet away and where he had his brief case. Clyde sat in the chair that was by the door.

"What is this test that y'all want me to take? I like things to be up front." She looked over at Clyde. "I'm sure y'all like the same thing."

"This is a very simple matter. But you may not be qualified." So far in his career, Coppedge hadn't put a bad witness on the stand – one of the keys to his successes.

"So if I'm able to do this, are you going to be able to provide me with what I asked for you?" When it came to her son, she wasn't about to take any chances.

"We'll definitely provide you with protection. We're working on the money. The application has been put in." Coppedge wouldn't be putting in the application until Monday, if he thought that she could handle the job.

"Mr. Coppedge, I don't like your answer. But let's get this test done." She didn't know that the way she answered, the question gave her points with him.

Coppedge reached into his briefcase and pulled out a seven page manuscript that detailed what they wanted her to testify to. "I want you to read this three times." She took it from him and started reading it. Clyde was liking what he was seeing and hearing.

Coppedge took out a legal pad and started writing questions that he would use for cross-examination if he were a defense attorney – something he should have done earlier. With his peripheral vision, he kept track of Diana's demeanor. Her not moving her lips while reading was a sign of good reading skills and perhaps good reading comprehension. He was also timing how long it took for her to read each page. Her rate was just over a minute and ten seconds. On the second and third times, she quickened her pace. Since it wasn't a drastic change, he felt that she was still actually reading. It took her juts over twenty minutes to finish.

Coppedge started her out with some introductory questions that had nothing to do with the situation. She sounded good and convincing and knew what to say. Coppedge starting pacing the width of the room. He was along side the bed that he was sitting on. She was putting the story back to him just like he had it written. After about twenty questions, she had completed that part of the task with flying colors. There were only slight improvements that had to be made. So far, she was a natural.

"You did well with that Ms. Smiley. Now cross-examination is the real test. Are you ready?"

"I don't see why not. I've seen a lot of Perry Mason shows." She looked at Clyde to see if he was still smiling. He was.

Coppedge started out by making the kind of introduction that a defense would make. She handled the questions with ease. With the next few questions, she started to crack a little bit. His tone was changing from friendly to aggressive. On a few questions, she felt like cursing him out. Though she didn't do it, her agitation was heard in her voice and seen in her face. She didn't think it would be that tough. To get that money, she did her best.

"Is that it? I thought you were going to ask me about the color of my underwear next." It was mandatory that she scream on him.

"That's how Shadika Jones is going to do you in the courtroom and on international television." Coppedge sat back down on the bed.

"So what about the test?" She almost said something about the trial being on television. She knew that the case was important, but not *that* important. She was thinking about changing her mind because the entire world would know that she had testified against somebody.

"You did good, but we are going to have to practice a lot. I do mean a lot."

"If I can't get $100,000 and my family relocated, I'm not going to do it." She looked at Coppedge. Coppedge looked at Clyde. Clyde looked at her. "That's a lot of abuse that I'm going to have to take. And on television."

Coppedge looked at her. His expression didn't resemble any negative thoughts. She couldn't have been a bit more serious. And she was still mad about the cross-examination.

Coppedge didn't have a lot of leverage. "I'll make sure that I get all that I can."

Clyde stood up. "I'll make sure that it all equals $100,000." Clyde wanted to make sure that there were as few complications as possible.

"I'd also like to move as soon as possible."

"I can make that happen in the next two weeks," Coppedge responded. "But we have to meet for at least twice a week." It was a matter of cleaning up her rough edges.

The rest of the meeting was about installments for the money to be paid. She could have boosted her price up to $200,000 and received it. Coppedge was feeling that good about her performance. So was Clyde. With fifty-two days to go, they were in accord and feeling good.

Chapter 13

Tyrone was in the law library on Monday morning at about eight-thirty when he heard, "Tyrone Taylor, report to R & D immediately."

In the law library, the P.A. system isn't that loud. He went into the library to see if anyone there had heard his name called. They confirmed that they had heard it. He made it through the hallway just before the compound was closed for the move.

After he got to the mailroom, he had to go down two more hallways to get to his destination. A split second after he walked through the door, he came to an abrupt stop.

"Mister Tyrone Taylor, you are under arrest for the murder of DEA Agent Larry Atkins." Clyde was playing with his handcuffs and grinning.

Tyrone quickly took the surprised look off of his face. That wasn't what he wanted Clyde to see. "So you plan to take me back to Ohio? You made this special trip for me?"

"I sure did." The complaint was filed on Friday, along with the indictment. Clyde read him his rights. "It won't be necessary for him to change his clothes. I'm in a rush."

This made things easier for the officers. They just patted Tyrone down to see if he had any weapons or contraband on him.

"Let him keep his legal material. He's going to need

them." Clyde cuffed him with his hands in front. "We're going to have a nice, long talk while we have this ride." He put Tyrone's note pads and legal papers in his hands. "Let's go."

Ordinarily, the shackles would have been put on Tyrone. Clyde would pay for him to start running or make an attempt to escape.

******

When I saw Clyde's face, I knew that there would be trouble. Ya know what. I'm not mad one bit. What else could he do but charge me? The prosecutor isn't going to want to try me with all the dirt that I have on Larry Atkins.

I was a little mad at first. Now that we are on the highway and moving, I don't feel that bad. It had taken me a few years to develop my thinking so that I can handle situations of this nature. It is a matter of simple math – if they can't convict Tina, how are they going to be able to convict me? With that settled, let me guess what he might be thinking.

It had to have been a spur-of-the-moment thing – like when he found out that I got a new trial. My new trial would be reason to give Tina, Shadika, and the community confidence. That's the last thing that they want.

Now I know that this clown isn't thinking that Tina or I is going to testify against the other. That isn't happening. But, of course, he'll try it. Maybe he also thinks that this is going to scare us and make Shadika slip.

On the real, this is better for me and Tina. As a co-defendant, I'll be right there and be able to coach each and every move that Shadika makes and assist her. What could be better? Plus, I'll be sitting right next to the lady that I love. Oh yeah. Now I don't have to wait to get a visit.

Now Clyde isn't thinking that I'm doing serious thinking. He figures that I'm just some big, dumb, black guy. He probably thinks that I'm helpless because Steve disappeared. I know that he had something to do with Steve disappearing like that. Steve's family hasn't even heard from him.

I'm looking at it like this. In less than ninety days, Tina and I are about to be free of all this federal trial mess. And it's only going to take a day for Tina's letters to get to me and vice versa.

Now, let me see how dumb and scared I can act for this blood thirsty cop.

******

It had been about five minutes that they'd been on the highway heading west. "So Clyde, why did you have to charge me with this?"

Clyde was still tired from all the drinking and drivinging that he had done over the weekend. It's what should have happened a long time ago."

"Wasn't I in prison when this murder took place?" Tyrone had to wonder why Clyde didn't resemble Atkins. He, at least, expected them to have the same beady eyes.

"That doesn't matter and I'm sure that you know this." How good Diana would be on the stand after she practiced for thirty days was the main thing on his mind.

"So what is the theory that you have?"

Clyde looked at him in the eyes. "You must truly think that you are going to beat this case. I know that you stay in the law library all the time. You didn't know that, did you?" Clyde wasn't knowledgeable enough about the law to know how to convict Tyrone. He changed the subject to keep from sounding weak.

"It doesn't surprise me that you know that. You probably know what time I go to bed and what my mail says." Steve had taught him the benefits of critical thinking and thinking like a cop or prosecutor.

"Yes, I do know a lot about you and Tina. It's part of my job." Now that the deal had been sealed with Diana, he wasn't placing as much significance on Steve. But he still planned to put all the pressure on Steve as possible. He planned to check if Steve had been transported yet.

For the entire ride, they talked and jived each other. Each felt that they had the upper hand.

******

"How did you get in my room?" Shadika hadn't seen Maurice in four days and hadn't returned any of his phone calls. She had also changed up her schedule and hotels to keep him from surprising her. Though she sounded mad and felt slightly insulted, she was happy to see him.

"It's simple. I told the bell boy that I was your husband. There is the possibility that we are still getting married, correct?" Maurice wanted to end the suspense.

"I want you to get out." She placed her briefcase and purse on the first bed.

Maurice hadn't taken his eyes off her eyes. He was searching to see if she meant what she had said. He got out of the chair and slowly approached her.

It seemed like it took an hour for him to walk seven feet. She did her best to maintain her gaze into his eyes. When he got to about a foot of her, she started batting her eyelashes. Her temperature rising made her step back a bit.

"Is this how you like to treat a man after you get his heart open? Just disappear and what not." He had let her have all the space that she wanted.

As usual, he said the right thing and got her attention. "That's almost an insult. Is it?" She wanted to delve into the part about his heart opening.

"You tell me what it should be. You are the one doing all the avoiding like a teenage girl."

She flexed her lips towards the ceiling and gritted her teeth. "I'm not a teenage girl. I just needed some time to myself." She walked around him so she wouldn't be trapped by the door.

Tina

"You could have told me if I made you mad. There - " She had grabbed him and gave him one of those kisses that stated one intention. He held her as tight as she was holding him.

"I missed you Maurice. I did need time to myself." She pulled his jacket, it dropped to the floor.

He picked her up and started carrying her to the couch. She kissed him all over his neck and face. He missed her just as much and didn't want to talk.

She felt foolish and thought of how dumb she had been being as she looked into his eyes. As she felt the couch, she grabbed his pants and started taking them loose. It excited her that much more feeling that he was just as excited.

"I don't have on any underwear. I was praying that you would show up." A female loves to see how bad a man wants her by seeing how far he'll go.

"Is it that serious?" What she said stroked his ego and turned him on. It was nice to know that he had made the right moves. He was pulling up her skirt to see if she was for real.

"I missed your touch Maurice. I need you inside of me." He had just positioned himself. "Oooh Maurice, it seems like forever. You feel so good inside of me." She had started getting moist from the moment that she had seen him.

"I missed you also." He was stroking fast like he hadn't had sex in years. "I couldn't take it any longer."

"Oh yes, that's it. You are such a good lover." She moved to the right for him to hit that spot again. "Yes, that's it."

"Shadika, I couldn't get you off my mind. That has never happened to me." He thought to himself if he meant what he had just said.

He had hit her mental spot. "I'm coming Maurice. Maurice. Maurice." They climaxed together.

Maurice had almost fallen out after that. He had just enough energy to make it to the chair and to pull his pants up.

Shadika felt like she had been given a new life. She was glad to be over with the feeling of wanting to see him and wanting to not see him.

Two hours later, they had eaten dinner and made love again. This time they used the bedroom.

It was nice, once again, to be lying on his chest and thinking about how things could be. She wasn't scared like she was before because she felt like she knew what she was dealing with. Instead of it being all up to him, it was all up to her.

"So, are you going to tell me what the problem was? I think that I have a right to know." He wouldn't have asked if his emotions hadn't been involved.

She kept playing with the hair on his chest.

"So, Shadika Jones, the great lawyer, is stuck for words. What's the problem?"

"Why do you have to keep challenging me?" She was spelling his and her name in his chest.

"I wouldn't have to act this way if I knew what was going on in your head. Playing with my feelings ain't happening."

She sat up and got comfortable next to him on the pillow. "Tell me about your feelings." What he had said during the first sexual episode was still fresh in her mind.

"No, Shadika. I'm not going to let you change the subject." He sat up a little straighter.

She sat up straight also. "I have some concerns about all the influence that you have in the community and what you may do with it." It had taken her days to figure out how to say it.

"Please say that again."

"We might have issues because you are a gangster." She crossed her arms.

He thought to himself that she had checked the public records to see what things he'd been investigated for. Asking her that though would seem very defensive.

144

Tina

"Let's just say that I'm a gangster. What is the problem supposed to be?"

"I'm scared that you might do the wrong thing to make the right thing happen and that may affect me." She had preferred to have this conversation after the trial was over.

Maurice hadn't prepared himself for this kind of situation. She was absolutely correct and he didn't feel like admitting it. At least not directly.

"Is there a chance that you might be exaggerating a bit? I served my time for my case."

She had to clear her throat on that. "You still think that I'm that teenage girl, huh?" She hoped that that would be enough.

"Maybe you need to explain what you mean."

"If it came down to kidnapping that girl to keep her from testifying, would you do that to keep Tina free?" She said this quickly to throw him off and get a quick answer.

"That's a rather interesting thought. Do I look like an evil dude?" Her expression was saying that there wasn't a right thing for him to say.

"I'm sure you can have it done. Some of these people would stop breathing if you told them to."

"By the way, since you brought this up, she met with Clyde at a hotel in Pennsylvania on Friday night. We can prove this. What does that mean to you?" This was the reason he made sure that he showed up tonight.

"How do you know that? You see what I'm talking about." She was still stuck on the other subject.

"Isn't Tina's case the most important thing here?" He got up and grabbed his pants out of the chair.

"Why do you always start putting on your clothes when we start talking about certain things?" Just like a lawyer, not missing a detail.

"I'm expecting you to ask me to leave at any minute. You don't seem to be thinking about Tina's case."

Letting him win for now wasn't a problem. "You are right Maurice. How do you know that they met?" She rubbed her left hand up against her thigh.

"Some people I know followed her and checked the hotel records. The hotel in Pennsylvania and it's not that far away." He would hit her with the rest later.

"That's rather strange. What would they go that far for? There has to be more to it than that." Her instinct told her to get up. She wanted to pace to think. She still wanted him to come back to bed.

"They were in the room for a very long time. Like three to four hours." This is the part when he had to decide if he would kidnap her or not.

"What do you know about her?" The key was to find an angle that would help her beat the case.

"I'm not that familiar with her. She hasn't lived in Westlake for a real long time and doesn't come to the Elk's. She's like an outsider that just lives there." He sat in the chair to wait for her conclusion.

"Off the top of my head, they are about to violate a discovery order. Coppedge said the other day that they did not have any eyewitnesses yet." There were many other things on her mind that she didn't mention, like perjured testimony and government misconduct.

"What can you do and what are you going to do?" Maurice sensed that she was right at making a great move.

She was tempted to bring to his attention how he had smoothly changed the subject. "It's interesting that she hadn't come forward until now. That has to be the key."

"Let me give you a little bit of information. A few weeks ago, she was at the club partying hard and spending quite a bit of money and wearing a brand new outfit. She had talked to Clyde and went to meet with him." He had wanted to give her that information before. Thinking that she might start tripping made him hold back. Since she had brought up the gangster thing, he felt that he might as well.

She squinted her eyes to the point that she almost showed her anger. "So you sound like you know that she's about to tell some lies." She didn't speak her mind because of the mission at hand. But she wouldn't forget.

"There is no doubt in my mind that she's going to lie if she takes the stand. But you are now ahead of the game and can deal with it." It had to be one of two things. If he didn't feel like she could make significant use of the information – then he planned to do what he had to do. Whether she approved or not didn't matter.

"If you have something concrete that I can show a jury then I can slam the entire case. Do you have that?" She knew exactly what to do if he provided what she thought he'd provide.

"I'll have what you want and more. Like I already told you, we have some stuff already. Does that mean that Tina is going to be safe?" He liked what he had heard.

"It should be an easy thing to do." She knew what she wanted to do. She didn't know if she'd be able to do it like she wanted to. "So now that we've resolved that, would you mind coming back to bed? I know that you aren't going to leave in the middle of the night."

In his eyes, she could see the gangster in him. It was like he was waiting like a cobra, ready to strike in an instant. His voice and body language told her that he was willing to do whatever to get Tina back to the streets. His intensity was turning her on as much as it was scaring her. She hadn't made up her mind if she'd be able to deal with his style of possibly handling the situation.

What he had provided – and would provide – had the potential of an acquittal. She decided to play her hand with finesse on two fronts. For the time being, she had to keep him convinced that she could win the case. This would keep him from committing a crime. She would also enjoy him until the trial was over with if that's as far as their relationship went.

At the least, she had to please her desire for him until it was time to make a major decision. She was pleased with her decision to wait because it was based on logic, though it had a lot to do with her being turned on.

******

I could just holler at the top of my lungs considering what the guard just told me. I can't believe they charged Tyrone with the same case that I have. There's no doubt in my mind that Clyde is serious, but not this serious. Hell, Tyrone was in jail when the murder occurred. There is nothing for them to be able to put on him.

Oh yeah, I'm emotional at this point. On one hand, I'm angry that he's being charged. On the other hand, I know that he can beat the case, though I don't know that much about the law. I should be laughing that they made a mistake.

Well, like I told you before, I love my man more than I love myself. I'm feeling like Clyde needs to have a few bullets put up in him also. He can't be happy with just killing me; he wants to kill my man also. If I had the chance, I'd show him how I feel about my man.

I'm just pissed. And to think that I was feeling good the other day. Now my man and I have got to beat this case.

Let me calm down and think. Spazzing right now is out of the question. Pacing this small space isn't helping me to calm down. All I can think about is what I'd like to do to Clyde. He deserves to die for the abuse of power that he has committed. I know that I'm wrong to think this way, but I can't help myself.

Okay, maybe Shadika is going to show up. She only has one case. She needs to get here before I walk myself to death. I would go to that crackhead across the hall, but she'd be so damn envious that I might end up going off on her.

Shadika, I need to talk to you. I need to talk to you now.

******

Tina

It was about five hours later that Shadika made it to the jail. She had called ahead of time so they'd let Tina know that she was coming.

"You don't look so cheerful, Ms. Thompson. It isn't as bad as it seems." She didn't bring any food because she figured that a woman in love wouldn't be in the mood to eat.

"It's bad. It's as bad as it can get. You must not know that they charged Tyrone with the murder also." She felt that it wasn't necessary to talk too loud.

"I know and that's why I'm here. Maurice called me and told me." She was suspicious that he knew so much.

"Why then--. Why does Clyde want to do this when we have forty-seven days before we go to trial?"

"Thanks for lowering your voice. It isn't as bad as it seems. They're just trying to scare us. They are going to charge him as an accessory after the fact and conspiracy. That's all hard to prove." Shadika had expected what they would charge him with long before they thought about it.

"How can you be so calm at a time like this?" If she had to explain why she asked the question, she would not have been able.

"I'm going to represent you and him. They don't have a good case against you. So they definitely don't have a good case against him." Part of being a good attorney meant dealing with a client's emotional side.

"That makes sense. I'm still scared."

"I understand and that's one of the reasons that I came to see you. I also have some very good news." Shadika was a little envious of the love that Tina had for Tyrone. Meeting Tyrone was a must.

"I need some good news. Tell me. Tell me." Her patience was nonexistent.

"Tyrone is in this building and I'm going to make it so that you can see him."

"Stop playing Shadika." She was thinking to herself that she wasn't ready to see him. She wished that she could do something to make herself look better – at least get her hair done.

"I'm serious and I have some news that's even better." Shadika felt like her mission was almost complete.

"You just told me about a fantasy. What else is there that you can tell me?" The thought of hearing two pieces of good news back to back made her suspicious.

"They have a witness and I have the drop on her. If she takes the stand, I'm going to get a murder charge." She had done enough research to be sure that the trial was in the pocket.

"Stop Shadika."

"That gangster of mine did all the investigating. I did the most important part today. Be ready to go home." Shadika had a smile that said she was ready to go to war.

"I told you that Maurice loves his people. You got to marry him. Y'all are perfect for each other." She could see them walking down the aisle.

Shadika smiled and laughed. "I must admit that he has made a difference in my life and this case." She was uncertain about the rest.

"I know that if you would just accept him for being him – that y'all would be great together." A woman can tell when another woman is experiencing something good with a man. "When I see him, I'll be thanking him."

"Okay Tina. I have to get Tyrone in here so that I can talk to him too. You be good. His preliminary hearing is going to be in the morning. The both of y'all are going to be there in the morning."

"For what?" She didn't exactly care. She was excited about getting to see Tyrone.

"You'll see when you get there. Just be cool."

Tina

Tina left the visit feeling like a brand new woman. Shadika had told her more than she had wanted to hear. Because of the way that Shadika had been acting, Tina had to believe in everything that was said. Having that kind of confidence in one's attorney can make all the difference, especially for an emotional person. Tina's frame of mind went to worrying about something else.

Knowing that she would be seeing Tyrone in less than eighteen hours had her happy and nervous. Going to the beauty salon wasn't a possibility. Neither was getting a new outfit nor some make-up. He'd have to see her in the raw. Though she was a naturally, good-looking female, she wanted to look her best for her man. It didn't have a thing to do with whether he loved her or not. It was about keeping his attention by keeping him happy, pleased, seduced, and desiring her.

"They just had your boyfriend on the news. I thought that you'd like to know." Joann had just lit up a Newport with an old one. The guard had just opened Tina's cell door.

Tina waited until the guard left. "I know. It's going to be okay. So what is up with you?" The last few times that they had talked, Joann had complained about how her attorney never came to see her.

"I was just thinking that maybe you needed to talk about the situation. I know I'd be stressed if my lover was charged with murder." Joann had grown so bitter that she wasn't able to hide it.

"Shadika just told me that it would be okay. She's going to represent the both of us."

"So you think she's going to be able to beat the case?" She was doing her job for Clyde and Coppedge.

"She talks like it and I have no reason to think that she's lying." Nothing in the world let her tell Joann the truth or any of her business. She knew that they let her out a little bit too much for sick call.

"I asked because the news made it sound like Tyrone had you kill Larry Atkins." She put her little twist to it.

"Most of the time they do that. They made me sound like the most infamous female to come out of Ohio." She was thinking how nice it would be to have Tyrone across the hall from her, instead of Joann.

"They do have a tendency to do that. I hope that she beats the case for both of y'all. I wish I could pay her to be my lawyer." Joann was trying her best to be nice so that she could get some useful information.

"Shadika seems to be really busy these days. But I'll see what she says later on." Tina was saying something nice just to return the comment.

"You'd do that for me?" She took a puff off her cigarette.

"I got you. For now, I need to get some rest. I have a lot of things on my mind." Tina stepped away from the door.

Joann had intentions of getting inside of Tina's head. If she could only get her to say something about the murder, things would be lovely. Joann didn't know exactly what she'd get for the information, but she knew that she'd be getting something.

Tina was overwhelmed by all that had happened in the last week. She had been up and down the emotional spectrum. On a daily basis, she had been thinking about what it would be like to be strapped to that gurney. This was one of the thoughts that she wasn't able to keep out of her head. Whenever she saw a crime show on television, it reminded her about her situation. On the days that she felt confident that she'd beat the case, she still thought about the possibility of death.

But there was no fear. There was no "let's prolong this thing so that I can live longer." Tina had it naturally built in her to deal with whatever. It's not a matter of wanting to die. It was recognizing what was at stake and accepting the consequences without backing down. What mattered was that Tyrone loved her as much as she loved him. Tina's love had that much value.

There was no doubt in her mind that she'd die for him and kill for him. Of course, with the preference of being with him until the both of them were old and gray.

The largest of her emotions was nervousness. She would soon see the man that she had given her heart, mind, body, and soul to. She had visions of them sitting at the defense table together. She was in a rush to go to trial.

******

Shadika forgot her manners when Tyrone walked into the room. She couldn't help but wonder what Tyrone was made of. It was a matter of intrigue, not attraction.

"Are you okay Shadika? I'm Tyrone." He put his hand out.

She stood up and shook his hand while looking deep into his eyes. "I'm sorry. My mind went to another place. Please sit." Her thoughts went to her relationship with Maurice.

"I hope that you plan to represent me along with Tina. There isn't going to be a conflict of interest." He was pretty sure that Clyde had an attorney waiting to get appointed to his case – an appointed attorney that would sell him out.

"That's exactly what I plan to do, Mr. Taylor. That's why I called you in here." She appreciated how he put things in a legal perspective. Hearing him say something of that nature impressed her more than what he wrote about the Witness List. If she could get Maurice to speak in those kinds of terms, it would be nice.

"That means that Tina and I should be free in a matter of months. Why do you think that they charged me?" Tyrone was thinking about the good vibe he was getting from Shadika.

"They got mad because they know that you are going to beat the drug charge. There were a lot of bad things that came out about Atkins. We all know that you are going to beat it. I'll make sure that you beat it." It was mandatory that she handle that also.

"You are going to hold us down like that?" It was more of a statement than a question.

"Yes, Mr. Taylor, I'm going to see you through this." She was feeling him on the strength that he was doing the right thing when it came to Tina. It was just that rare of a thing.

"I was thinking would it be possible if I was placed at a BOP Institution so that I'll be able to do some legal research." So far, he had no idea of what was necessary to prove Conspiracy to Murder (18 U.S.C. 1111).

She was thinking that he could make a good paralegal. Knowing that he wasn't the most intelligent big man, she was impressed even more. "That's a good idea. Do you have anything else on your mind?" She had given him a certain amount of respect.

"No. I'm good. I just want to do what I can."

"I understand."

"I can see why Tina thinks so much of you. You act like a lawyer is supposed to act. I appreciate what you are doing for us." Tyrone felt like he was about to have a title bout with a thirty million dollar purse and he was favored to win in the third round.

"You may not believe this, but y'all are doing just as much for me. In the morning, they are going to have your preliminary hearing. Do you have any suggestions in the matter?" She wasn't expecting him to have much to say about a simple hearing.

"Tell me this first." Shadika nodded her head. "What is up with the witness list and them having a witness?" He was rubbing his chin to assist in his thought process.

"They haven't turned over a witness list yet and we aren't expecting them to. But we know who the main witness is going to be." She just wanted him to keep asking questions like that.

Tyrone grinned at the results of his work. "This witness must be getting ready to tell some lies on my lady. Witnesses just don't pop up eighteen months later."

"We already have a bomb to drop on them if they use her. This should be real simple. She certainly can't say that she met you." Shadika had just come up with her next move, which would be made at his preliminary hearing.

"That sounds like a winning strategy. All we need is a jury that isn't racist and biased towards police officers and we'll all be happy."

The rest of their discussion was short and to the point. It's like that when a defendant has an understanding about what's happening, especially if he knows that he can win.

Though Tyrone hadn't realized it, being in prison had done him a lot of good. He was wiser, more mature, smarter, more responsible, and disciplined. When a person's freedom is on the line and they look at it as a matter of survival, things happen. Tyrone had dug in as deep as he could; starting the day he arrived in the federal prison. Other than having to do homework for his G.E.D., he hadn't done a lot of reading. Reading law books was extremely difficult when he started.

After reading for about an hour, he would get a headache when he started. As he pushed forward, he extended the time to two hours – then three – then four. Soon, he didn't have any headaches and started to enjoy reading law materials.

All of the reading and thinking had made Tyrone into a new man. His pay off was the moment he was experiencing. It felt good to him to be able to understand what was happening. It didn't matter that he had to ask a lot of questions at times. What mattered was that he got to where he was going. Wisdom and common sense had gotten many further than intelligence and talent.

Tyrone feeling good made Shadika feel good. Forty-seven days to go before the trial.

Chapter 14

Steve had been placed in the one-two day program. He wouldn't be spending any more than one-two days at any locations. So far, he'd been traveling for a week. The first night he was in Oklahoma; the second in Tallahassee, Florida; the third in Marianna, Florida; the forth back to Tallahassee; the fifth in Butner, North Carolina; the sixth in Petersburg, Virginia; and finally Lewisburg Penitentiary. The only inmates that he got to see were the ones he rode the buses with. They intentionally put him on the bus with people headed to camps or going to another camp. He'd be the only inmate on the bus with handcuffs and shackles. Not a very good feeling.

Steve was placed in a cell with a guy who looked like a homicidal maniac. He weighed about four hundred pounds and smelled like he hadn't taken a bath in a month. Steve was slightly relieved that he was still sleeping; even hours after Steve had been placed in the cell. Steve had no choice but to think about all the horror stories he'd heard about penitentiaries.

With the smell, he had to deal with the heat that was coming from a steam pipe that was located in the corner across from his bed. For fear that the guy might wake up, he wouldn't open the window.

It was tough to lie there and think about pleasant things. There was nothing to do but think. It would have been nice to be able to get his hands on a book, just to keep his mind occupied. Just lying there was the worst part about the situation. Boredom ends up being the worst thing that can happen to a prisoner, especially a prisoner in the hole.

A mind can run rampant when there's a combination of boredom and fear. Steve started to imagine what he'd do if the big man woke up and started assaulting him. He was hoping the yelling would cause the guards to get there before he was pounded to death or raped.

Clyde's offer started to come to his mind also. The activeness of his thinking had sped up to the point that he started sweating. Most of the time, he had been in the hole by himself. Being lonely and alone all the time was also having an affect on him. He would have talked to some of the inmates on the buses if he thought they would have understood what he was going through. If he asked any of them to contact his family, they would have probably thought that he was going crazy. If word got back to one of the guards, then they might send him to the psychologist. Getting medicated would be disastrous – a new fruitcake.

He had to think about giving in. The vision of him testifying made him sit up in the bed. If he had been in a room alone, he would have screamed. He was mad with himself for having that thought, though it was a thought that he had to have because it was the only way that he could be relieved from his condition.

He would have put his feet over the side of his bed if he hadn't been scared of the man underneath him. Instead, he looked out the window, into the darkness, where there was nothing but a chain link fence and a fifty-foot wall. Just for a millisecond, he thought he saw Clyde's face and heard his voice.

Tina

With his hands pressed together in front of his chin, just below his lips, he started to pray. He asked God for the strength to endure the mental torture and for it to all end soon. He said the same thing, silently, for about twenty minutes. He added a part in there about keeping his sanity.

Some time in the midst of praying, he fell asleep on his knees. He woke up at the break of dawn when they called him out of the cell. He tip-toed out like he had gotten away with his life.

******

United States v. Tyrone Taylor had the world's attention. Though it was only a preliminary hearing, media were interested in letting people see Tyrone live, at least for a few seconds. The popularity of the case had grown since Tina's arrest. When Tyrone got arrested, things had already shot up to another level.

Cameras and microphones had been placed in every possible spot of the courtroom. It was a matter of people wanting to know who Tina supposedly killed the cop over.

Shadika intentionally had Tina brought into the courtroom first because she wasn't the main attraction for this hearing. Though she wasn't for sure, she figured Coppedge would have a press conference before the preliminary hearing. This also meant that she planned to use the publicity to her advantage, just as Coppedge had planned.

Clyde and Coppedge walked into the courtroom with smiles on their faces. The night before, they had tested Diana again in a grueling cross-examination session. She almost had the act down pat. If the U.S. Attorney's office in Washington, D.C., approved to relocate her, they planned to move her and her family by Monday. The money issue had been taken care of in Ohio. The U.S. Attorney's office in Ohio would give her $50,000. Clyde would take care of the rest. She'd get $25,000 when she was moved. The rest would be provided if a conviction was obtained or it wasn't her fault if one wasn't obtained.

When she was moved, Coppedge planned to submit the witness to Shadika.

******

Now, we have to stop the press and whatever else, put the tape on pause, and show our respects. My man just walked into the courtroom.

He's wearing a dark brown, pinstriped suit that fits him to perfection. I mean like it was tailor made. I can't forget about the light brown, silk tie and light brown, silk handkerchief to match. To make everything just perfect for the situation, he has a writing pad in his hand.

Just seeing him makes me have the hooey-gooey feeling all over and getting moist by the second. And he's wearing a smile that looks so sexy that if it wasn't for me that I'll be jealous.

If I could get up and run out of the room, I would. A female can't stand for her man to look sexier than her. I have a nice, dark blue, skirt outfit on that isn't doing my any justice. If I had just a little bit of make-up on, I'd feel better. It's a good thing that I'm a natural beauty that can shine with just a few tricks with Vaseline. A little Vaseline and water can do wonders if you have something to work with. I feel bad for those scarred chicks.

Though I feel a little less than up-to-par, I'm still going to enjoy my man like we were free.

All eyes are on him and he's about to sit down. Here we are, live on television, and we can't stop smiling at each other. I guess that's just how it is when two people are in love with each other. We're acting like there's nobody else in the courtroom. I don't care and I'm sure that he doesn't care either.

Damn, he's almost to the table. I have to make a decision. I want to get up and just hold him for a few seconds, but I don't want to embarrass myself, my man, or Shadika. Humph. Forget all of that. I don't care if the world knows how I feel about him. In fact, I want them to know.

Tina

I'm doing this real casual-like. I'm getting ready to just shake his hand. All of the onlookers just started looking at me. So what. He just walked past the prosecution table. When he gets close to the table, I'll put my hand out. He put his hand out when I put my hand out.

He's on my side of the table and we're about to touch hands. His brown eyes are so beautiful. The touch of his hand is sending chills throughout my body. I'm paralyzed and I can feel my mouth hanging open. It feels like I've died and gone to heaven.

I can't believe that he's kissing me right here on television, without any regards to what's happening. Naturally, I kiss him back.

Damn, I wish that he hadn't done this. Now, all I can think about is having that big thang of his going in and out of me. If Shadika hadn't told us to stop and sit down, the marshals might have made a scene. Then again, what could they have done? Give us some more charges.

It's nice to be sitting to his left and holding his hand. Let them do what they like. I have my man by my side.

******

Tina and Tyrone didn't know that they had boosted up a lot of people's confidence. That show of affection had caused many observers to take their side in the case.

Many were thinking that she had to have done it if she had that much love for him. Coppedge was thinking in the same vein. He had to tell Clyde this to keep him calm.

"All rise," the bailiff hollered.

Judge Grumpfree entered slowly with a smile on her face. She had watched the show in her chambers. She had been waiting for Tyrone to enter and be seated.

"You may all be seated."

Judge Grumpfree looked around the courtroom to get a good feel of the situation. What was happening in her courtroom was the talk of the town already. "So good morning, Ms. Jones. Good morning, Mr. Coppedge. We might as well get down to business." She read the charges in the complaint: Conspiracy to Commit Murder; Accessory after the fact; and, Misprision of a Felony. Tyrone was the only one still standing along with Shadika. "How does the defendant plead?"

"The defendant pleads not guilty." This was to be expected.

Next, Coppedge went over some of the evidence that supported the charge. Shadika already knew that Judge Grumpfree wasn't inclined to throw the charges out at this stage. Thus, she laid back a little bit with her argument. All the complications that could have gone with her argument would have worn out the court's attention and taken attention from her main objective.

"I feel that there is enough evidence to take Mr. Taylor to trial." Judge Grumpfree was extremely interested in how the defense and case would be presented. It was a rather close call. Very little would still make her spoil the show. "Are there any other matters that need to be taken care of Mr. Coppedge?" She wasn't expecting him to say anything.

"Yes, there is your Honor." Her ruling had given him the impression that he was back in her favor to some degree. "I motion that Shadika Jones not be allowed to represent Mr. Taylor because of a possible conflict of interest." Shadika, along with Tina, cut their eyes at Coppedge. Tyrone sat with Tina.

"Please present your argument Mr. Coppedge." It was a matter she would have had to resolve if he hadn't brought it up.

"Ms. Thompson and Mr. Taylor are charged with different charges that pertain to the same act. Surely their defenses are going to be different and could possibly cause Ms. Jones to favor one client over the other. Under the Sixth Amendment, a conflict of interest could cause the trial to be overturned. I'm sure your Honor doesn't want that." This was somewhat a fishing expedition. He was hoping that he could find a way to have another attorney appointed to represent Tyrone. Preferably, an attorney that owed him a favor.

"I appreciate your bringing that to my attention, though I had put some thought into it already." Judge Grumpfree wasn't about to let a prosecutor make her look like an inept judge on television. She was being nice because of the cameras. "Ms. Jones, what do you have to say about this matter?"

"My clients and I have already discussed this matter in depth. They insist that I represent the both of them and they are ready to waive any future arguments concerning a conflict of interest." Shadika was going to mention it, if they hadn't, so that Coppedge wouldn't be able to do something dirty.

Judge Grumpfree looked at Tina and Tyrone. She paused on the thought that they might be holding hands under the table. "Would you two please stand up?" The way that their arms parted told her that she was correct. She read them a boilerplate waiver about having the same attorney. This stated that they understood their rights and they waived all their arguments that could possibly come up concerning a conflict of interest. She made herself look very professional the way she had handled it. It was easy to see that she was prepared. Tina and Tyrone waived their rights with smiles on their faces.

"Does the prosecution have any other matters that need my attention?" Judge Grumpfree had a pretty good idea of what was about to happen.

"No, the government doesn't have any other matters of concern. Maybe the defense does." He looked towards Shadika like they had been friendly adversaries for the longest.

"Yes, I have reasons that I can't reveal to the court that Mr. Taylor have a separate trial from Ms. Thompson. It's rather suspicious that they decided to try him all of a sudden. All of this comes under Rule 14 and 8 of the Federal Rules of Criminal Procedure." Shadika had laid a seed with the statement about the government possibly doing something slick.

Judge Grumpfree wanted to ask her about what she knew. Instead, she preferred to experience the surprise and suspense. "It's your turn, Mr. Coppedge." Inside she was laughing at him because she could see he had taken some bait.

"Your Honor, I think that Shadika Jones plans to have two shots at the apple. Both cases have the same evidence. There will be no prejudice in both defendants being tried together. In fact, it's this court's practice to try co-defendants together." Judge Grumpfree would have to agree. "If she has evidence of the prosecution doing some kind of wrong doing, then we urge her to bring it forward. We intend to give her a speedy trial as she asked for. If she likes, we can have the trial in two weeks." He thought that he was being slick.

Coppedge took what she had said as a sign of weakness. With a star witness and a back-up witness, he felt like they had an advantage. He had to take the chance of making himself look good while making her look bad. Clyde was at the table shaking his head. He could taste blood.

"Umm." Judge Grumpfree hummed into the microphone, making sure that she was heard. "Ms. Jones, do you have anything that you'd like to say?" This was the kind of action that she wanted.

Shadika smiled – then looked at her clients. To let them know that she was in control, she winked her eye at them. "Your Honor," she said and paused and looked around to make sure that all eyes were on her. "If it isn't a problem, would you schedule *this* trial in two weeks for both defendants, just as Mr. Coppedge just motioned for? We are ready to proceed today, if necessary."

Tina

Things had gone far better than she had expected. She had worked him without him knowing that he had been tricked.

"The motion is granted. Trial will begin in two weeks from today." She knew that Shadika had a trick, but that was something that she hadn't expected. "This session is over."

Coppedge could have hollered that he hadn't made a motion, but that would have made it look like he was backing down. All he could see was that he had an advantage. Plus, his ego had been salved. Because Clyde was in a rush, he was excited and felt that the sooner the better.

The media were hard to explain to what had just happened. Some were saying that the defense had the advantage. Some were saying the same for the prosecution. All of them had different theories about what had happened and what would happen next.

Shadika looked at Coppedge and laughed about how she had used his male ego against him. She had accomplished several things at one time. She had them feeling like they had the case won. She had set the stage for what she had planned for the trial – one hell of a surprise. She had also put the press on them again by forcing them to present their witness a little sooner.

*****

I just got to kiss my girl. I just got to hold her hand and talk in her ear. I just had the chance to see some of the slickest legal maneuvering that I have ever seen. Shadika had to explain it all to me.

She's so far ahead of the game that she knows who the key witness is going to be. She also knows everything about the witnesses. I couldn't ever think to ask how she came up with all the information. If she says that she has it – then she has it. And I don't care how she got it. I just can't wait to see her use it.

You see, I knew that she was up to something when she said that she suspected that the government might do something dirty. If a person doesn't know anything about the law, he might have thought she was tripping. She just threw something out there to be saying something. She's the kind of lawyer to have something fully investigated when she presents a motion. And you have to understand that I'm not the kind of man to underestimate a female, like Coppedge or Clyde. They underestimated the wrong female. I'm glad that she's our attorney.

Now I have to talk about my lady. My lady and I are facing the death penalty together. I would never say that she's a soldier because she's way more than that. She's a female general and though she's that, she respects my position as a man. I think that we have an unheard of relationship.

When I saw her today, I realized that I didn't know how much love I have for her. If I could, I'd take the death penalty and let her go free, though I feel confident that Shadika is going to beat the case. What can I say? That's just the way I feel.

Now half of you cats would be down for using and abusing a female like her. I don't know what that is, but it isn't love. If any of y'all ever get to experience the kind of love that I have for her – then you'll understand that there isn't any turning back.

Tina and I had to be made for each other. There just isn't any other way that I can explain it. All the other females that I had didn't know how to keep my attention and motivate me to do certain things.

I love the most how she handled the Atkins situation. She kept emphasizing to me, on a daily basis, how much she loved me and didn't care about the situation. She told me everything that she could think of to make me feel good. She told me she understood that I needed some kind of redemption for what Atkins had done. I felt like a little boy because it happened right in front of her and in front of her house.

Even after I went to prison, she was right there each and every step of the way. I mean she just wouldn't give up. It was like she stayed mad at me for not upholding my end of our relationship. I didn't think that a woman could stay in a relationship with an incarcerated man. She taught me differently and so many other things. I'd be a fool to not return her love. She has definitely proven herself to me. It doesn't hurt that she's all of it when it comes to sex. I mean the best pussy that I've ever had.

When we beat these cases, I'm going to make her feel like she's the most special female in the world. I plan to stay on top of her like she's been staying on top of me. Us beating these cases will be my redemption. With Shadika, how can we lose?

Chapter 15

Ten police cars came up in Westlake Projects like there was some kind of terrorist attack. Everything came to a pause to see who was about to get arrested. Most figured that there was about to be a drug bust.

Diana was looking out of her window just like the rest of the people in her building. She was surprised when she saw them surround her building. She was even more surprised when they busted her door down. They escorted her out of Westlake like she had done something. They even put the handcuffs on her to make it look good. Her son was at her mother's house. If she had known what was happening, she wouldn't have been acting a total fool. She cursed at all of the cops. Many of her neighbors did the same thing.

She calmed down a little bit when they got her in the car. She was still a little upset because she didn't know that this was going to happen. When she saw Clyde, she'd have some very serious words for him.

While all of this was happening at her spot, the same thing happened at her mother's house.

Coppedge and Clyde had agreed that they had to take every precaution and make sure that nothing went wrong. That meant getting her out of Westlake and training her every day to get as close to perfection as possible. What Shadika had said may have meant that they knew who the witness would be. They figured that she was bluffing, but they had no way of knowing what she had on her mind.

By the end of the day, they'd have Diana and her family in the Witness Protection Program.

******

"Oh boy, did you show off today." It was about five o'clock in the evening when Maurice arrived at Shadika's hotel suite. He hadn't walked in the door yet.

She just stepped to the side to let him in. This was a side of him that she hadn't seen. If he wanted to express himself, she would just let him do that. As she walked in suite, she paid attention to all details about his body language to assess his temperament.

He went and sat in the chair.

She approached him with her hands behind her back to be humble. He definitely had something on his mind. She was looking directly into his eyes. He was looking into the distance as if she wasn't really there. She parted his knees and stepped in between them with the intention of sitting. He was still looking into the distance. She sat in his lap and hugged his neck.

"The Maurice that I know would say why he's mad with me." She started gently kissing him in his right ear.

There was a bridge that he needed to cross with her. It wasn't that easy with all the things that were happening, including their relationship. "I wish that you would have told me what you had planned to do." He stuck his right hand behind his neck.

She stopped kissing his chin and looked straight up at the ceiling. "So my man wants to approve my legal strategies." She wanted to find a way to change the subject. What he said didn't fit well with what she was made of.

"The police just picked up Diana, along with her mother and son." Maurice was having a dilemma: He wanted her to know exactly what was on his mind and for them to have a meeting of the minds. He knew that it would be a monumental task – really, impossible.

"I love you Maurice. Let's not go in that direction at this minute." She hugged him as tight as she could.

He stood up and took her over to the couch. "Sit on the couch. We have to talk." He placed her on the couch and sat back down in the chair.

What he had just done was right up there with things that would insult a female's womanhood. She took her hair loose to let it hang. With her feet on the carpet and her hands by her sides and pushing up on the couch cushions, she looked at him with a caring look.

When she looked at him, he looked up at the ceiling. It was a unique situation. Here was the lady that he had adored all his life and he just needed her to understand what he was all about. The closer that it got to the trial, the more intense the situation got. If he didn't have feelings for her, it would be easy for him to be able to communicate with her.

"I need to know what you have planned for the trial and what you plan to do when it comes to the case." He wasn't sure if this method was the right course.

She put her head down just a little bit and leaned forward. "Is this about this case or is it about Shadika Jones answering to Maurice? Please tell me." She had experienced this with many men and had quickly departed with them. She didn't want it to happen that way with him – at least not yet. Being less than the woman than she is was out of the question.

"It's not about Shadika answering to me. I have far too much respect for you and that isn't going to change." Maurice didn't want to say that he had intentions of committing a crime, if needed. He just wanted to make it so he wasn't hindered by her actions. There was no way for him to say that directly. "I feel that we are supposed to be a team. Can a man feel left out?"

She looked to the side and started moving her head up and down. She felt that she could go for what he had just said and be peaceful or she could delve deeper into the issue.

"Maurice, I love you and care about you and have much respect for you. This is the first time I feel that you aren't being straightforward with me. I can't deal with that. Please say what's on your mind." It was a matter of them being able to communicate about things – meaning anything and everything.

It seemed that not saying what was on his mind would cause as much of a problem as saying what was on his mind. She wasn't the kind of woman that he could just say anything to. Nor could he not say a thing.

"I just need you to do one thing." He stood up. "I'd appreciate it if you kept me in the loop about what your moves are going to be."

She was getting ready to ask him why when she saw his body turn and head towards the door. She didn't know what to make of him walking out like that.

Shadika crossed her legs up under her so she could make a decision of what to do and what to think. What had happened was one of the things that she wanted to avoid – not that she was specifically thinking about him walking out. She knew that he wanted to have that control of making sure Tina and Tyrone didn't get convicted. If he was mad about Diana being picked up by the police, it meant that he had intentions of kidnapping her.

Shadika didn't try to bring these things up in their conversations because she didn't know how to make things work. Her plan had been to handle the trial and take it from there with him.

She had come to accept that he was a gangster, but she would never let that or anything else dictate how she did her job.

Though she wanted him to come back so that she could

love him and all other kinds of things, she chose to remain focused on her first priority. She understands that a man's pride could make him act certain ways at certain times.

Maurice rode around Youngstown trying to clear his head. He didn't like that he wasn't in control of the situation, especially when lives were at stake. He had vowed that Tina wouldn't get executed. He felt that he had been in total control until Diana got picked up. Kidnapping her was what he had planned to make sure the prosecutors didn't have a chance. Now that he couldn't do that, he was mad at Shadika and feeling desperate to find a solution.

Not being able to tell her what was on his mind had him frustrated as well. Maurice was holding himself solely responsible for what happened to the people in Westlake. Tina was his special project.

It was a matter of his emotions getting the best of him. If Shadika was the kind of female that would accept that he was a gangster and what he might do if he had to, things would be easy. Instead, he knew that she'd do her best to make sure that he didn't do anything to scar her reputation. Convincing her to compromise her ethics wasn't something he'd try to do.

With all of this in his head, he also had his feelings for her to deal with. He had adored her for his entire life and she had turned out to be far more than he could have imagined. She was definitely the one. The one that he had to wife.

It was a big thing in the community that they were having a big romance. He kept telling people that it was just a thing that would end when she decided to leave town. He was going to make sure that she didn't leave town again.

One way or another, he was going to have to explain himself to her. He also knew the sooner the better. He wasn't the kind that would let the lack of communication spoil a wonderful relationship. Nobody had to argue to him that the problem was within him, not her. She was doing all the things that she was supposed to.

Tina

******

"Steve, you look like you've been dragged through the mud." Clyde had Steve at FCI Elkton – a federal joint in Ohio.

Steve had a black eye, a swollen lip, and a concussion to the head. His life had barely been saved when they had him in U.S.P. Lompoc in Lompoc, California. Steve didn't have a chance with the lunatic that they had put him in the cell with. If they hadn't thought that the guy was going to kill him, they would have let him get raped – the original plan.

"Let me tell you a little secret, Steve. We've charged your man with Conspiracy to Commit Murder and Accessory after the Fact. He's going to trial in two days." Clyde didn't want him to testify as badly as the last time they had met.

Steve was trying his best to stop shaking. There was nothing that he could do. The near-death experience had left him psychologically damaged as well. A lot of what he was dealing with was shock. Five punches to the head on a metal toilet, from a muscle bound man weighing two-fifty, have serious implications.

"We have a star witness that is going to send Tina and Tyrone to their deaths. She's going to make about $100,000 and get relocated. We could have done the same thing for you. You fool."

Steve felt like he was past the point of no return. He felt that he had endured the worst of it. If he had possessed the strength, he would have spit in Clyde's face. He still had a headache from two days ago and all he felt like doing was sleeping.

"Wake the fuck up. I'm talking to you." Since Clyde was feeling nasty, he slapped Steve with a hard right hand. Steve fell to the floor like he was dead. A few seconds after his head hit the floor, he was dead.

Clyde hollered at him for about five minutes thinking that Steve was faking. When he kicked him a few times, he knew that something was wrong. There was no pulse.

Clyde's father had taught him exactly how to handle these situations. He'd say that Steve fell out of the chair while they were talking if any questions were asked. Since it happened in a prison, there would be very few questions.

Clyde called the guard that was waiting outside the door and headed to another part of the prison to check out what Tyrone had been up to. As he had expected, Tyrone spent most of his day in the law library. This didn't surprise Clyde. He just checked up on him because he could.

As far as Clyde was concerned, all things were just perfect. He didn't really care about Steve not helping him. In his opinion, Diana had worked out perfectly. She had come to the point that she was able to anticipate what the next question would be. Clyde wished that the trial would start the next day. It was time for a few drinks.

******

Shadika had been doing nothing but researching the law that pertained to her defense strategies for the entire week. Tyrone had been of great assistance and she had visited him a few times.

"Since the trial is a week from today, I had to come check up on you. What's happening Tina?" Shadika was pretty close to being exhausted.

"I'm good. I've just been reading, writing, and watching television. They are really making a big deal about this. That makes me a little nervous." She was still looking forward to sitting next to her man and holding hands.

"I need you to look at this witness list." She had gone to Coppedge's office to get it. She did that instead of filing another motion to let him know that she had that much spunk. By the way he had laughed, she could tell that it had worked.

"This Joann is the female that's downstairs with me. That

bitch is trying to get a time cut off of me? I knew that she was trifling." Tina passed the list back to Shadika before she balled it up.

"Just calm down. Tell me a few things about her. I already know that she's up for murder." Shadika wasn't going to take the witness for granted just because she was charged with a murder charge.

"She's a crackhead that smokes cigarettes all day. I've always wondered how she's able to keep all those cigarettes and she'll have to lie. What am I getting mad about?" Tina was thinking about what she'd do to her if she had the chance.

"It's real simple, just like you just said. She's going to say that you admitted the murder to her. It's nice to know that she smokes cigarettes in a smoke-free jail." She had a hunch she needed to investigate.

"So that means that Steve is going to say the same thing about Tyrone?" She didn't want to believe that Steve would go out like that.

"Don't worry about that. My investigator found out that Steve died in the same prison that Tyrone is in right now." Shadika knew that Steve's name was put there as a diversion and a scare tactic, or both.

"Whoa, that was Tyrone's best friend in prison. Did you tell Tyrone? He must know because he was there." Thinking about Joann testifying against her made her emotional.

"From what I gather, Steve had been in the hole there. I understand why. I'll speak with his family when I get the information." If she called, it would be out of general principle just to see what could be scratched from the surface.

"Well, I'm not worried at all. Tyrone told me in a letter that y'all have put the case under a microscope. So what's happening with you and Maurice?" She planned to tell Joann a few lies to have fun with the prosecution.

Shadika took a few seconds to think. Maurice's name changed her demeanor. It was a look that spoke of uncertainty.

"Damn, Shadika. Is it that bad?" She wished that she hadn't asked.

"I shouldn't tell you this, but he got upset with me because they put Diana in the Witness Protection Program. We haven't talked in a week." She had hoped that he would come around in a few days.

"Maurice is definitely out of his character. By the time that this trial is over, I'm sure that y'all will be on the best of terms again." If it were possible, she would definitely call Maurice and give him a piece of her mind. As a female, she felt that it had to be his fault.

"I've been thinking that Maurice and I don't mix."

"Stop Shadika. What are you talking about? I know that you aren't going to give up just like that. Y'all just need to talk it out and get it together."

"That's the main problem. He didn't want to tell me what was on his mind. I can't see myself dealing with that." Shadika didn't mind talking with her about it, but she preferred waiting until after the trial to deal with him.

"Can I make a suggestion?"

"Go ahead."

"Girlfriend, I care about you and him. I want to see y'all together. He's a gangster and gangsters do what they do." Shadika leaned back in her seat as she sat up. "I'm sure that he can accept you for what you are. You have to let him know that you accept him for what he is."

"That means that I have to accept the consequences of his actions. I'm not a gangster. Why should I suffer?" Shadika had thought about it from every possible angle. Love didn't pan out to be worth the possible fall out.

"Maybe it isn't as bad as you put it. What do you think could happen?"

Tina

Shadika crossed her right leg over her left. "Suppose he had kidnapped and murdered that girl." Tina's mouth fell open. "He would have had to kill her. Suppose he had gotten caught, charged and convicted. What do you think would have happened to me? Lady Lawyer and boyfriend get life sentences." She hated to be so caustic and descriptive about it, but that was the present risk.

To Tina, these things didn't seem to be such a big deal because these are the things that happened in her projects on the regular. Tina couldn't expect Shadika to put her freedom at risk like that.

"I think that you should bring all of that to his attention. What do you have to lose? I have to agree that a man shouldn't put his lady at risk at all like that." She also wanted to say that Maurice wouldn't do anything like that if she was at risk. But then again, she knew that Maurice loved the community more than he loved any female.

Shadika took a deep breath. It was not easy deciding what she should do next. "Not to be nasty, but what do you think that he's going to do and say. We have to remember that he's a man."

"What can you lose? At the moment, y'all aren't together. So what's the difference? Can you tell me that you know what he's going to say?" She was betting that Maurice also wanted things to work out.

Shadika didn't care for the idea because it was Maurice that walked out on her. "I don't know what to tell you Tina. What I plan to do first is to make sure I win this trial. I can always find a man." Her ambitiousness was talking. Man or no man, she kept her priorities in check.

"After the trial, you promise me that you are going to bring it to his attention?"

With reluctance, she answered, "Yes, I'll do that just for you. What do I have to lose? Can a lawyer leave now?" She cracked a smile to make Tina believe her.

******

"So can a brother come in? I've been waiting all day for you to get back." Maurice was at Shadika's hotel suite.

Shadika had been thinking she should make him wait a few weeks before she decided to see him. When the front desk told her who came to visit, she made Maurice wait ten minutes before she called the desk back.

"You aren't going to stay that long. I guess its okay." She was wearing a white robe and had a towel around her hair. "Make sure you close the door behind you." She walked into the suite with a nasty walk.

Maurice knew this routine and he felt like he deserved it. By the time he walked in the room and closed the door, she was out of sight.

With the lights on dim, he could barely see her face. She was sitting on the couch with her legs crossed. With a slow pace, he walked to her and sat on her right side.

"You had better have something good to say Mr. Maurice." She growled at him because the smell of his cologne had started biting her.

"I'm coming in peace. I should not have walked out on you. Do you accept my apology?" Apologizing was the easy part.

She kissed him on the cheek. "That was sweet of you to apologize. But we have bigger things that we have to talk about." She wanted to resolve the issue that they had or just have sex with him until she left town.

He sat up in his seat and was still facing her. "Since I'm not able to do what you do, I do things that get the same results. I can't change the way that I was taught." She almost hollered that he could. "How you feel about me being a gangster is understandable, but you can forget about asking me to change. But I promise that nothing I do is going to make you look bad or cause you to go to jail." It had taken quite a bit of time for him to be able to figure out how to put his feelings in words. There was also the matter of taking the risk of not seeing her anymore.

She put her right arm across the back of his shoulders and put her right hand on his right shoulder. With her other hand, she placed it on his left shoulder and pulled him back into the couch. By the time that they had leaned all the way back into the couch, she had her arms around him and was rubbing his chest with her left hand.

"Maurice," she whispered in his ear. "I've always known that you are the kind that handles his business." She worded things to fit the situation. She started climbing on top of him. "There are a few things that I need to know."

He wondered how aggressive she would be if she was in her twenties. "What do you need to know?" He was also thinking about how beautiful she looked.

"Though I'm scared that you might end up dead or in jail, I need to know that you are going to protect your woman." She was grinding against him like they were teenagers.

"I promise to do that." He was happy to be past that part.

That merited a kiss on the lips. "Do you promise that we are always going to communicate and you are never going to walk out on me when we are talking?" Being ignored was the last thing that she'd tolerate.

"I promise that we'll always have an open line of communication. Is there anything else?"

"You know what I want." She stepped back and let her robe drop to the floor. His smile was exactly the reaction that she wanted. "It's been over a week. You know that I got to have it."

"You can get what you want and a whole lot more." He stood up and kissed her. She wrapped her arms around his neck. "I have something very special for you."

She was rubbing her body up against him. "Is it hard, long, and a part of you?"

"I have to show it to you. I have to get on my knees."

She smirked, stepped back, put her right hand on her hip, took the towel from around her hair, put her left hand on her left hip, and struck a sexy pose.

The way that she pulled that off made him want to applaud. No doubt was left in his mind that she was all that he wanted and needed. He reached into his jacket pocket and pulled out a small jewelry box.

She wanted to holler. "Oh Maurice," and grab the box. It had been almost two life times that she had waited for this moment. When he took the ring out of the box and held it up in the air, all of her insides started turning to jelly. She couldn't take her eyes off the ring. If he hadn't gotten on his knees, she wouldn't have known. Her eyes were the only things that had moved since he had taken the ring out of the box.

The moment felt just perfect to him. He felt great about making the big step and making a commitment to one female.

"Shadika, will you marry me?" He grabbed her left hand and slid the ring on her finger.

"Oh my goodness," she hollered as if the ring being put on her finger gave her brand new life. She had her hand up in the air to look at the ring, though she couldn't see it that well. "Yes, I'll marry you." She got on her knees and started kissing him.

They were having one of those kisses that meant a romantic relationship had been taken to a brand new level. Their lips and tongues were moving at a medium pace as they stood up at a slow pace. She almost had him out of his jacket. In sync, they moved and balanced each other, trading breaths, energy, and affection.

After they had fully stood up, she used her right pointer finger to put her hair behind her ear. "I love you Maurice like I've never loved a man. I'll never hold back on you." Her hands were loosening his pants.

Tina

"I feel the same way about you." He was rubbing his hands up and down her backside and nibbling on her left ear lobe. She had started caressing the shaft of his tool, just the way that he liked. "That feels good."

"This is going to feel better." As she was getting on her knees, she pulled his pants and his underwear down to his knees. With the smoothness of a swan, she started licking the head of his tool.

With her right hand, she started caressing his balls. Her left hand was gently pumping his shaft.

"Yes, that feels good." His head was looking straight up at the ceiling. He just relaxed with his hands on his hips. He had no idea that she knew how to give head.

She took meticulous care to concentrate on the head of his tool with her tongue and lips.

"Ooh, Shadika. That's the spot." Sweat had started to form on the top of his head. The sensations had him to the point that all he could do was make sounds and grin.

To let him relax and extend the pleasure, she started taking all of him in her mouth. She was still looking at him to see his facial expressions. With ease, she had deep-throated him.

When they made eye contact, an unbreakable bond had been formed. She had saved this to make him feel that she would do anything for him. The pulsing of his heartbeat made her feel like he had reached the special place inside of her.

"Stand up, Shadika." Though he hadn't ejaculated, he was ready to make her feel as good as she had made him feel. As she was standing up, he finished getting out of his pants and underwear. She helped him take off his shirt. "Get on the sofa and open your legs as wide as you can."

"Can you handle it like that?"

"Of course, I can handle it like that." He stuck his tongue out of his mouth in a stroking manner.

"I'd rather lie right here on your clothes and mine." Before she finished talking, she was sitting on the floor and about to get on her back. With her hands on her knees, she spread her legs wide open. "You had better lick until I climax or I'll sue you."

He walked in front of her and got on his knees. He stopped for a few seconds to look at her face, hair, and body. It was hard for him to believe that she was in her forties and looking that good. No one could have told him that he didn't have a hell of a lady.

With the crawl of a panther and the gracefulness of a playa, he crawled in between her legs, up to her face. He stopped moving forward when their tongues touched. In rhythm, they began to suck on each other's lips. She was also massaging his ears and the back of his head. With delicate kisses, Maurice worked his way over to Shadika's right ear.

A chill went all through her body. "That feels good Maurice." She had never experienced this amount of openness while making love. She clutched both of her hands around his face as her legs wrapped around his back. "I can't wait any longer for us to make love." Before she finished her statement, she had the head of his tool at the entrance of her love box. "Oh yes. Please take your time."

"I'm going to treat you like a queen Shadika." This was the wettest that he had ever felt her to be. It also seemed like he could feel every part of her love box clutching and pulling at him with more warmth than he felt from her than usual.

The intensity of the instant orgasm caused her to wrap her arms around his neck. "I promise to treat you like a king until we die. Just don't stop loving me."

Her eyes were pressed tight. But not tight enough to keep her tears of joy from running out. She had reached the place of joy and ecstasy that every female dreams and fantasizes about. Her soul, spirit, mind, heart, along with all the pores in her body were as open as a starry sky. She was as

Tina

scared as she was happy. It was the first time in her life, also, that she had thought about losing a man. Her mixture of emotions made her put her all into making love to him.

It was feeling just as good to him. Now that they had come to an understanding, he felt that much more comfortable making love. He was in that zone that his erection would last until he had four orgasms. So far he had had three. Their bodies had danced for almost an hour.

"Oh yes, Maurice. This is the best loving that I've ever had." She had lost track of how many orgasms she had had.

"It's also the best that I've ever had. You are the best woman that I've ever had." He was stroking at a medium pace.

She kissed him on the lips – then on the chin. "You are the best man that I've ever had. I feel so safe with you." Their eyes were locked.

"We are going to be together forever. Nothing is going to come between us. I have that kind of love for you." Something kicked in and caused him to stroke faster.

"Do you really mean that?" She felt herself getting closer to another climax. She wanted to hear him confirm what she was feeling from his love making.

"I mean it. It feels so good to be making love to you. We'll be together forever."

They climaxed together.

Like a great lover and protector, Maurice appropriated a blanket and some pillows so they could get comfortable on the floor and enjoy the energy that they had created. They had made love in the same spot that he had proposed to her. All that energy was in the air. All that passion was in the air. It was all right there for them to relax and sleep in. It was that feeling of pure satisfaction that makes a couple know that they belong together. They didn't wake up until the next morning when the maid opened the door. They made love again after she left out.

Darrell Debrew

Over the next few days, they searched for a house that would fulfill all of their needs. Maurice didn't mind moving. He respected that she didn't want to sleep with him in any place that he had slept with another woman. Since that was her main concern, she let him choose the house. Her only requirement was that there was lots of space.

After they picked a house, they flew to California to get all of Shadika's things packed. This was a test within itself. Just her jewelry along was worth over half a million. She hadn't told him that she was worth over twenty-five million. What she had didn't bother him and he didn't mind signing a prenuptial agreement.

It was the lawyer in her that made her bring up the agreement part. There was nothing that wouldn't make her protect what she had worked so hard to achieve. Him doing it without having a negative thing to say meant the world to her.

When the trial was over with, they planned to get married and move into their new house.

Chapter 16

I've been reading so much in the past five weeks that I might know more about the Federal Death Penalty Act than most federal prosecutors.

Shadika and I came up with a great plan of action. I have to admit that she's a genius. When she first told me about what she wanted to try, I looked at her like she might be losing it. Once she explained it, I saw the logic and how it could work to our advantage.

So we both have been doing research to make it happen. We found out that it is possible to make it happen. She had me do most of the research and case reading. It makes all the difference in the world that we have the right judge on the case also. So be ready for a big surprise.

I must also tell you that I feel so good and confident about beating this case that I almost don't feel like I'm going to trial. A lot of this has to do with how great a lawyer Shadika is and the relationship that we have.

It has a lot to do with me not being ignorant. When I went to trial the first time, I was emotional and stressing because I didn't know what was happening. That's the worst feeling that a man can have. I felt like I was the only one that didn't know what was happening. Those feelings make me stay in the law books.

As a black man, I feel that every black man needs to learn the basics of the law. When I get home, that's one of the first things that I'm going to do with my son. I'm still going to teach him about sports and how to play them. But I'm going to make sure that he's *able to think about things in a legal manner. And, I'm going to make sure that he teaches his sons and daughters.*

No, I'm not saying that I want to have a bunch of lawyers for children and grandchildren, though it would be nice. I don't want them to be placed in weak positions. What African-Americans don't know about legal matters is a tragedy. I really couldn't see it until I went to prison.

They say that prison either makes you or breaks you. It made me. Clyde is about to find out.

******

"I can smell the liquor on you Clyde. What the fuck is wrong with you?" Coppedge was thinking to himself how glad he'd be to get rid of him. It had already been a long day.

They walked into Coppedge's office. Coppedge was glad that his secretary had left for the day.

When Coppedge got to his desk, he pulled a glass out of his drawer before he took his jacket off. "Pour me a drink Mister. I know you have a bottle in your back pocket." He had been thinking about the trial day.

Clyde pulled a brand new bottle of liquor out of his back pocket. What he had in his flask was just enough to get him started. "I've been needing to buy you a drink for the longest."

Coppedge looked at the liquor before he picked it up, as if a drink would solve all of his problems. It had been a hectic day. "Have a seat and let's toast." They sat.

Clyde sat and waited for Coppedge to pick up his drink. "What are we going to toast to?"

Coppedge leaned towards his desk, just far enough to toast. "This toast is for Diana. She is going to be a great witness." They had practiced that much.

"Damn it, I'll drink to that." They toasted, drank, and sat back.

Coppedge had put more work and thought into this trial than any other that he had conducted. Most of that work had been with Diana. Having her picked up was the best thing that he felt he had done. Without her testimony, he felt that he had a fifty/fifty chance. With her testimony, he felt like he had a ninety/ten chance of winning. Since he felt good about it, Clyde felt pretty good about it also.

"Coppedge, I have to hand it to you. You've done what it takes to make sure that they get the death penalty." Clyde was envisioning the entire thing happening. It was just over two years that his father had been murdered.

"If it wasn't for all the detective work that you've done, this case wouldn't be going to trial." He took a drink.

"Yeah, I ran her down." He felt that he had messed up because he had missed the chance to kill her. He had promised his father on several occasions that he would avenge his death with her life. He took a swallow.

"We've checked every angle that there is to check. It's just a matter of time. I feel like I can give you a money-back guarantee."

They toasted one last time.

******

"Oh, I thought that maybe you had forgot about your main client. You go see my man and forget about me." Tina had seriously been wondering if she was going to see Shadika again before the trial began.

"I know that you got my letters and postcards." Shadika was getting herself in the seat.

"Yeah, yeah, yeah. Let me see the ring." Shadika held her hand up. "Maurice got love for you girl. Oh yeah, I have to talk to him. When is the wedding?"

"Well Tina, this is what we decided to do. When you and Tyrone beat these cases, we were thinking about having a double wedding. I know that you want to marry Tyrone." Shadika had discussed this at length with Maurice. Shadika felt that if it weren't for Tina's case, she would have never met Maurice. She felt that that was the least she could do.

"Are you sure about that? What do Tyrone and I have to do with you and Maurice getting married?" Naturally, she wanted to marry Tyrone, but she hadn't made any plans. What Shadika said took her by surprise.

"All you have to do is show up for the wedding and the honeymoon. I got your back like that. So what do you say?"

"Well, if Tyrone likes the idea, then I like the idea. I have to follow where my man leads me." She felt that Shadika was doing a little bit too much for her. Saying no would have been like an insult.

"Okay, I'll put the proposition to him in the morning. So how are you feeling about the trial?" Shadika had already planned to start a law firm in Ohio and to make Tyrone one of her paralegals and partners. She'd work it out by paying him whatever.

"I feel good about it. Tyrone told me that y'all have a big surprise for them. Is that true?"

"Yes, that's true, but I can't explain that to you. When it happens, you'll understand." Shadika felt that she'd have to answer too many questions and Tina might talk to someone about it just because she didn't feel comfortable.

"Well, what about the crackhead downstairs? Do you think that she's going to testify?" On many occasions, Tina found herself ready to scream on her and ask her why.

"I hope that you haven't said anything to her." In all of her letters, Shadika kept telling her to stay calm.

"Nah. I've been able to just humor her. She really gets on my nerves." It was common for the feds to put their snitches with the defendants to tempt the defendants.

"She can't hurt you. In this situation, her credibility is going to get shot to hell. I'm ready for her to take the stand." Shadika had a rather serious trick for Joann. A little bit of money can go a long way.

Tina

"Is it a good idea for me to testify?" She hadn't asked until then because Shadika and Tyrone seemed to have all the angles covered.

"No. That's not a good idea. And let me tell you why it isn't a good idea before you say a thing." She put her finger in the air to stop her from saying anything. "If you get on that stand, Coppedge is going to ask you some extremely personal questions that you aren't able to answer."

"Like what?" Most defendants would ask the same questions.

"What are you going to say if asked: Are you willing to kill for your fiancé?"

"I'm going to say 'no' like I'm supposed to." She smiled like it couldn't have been any simpler.

"Nobody in the courtroom is going to believe you because we all know that people kill for their loved ones."

"So are you saying that I'm supposed to answer 'yes'?" It was just another question because she didn't have an argument to present.

"If you answer that, the prosecution is going to love it. He'll repeat your answer as much as possible. So do you get it?"

"That isn't fair Shadika. He shouldn't be able to ask me questions like that. Can't you do something about that?" It was a common thing for people's emotions to be used against them on the stand. Anything else would be unconstitutional and a limit on justice. The trick is for the defendant to use the emotions of the witnesses in their favor.

"No. And I wish that I could. Just relax. We're going to win this trial with the greatest of ease. A day hasn't gone by that I haven't studied this case."

"Okay. I'm just a little nervous. Can you blame me?"

"No, I can't. Let me get a kiss so that I can rest up for this trial." They hugged and kissed.

******

According to the polls, fifty percent felt that Tyrone and Tina were guilty of having something to do with Atkins' murder. Fifty percent felt like they were about to get convicted. Fifty percent felt that both would get the death penalty. Even legal analysts were bitterly divided about what the results would be.

The average individual feels that a person going to trial has to have done something wrong or else the government would not waste time charging him or her. This is more so when there's a murder charge that has a good motive. Many are just plain bloodthirsty and want to see somebody die. There are also those that root for the bad guy.

In "Cop Killer" cases, things are taken to a new level. People automatically want to know who this individual is that has the guts to kill an authority figure. The authorities will want the defendants convicted and sentenced to death to make an example, even if they didn't do it. How could the system function if cops are being murdered on a daily basis? Authorities want citizens to be scared to the point that they never even think about killing a cop. If the wrong person gets convicted, it's okay.

Now the police-haters and anti-government kind want to see an acquittal. For various reasons – some good, some bad – many want to see many cops – especially bad cops – put to death. Even if that defendant gets convicted, many want the satisfaction that someone pulled the trigger on a cop. To many, it's a sign of defiance and the ultimate revenge. Many would love to see it happen, but aren't willing to pay the price for killing a cop. The ultimate satisfaction would come if there's enough evidence that says she did it, but not enough for her to get convicted for it.

It seemed that all of Ohio was up earlier than usual. Every radio station and television had on lengthy discussions about the trial. It was almost impossible in Ohio to not know what was happening, especially in Youngstown, Ohio, and surrounding areas.

All other federal court proceedings had been postponed through acts to the judges. They wanted to see all of it as it happened. Nobody had a complaint. Judge Grumpfree even made sure that her courtroom looked like it was brand-spanking new. She had even toyed with the idea of selling t-shirts. Not wanting to start something that would make the justice system look like a circus kept her from doing it. Plus, she felt that she'd be amply entertained.

When Judge Grumpfree came to the courtroom, everybody had already been waiting for at least twenty minutes. It was a matter of appearance that all be in place as early as possible.

Shadika made sure that she, Tina, and Tyrone were dressed in black to make them look like a team. Shadika had been trained that all things matter in a trial. Appearance was at the top of priorities. Also, she planned to put on a show.

Clyde looked like he belonged in a suit. Most figured that he worked for the prosecutor's office. Clyde was making sure that he didn't miss a thing.

It was coincidence that he and Coppedge were both dressed in dark brown suits.

"Are we ready to proceed?" Judge Grumpfree said as she stood before her desk. She was ready to go. She didn't allow the bailiff to tell everyone to be seated.

"We are ready to proceed," Mr. Coppedge stated with a pleasant smile. He turned to Shadika.

"The defense is ready to proceed." Shadika had a pleasant smile that was sincere and appeared far more convincing than Coppedge's. She wished that she could have talked Maurice into being there. He felt that he belonged at the Elks Lodge with all his family. The Elks had several people there that didn't want to watch the trial at home or alone.

"You may all be seated. Please bring out the master jury."

What was about to start is what many call the most important part of the trial: jury selection. The right jury could make it easy for the defense or the prosecution. Looking deeper into it, one juror could determine the entire proceeding with the wrong comment to the rest of the jury. All it takes is that one juror to have a hung jury.

An attorney's job is to make sure the wrong kind of person doesn't end up on the jury. A prosecutor definitely doesn't want an anti-government person or someone that feels that the criminal justice system mistreats people. Prosecutors are given seminars on how to pick out problem jurors. They also have techniques of keeping them off the jury: It had already been provided that no one from the Westlake Project area would be chosen.

It was noticed by Shadika that Westlake's entire zip code had been deleted from the jury panel. She had the addresses of each potential jury member. This was a small matter that a winning issue could not be made out of. The prosecutor would only bring up that no one in the Westlake Project area would talk to the police about the murder.

What mattered to her was that the jury panel represented the racial composition of the community. Since close to fifty percent of the panel was African-American and minorities, she didn't raise any hell. The last thing that she wanted was trying the case before an all-white jury.

Shadika was looking for two kinds of jury members. She was mainly on the look out for a pro-government juror that had a strong enough personality to sway the other jury members. Shadika was smart enough to look past skin color to find this person. The second person would be the kind to be open-minded and maybe sympathetic to the cause of the defendants. All it would take would be one person to have a hung jury. That one person would have to be a strong person.

While Judge Grumpfree was asking questions of the jury panel, Shadika went about her business of making marks on her list. It was that time to be alert to anything that raised an alarm. Coppedge made notes as well.

The biggest thing that concerned Shadika was whether any of the prospective jurors had a law enforcement relative that was killed while on duty. She was also concerned about those that had kin in the military that had been killed in action. Shadika had Tyrone backing her up in this process. This made her job easier and made Tyrone look intelligent before the jury.

There were several that answered in the affirmative when asked these questions.

When the time came, Shadika made sure that all of them were removed for what they call "cause." Just the same, Coppedge made sure that he had the potentials removed for cause. One hundred and fifty people had been shrunk down to forty. It was twelve-thirty before that part concluded. Judge Grumpfree called for lunch recess.

The last stage of jury selection started at one-thirty. Each party could pick off just ten people that they didn't want on the jury as long as it didn't have anything to do with race or sex. This is what's called preemptory challenges. If a person talked like they weren't biased, but an attorney has that feeling that person is out.

Coppedge had to be careful not to strike all blacks with his challenges. Out of the twenty that he had used, ten were used for blacks. Most of them were the ones that seemed to have a slight edge to them. As a prosecutor, he had to be conscious about the possibility of issues for a direct appeal. Having to try the case again after two years could be to his disadvantage.

When it was all said and done, fourteen jurors were left. Twelve would sit on the jury. Two would be alternates. As Judge Grumpfree set them in the jury box, the attorneys watched them with the deepest of care to see if a bond could be established with one or two of them. The right kind of eye contact could mean the world.

Attorneys – including judges – know that no matter how well jury selection goes, there are going to be biased people that can make it through. An attorney wants to take advantage of this by establishing a rapport.

Shadika got a smile from Juror No. 2. Beatrice Smith was a senior citizen and a retired school professor. She had grown up in the South – the deep woods of Alabama. Her lifetime fantasy was to sit on a jury.

Mrs. Smith was a sharp, old lady that seemed easy going. She saved her energy for those moments that mattered. She already had an opinion about the case.

Mr. Stanley Sellers already had his opinion about the case also. He was in his mid-forties and had just retired from the military. He had never seen any action, though he acted like a tough guy. As far as he was concerned, they did it.

Coppedge hadn't noticed him. He had noticed Mrs. Smith and hadn't struck her because she had a book in her hand. It was a characteristic he had been trained to look for. All the neatly done gray hair left him with the impression that she was a well-to-do black lady that would be in a rush to get back to her social circle.

Judge Grumpfree finished the day off by telling the jury their duties and how they were not to discuss the case with each other. Nor were they to discuss the case with family members.

There wasn't a member on the jury that hadn't heard about the case or hadn't discussed the case. There were very few magazines or media outlets that weren't covering the story. Reporters had been crawling all over Westlake Projects,

Tina

though it was dangerous trying to get a story. None of them came up with anything. They had started calling Westlake Projects "The Invisible Fortress." This had drawn more interest to the case.

For the rest of the evening, the media discussed the importance of picking the right jury. So far, the world had heard about everything else that revolved around the case.

Chapter 17

Day two started out with more attention than the first. Those that didn't find jury selection to be worth their attention were very attentive for the opening statements.

"All rise for the Honorable Judge Grumpfree." It was nine-fifteen on the dot. All rose.

She was glowing and ready. "Mr. Coppedge, are you ready to give your opening statement." She was still standing just to strut her stuff.

"Yes, your Honor, we're ready to present the opening statement." Coppedge had the look of a cowboy. This was his way of making himself look like a hero. He was wearing another dark brown suit. In light brown, on the lapels, it had what looked like cattle horns.

"Is the defense ready?" It was only proper that she acknowledge the defense also.

"The defense is fully prepared," Shadika answered with a smile on her face. She, Tina, and Tyrone were wearing the same shade of dark green.

Judge Grumpfree liked the looks in their eyes. "Let us begin. All may be seated. The prosecution has one hour to present their opening statement." She sat down and reclined back to get comfortable.

Coppedge walked to the front of his desk. First he made eye contact with the jury. "Ladies and gentlemen of the jury, I need each of you to be attentive because this trial is going to go rather fast. I want to warn y'all that this trial isn't going to be boring like many of you expect. This is a cop killer case that's a rather simple case." Coppedge planned to hit them with the evidence in shotgun-like fashion – in a manner to make it hard for them to be convinced otherwise.

Coppedge turned towards the defense table. "Of course, you may wonder why would that nice looking couple right there – the defendants – murder a cop." He turned back to the jury. "When all the evidence is presented, you will understand their motive. You are going to find out that they're a couple that's madly in love in the worst way. For sure, Tina Thompson loves Tyrone Taylor enough to kill a police officer for him." He let a few members of the jury take time to look at the couple.

Shadika had warned them about making any kind of outburst or showing that they were angry. All three of them looked at the jury in the same manner the jury was looking at them.

"She wanted to get Tyrone out of prison like he's the greatest man that walked the earth." Any other circumstances wouldn't have allowed him to mention that Tyrone was incarcerated and convicted. It was a major portion of the motive. Shadika expected this and knew better than to make a wasteful objection. "We are going to show you proof that she loved him enough to kill a police officer for him.

"That's correct; he encouraged her to do it. Tyrone felt that he had been falsely convicted and that it was all DEA Larry Atkins' fault. When the courts disagreed with the theory that Atkins had lied on him to get a conviction, DEA Atkins ended up dead in less than thirty days. Yes, lover kills cop because lover can't get lover out of prison. Yes, they love each other that much."

Coppedge had managed to keep their attention by giving them one tantalizing piece, making it seem simple what he he had practiced.

With a foundation, he'd fill in the blanks. "We're going to show you their romance in the letters that they wrote to each other and their taped phone conversations." The taped phone call part was misleading, making the jury think that they had been under heavy surveillance. "You are going to see evidence that they constantly wished death upon DEA Agent Larry Atkins.

"I'll prove this to you by indirect evidence and direct evidence. What the defense doesn't understand is that we have a witness that saw her pull the trigger. That is correct. We have a witness that will make it clear that Tina Thompson is a cop killer." Coppedge walked to his seat as if he had given himself a silent ovation. He had only used up half his time.

Tina felt like jumping out of her chair. Tyrone squeezed her hand to make her calm down. A few members of the jury had noticed her facial expressions. Mr. Sellers had started rubbing his chin. Mrs. Smith took note of what he was doing.

"Thank you, Mr. Coppedge. That was rather brief and straight to the point." Judge Grumpfree couldn't help but to compliment him. Shadika almost objected. She knew this would make the compliment stand that much more in the minds of the jurors. Just topping what he had said would do the trick. "Ms. Jones, are you ready?"

Shadika already being a famous attorney had an advantage. The jury as well as the rest of the world was ready to hear what she had to say and see what she was made of.

"Yes, I'm ready," Shadika said as she stood up like she was a female tigress on a mission and ready to use her claws. "You may trust me when I tell you that Mr. Coppedge's story isn't as simple as he'd like for you to believe. Don't you think that my clients would have avoided the death penalty by pleading guilty?" She paused to let the jury and audience think about the question.

Tina

It was a low blow that even Coppedge had to respect. Good or bad shot, he didn't appreciate it.

Shadika continued. "He was at least correct about one thing. My clients are very much in love and I'm happy for them. I think that they make a handsome couple. Yes, it's also true that Mr. Taylor has been convicted of a drug charge, which he's going to beat in the near future because of a new trial. Mr. Coppedge was absolutely on point with these matters.

"As far as my clients having DEA Agent Larry Atkins killed, we're talking about a horse of a different color. While he's presenting evidence really fast, I'm going to be tearing it all down very slowly so that you can see the things that he doesn't want you to see."

Clyde nudged Coppedge to make him do something. Coppedge acted like he didn't exist.

"It's going to be hard for Mr. Coppedge to prove a few things that just aren't true. Sure, it sounds like I'm just saying a few things to make you think that they don't have a case. That is my job. But I plan to take this much further than he expects. Just be prepared to have a few surprises and a lot of glitches for this trial. I hand your attention back to Mr. Coppedge."

She had managed to prepare the jury to expect a surprise and a few more things. What she needed to do was simply make her presence felt.

She also prepared the jury to accept that Tyrone had a conviction for a drug charge. She'd get into that later and use it to her advantage.

Judge Grumpfree liked what she had heard, knowing that she would be experiencing an exciting trial with a few surprises. "Mr. Coppedge, are you prepared to call your first witness?"

"Yes, my first witness is prepared. I call Detective Larry Johnson to the stand."

First, Coppedge established that Johnson had fifteen years of experience and specialized in homicide to establish a format. Detective Johnson was a black officer that just cared to do his job and go home.

"Can you recall what you were doing the morning of January 19, 1982?" He could have asked directly about the murder, but that would have meant moving a bit too fast and sounding like the testimony was fabricated.

"I remember that night rather vividly. That was the morning that we got a call for a dead cop in Westlake Projects." He put a little more into it than he had to because it was a cop killer case.

"Can you recall the name of the officer?"

"Yes, I can. It was DEA Agent Larry Atkins."

"Would you please tell us where the body was found?" He was just making sure that he didn't miss anything.

"His body was in the street on the main strip of Westlake Projects."

"When you got to the scene, what reason did you have to believe that he was dead?" It was a must to make them see a picture, though he was doing it improperly. Cops aren't allowed to say that people are dead.

"When I arrived, there was a pool of blood around his head and he didn't seem to have any life in him." What he stated was, again, more than necessary. Shadika didn't object because it wouldn't have any affect on her plans.

"As the case agent, I imagine that you investigated this matter thoroughly."

"Yes I am. And, yes I did." This was what Shadika wanted to hear. That's why she didn't mind him going so fast.

"Did you have many suspects for this crime?"

"Yes, I did. We had a lot of leads."

"Were there any names that continued to come up?"

"Yes, there was. The name Tina Thompson kept com--"

"Objection," Shadika stated. "That is hearsay."

Tina

"Sustained." Judge Grumpfree saw the hearsay coming. It was rather obvious in the last question. "Please rephrase the question."

"Did you happen to investigate any of the defendants as suspects?" Coppedge didn't let the objection faze him.

"Tina Thompson was the prime suspect because she had relations to a case that Atkins had worked on that originated in Westlake Projects." Making it so that Coppedge didn't have to drag all kinds of information made him sound more credible.

"Would you please tell us about that case?"

"Yes, I will. Her boyfriend, Tyrone Taylor, was arrested in Westlake Projects with a large amount of crack cocaine."

Coppedge felt like he had arrived at first base. "Was Atkins the arresting officer for this case?"

"Yes, he was."

"Is Tina Thompson in the courtroom?"

"Yes, she is." He pointed at her. The stenographer made a note of this.

"Is Tyrone Taylor also in the courtroom?"

"Yes, he is." He pointed at him and it was noted in the record.

Coppedge finished out his direct testimony by placing relevant police reports into evidence as exhibits.

"I'm finished with this witness, your Honor." It seemed that he had established a fabulous foundation for some convictions.

"Ms. Jones, are you ready to do cross-examination?" Judge Grumpfree was thinking to herself that there should have been more to his testimony.

"Yes, I'm ready and prepared." She looked at a writing pad that Tyrone had written something on. Many were looking at Tyrone.

"Good morning, Detective Johnson. I take it you are very familiar with cop killer cases." She was still formulating a few things in her mind.

"Yes, I'm very familiar with these cases. I headed it up." He was expecting her to be a little more aggressive than that.

"When this investigation started, you had more than just my clients as suspects, did you not?" She was tempting him to say "no."

"There were several other suspects."

"I imagine that none of these suspects proved to be that good as leads." She had asked a question that didn't sound like the path that a good defense attorney would take.

"That is correct ma'am." He didn't suspect much of the question.

"So you concentrated on my clients because the other leads didn't pan out so well?" Shadika placed him in a position that his answer would lead to a question that he didn't want to answer.

"That isn't exactly what happened." He knew better than to let himself get caught in a lie.

"Thank you, Detective Johnson, for being so honest. Were you the officer that took this case to the grand jury?"

"No, I wasn't." Coppedge had just realized where she was going with her line of questioning. He felt that her strategy couldn't cause that much damage.

"Were you the officer that arrested any of my clients?" She had taken him to where she wanted him to be. Now, it was time to mix.

"No, I was not."

"You did say that you were the person that was in charge of the investigation." From his answer, she planned to build up her surprise.

"Yes, I was."

"Can you tell me who the arresting officer was?"

"Sure, I can." He practically felt like he had given him a way out. He couldn't say no. "I believe that Officer Clyde Atkins made the arrest." The name registered with the jury.

"Was he the one that also went to the grand jury?"

"Objection." Coppedge was not sure of where she was going, but he had to try something.

First blood had been drawn. "Your Honor, this is part of the chain of events that lead up to the arrests of my clients. It's just a matter of procedure." Shadika had her response prepared way in advance.

"Overruled." Judge Grumpfree was surprised to hear Coppedge object to this. She started to ask a few questions herself.

Coppedge had made his first mistake in front of the jury. The look on their faces revealed that they wanted to hear more. Clyde hadn't moved yet.

"Was Clyde Atkins the one that went to the grand jury?" Shadika was glad to repeat the question and to throw Atkins' name out there again.

"I don't know who went to the grand jury." Johnson was rather confused by the line of questioning.

"That is all." Shadika took her seat. She could have made a far bigger deal of it by asking questions from other angles. She had made her point. A vacuum had been created.

Clyde was asking Coppedge why she was bringing up his name. He also wanted to know what could be done about it. Coppedge had to tell him that she was just picking at the edges of the case.

Judge Grumpfree, along with the jury and audience, just watched and listened with deep interest, thinking that there must be a problem.

"Your Honor, I'm ready to call my next witness." There was nothing he could do about the attention Clyde had attracted. A few reporters recognized him from the night of Tina's arrest.

"Please do that." She had her chair turned sideways so that she could see what the jury was doing and how they were reacting.

"I call Stacy Darnell to the stand." Coppedge knew he had to get back on track and that he could do it with this witness.

Stacy Darnell was a veteran pathologist. All that she was capable of doing was talking about dead bodies.

"Ms. Darnell, did you have the opportunity to examine DEA Agent Atkins' dead body?"

"Yes, I did."

"Would you tell us about your conclusion about his body?"

"When his body arrived at my office, he was already dead." This established for the record that he was dead.

"Would you please tell us the cause of his death?" Coppedge felt like he had regained control of the situation.

"He suffered brain malfunction because of two bullets in his head."

"Do you know what kind of bullets they were?"

"The ballistics report stated that they were from a small caliber .22 gun." Shadika could have objected to the authenticity of the report. One way or the other, it would be proven, so she didn't want to waste the jury's attention with this.

"With your experience and training, were you able to determine how close the shooter had to be to Atkins?" He was still painting the picture with one stroke at a time.

"The shooter had to be rather close – within less than a foot."

"That would be point blank range."

"That is correct."

"I have no more questions." Coppedge felt that he had rehabilitated himself in front of the jury. Even Clyde felt better.

Tina

Judge Grumpfree called for a lunch recess. She figured she could enjoy a good lunch, saving Shadika's cross-examination for dessert. Judge Grumpfree had Shadika ahead on the score card, just as many others did.

Mr. Sellers could barely wait for the jury to be alone in their chambers. They were waiting for their lunches. "I can tell already that they are guilty. This isn't going to take that long."

The rest of the jury members had been in the midst of having small talk to pass the time.

"We were ordered not to talk about the case amongst ourselves." Mrs. Smith didn't like the sound in his voice.

"I'm just trying to make this thing easy for all of us and we can all get back to our lives much quicker. I'll just be our foreman and that'll make it easier." He figured that he had the most experience at leading people and that this entitled him, especially as a trained military man.

"We must have voted for a foreman in our sleep last night. We didn't do it this morning."

"Is there anybody else here that wants to be the jury foreman?" Nobody raised a hand. Most didn't want the responsibility for a human being's life. It felt better to stand in the background.

"Well, I'd like to be the fore*lady*. What do you have to say about that?"

"I don't think that you have the qualifications for that job." He had an arrogant grin that made it seem like this had to be a joke.

"Would you pull out the rules that you read that no one else has?" Mrs. Smith couldn't help but be reminded of the many racist bigots that ran the country that she grew up in.

"I don't want to fight with you lady. I just want to make this simple. I feel that I'm able to do that." Mr. Sellers wanted to see them hang. He felt that it was his patriotic duty to make sure that cop killers got punished. Changing his approach was mandatory.

Mrs. Smith leaned back in her chair. "Since our lunch is here, let's eat and take this matter up another time."

So far, the rest of the jury had not made decisions about which way to lean. All they knew so far was that most of them didn't want to be foreman.

Mrs. Smith hadn't made up her mind about the guilt of the defendants. She still liked the idea of a black female attorney representing a black couple against the powers to be. She was a lady that cared about things being fair and just. For sure, she didn't want to see them get railroaded like she had seen happen in Alabama. That's what made her speak out against Mr. Sellers.

******

Lunch recess seemed more like fifteen minutes than the hour and fifteen minutes that it actually was. The topic of lunch was what Shadika Jones would make relevant during her cross-examination.

Shadika asked a lot of preliminary questions to make the murder more vivid. She had her reasons.

"Ms. Darnell, you've been a very cooperative witness. I only have a few more questions for you." Shadika was signaling that she was about to bring the situation to a close. "After you thoroughly examined the body, what was the time frame of death that was determined?"

"It had to be between two a.m. and two-thirty that the brain stopped functioning." Ms. Darnell was used to this also being asked by the prosecutor – and for most defense attorneys to argue the time of death.

"And being that the bullets were shot from point-blank range, how long before the time of death had the deceased been shot?"

"No more than a half an hour before the death."

Tina

"So that means DEA Agent Atkins had to be shot between the time of one thirty a.m. and two a.m.?"

"That is correct."

"Thank you for your time." Ms. Darnell left the stand.

Clyde started smiling and wasn't trying to hide it. It got so good to him that he even patted Coppedge on the back. Coppedge was thinking to himself that she hadn't done anything spectacular. He didn't mind her going deeper into the situation and making his job easier.

Many that were watching thought that Shadika had slipped up. No one was expecting a defense attorney to use over an hour of cross-examination to establish the time of death and the time of the shooting.

"Mr. Coppedge, are you ready to call your next witness? Judge Grumpfree knew that something was up. She knew that Shadika didn't make mistakes and that if she did something, it definitely was for a good reason. It was just the kind of trail she had been hoping for.

"Yes, your Honor. I call Mr. James Green to the stand."

Mr. James Green took the stand. Green was the keeper for records at FCI Loretto. The first part of his testimony was about how he had worked for the Bureau of Prisons and what his duties called for. What mattered was the process that was used to monitor inmate's mail and phone calls. Mr. Green was simply being used as a link to get some evidence to the jury's attention.

"Mr. Green, would you tell us what that document is that I just handed you?"

"This is the print out of a phone conversation that took place at FCI Loretto."

"Would you tell us who this conversation is between?"

"The caller is inmate Tyrone Taylor from Loretto. The report states that he was talking to a female named Tina." This caught the jury's attention.

"Would you please read the second thing that Tina said to Tyrone?"

"I sure will. 'That dirty bastard cop is dead and I wish that I had killed him a long time ago'."

Tina wanted to shrink down in her seat. More than just a few eyes fell on her. Tyrone squeezed her hand to help her keep herself together. In several of his letters, he had warned her about the calls being used at trial.

"Would you tell us the date and the time of this call?"

"The called was placed on January 17, 1982, at about four o'clock in the afternoon."

"Thank you." Coppedge approached the witness stand and gave Green another report. "Would you please tell us what this report is for that I just handed you?"

"This is another phone call between Tyrone Taylor and Tina Thompson."

"Would you tell us the date?"

"It's January 24, 1982."

"Would you turn to page three and read the highlighted part?"

"Sure. 'I wish that I had somebody kill him before my trial, that way I wouldn't be here now'." Many eyes turned to Tyrone.

"Would you tell us who is talking?"

"Yes. That was Tyrone Taylor."

Coppedge introduced several more phone call reports and about ten of their letters before he finished. He stopped at the point where he felt he might overload the jury. It was two-thirty when he stopped and he was confident that Shadika couldn't have a good comeback.

There was no way of denying that the letters and phone calls hadn't occurred or were faked. There was also no way of even inferring that this had been fabricated.

All of Tina and Tyrone's "I could have done this, I wish I had done this to him, and, I'm glad that it happened to him" established a motive and was just below a confession. Shadika was aware of the strength of the information and planned to proceed as planned.

"Mr. Green, did you come upon these phone calls and letters because you gathered them together for your own purposes?"

He couldn't say "yes" because he had not been working at FCI Loretto in January of 1982. "No. I just made sure that all of these documents went through proper channels before they were brought into court."

"So this information was being gathered unbeknownst to you."

"That is correct."

"Do you know what agency or individual asked that these documents be gathered and tracked?"

Clyde had the feeling that she was trying to get at him. He whispered something to that affect in Coppedge's ear. Coppedge just cut his eyes at him and shook his head to say no. Coppedge couldn't imagine how she would be able to get at Clyde.

Shadika continued. "So you are just here to let us know that these are authentic BOP records?"

"That's basically it."

"That also means you don't have any familiarity with the defendants, except for those records?"

"That is correct."

"Thank you. I have no more questions."

"Trial shall resume at nine-fifteen in the morning." Judge Grumpfree was curious to the point that she wanted to ask Shadika what she was trying to do. So far, she only had an idea.

******

"I told ya'll that the two of them are guilty of killing that cop. This trial should be over within less than two more days." Mr. Sellers was excited and had a few of the other jurors agreeing with him.

"That's very patriotic of you, Mr. Sellers, to not allow them to put on a defense." Mrs. Smith had begun to really dislike him. It didn't matter to her that no one was agreeing with her.

The jury was waiting to be let out of the chambers. Judge Grumpfree wanted to keep sly reporters from getting at them.

"I think that you are just mad." Mr. Sellers felt that he could make her out to be an enemy and secure votes to be foreman.

"You act like you heard some confessions. Plenty of people wish death upon other people and say they wish that they had done it. It's a little early to make a judgment call." Mrs. Smith was hoping that Shadika had something up her sleeve.

All the other jury members turned to hear what Mr. Sellers had to say. "If they have an eyewitness, I think that this case is going to be a wrap. That is just my opinion. We'll see in the morning." He wanted to make her argue to prove that he had more self-control than her.

"That's what I'm talking about let's see what happens in the morning." She had a gut feeling that it wouldn't be that simple. On that statement, they were let out to leave.

Media outlets reported that it had been a great day for the prosecution. It was hard for anyone to argue that the phone calls and letters weren't damaging.

Shadika didn't get the warm reception that she had been getting when she got to the Elks Lodge. Still, her dinner and her man were there waiting for her.

"Why is this place empty Maurice?" She kissed him and sat down.

"They started leaving when all the confessions started being introduced." He was going to save that topic for later, but it was too heavy on his mind.

Tina

"I must admit that it looks rather bad. But this thing is far from over. I mean far from being over." She took a sip of wine to calm her nerves. The evidence had hit as hard as she had expected.

"Let's say a prayer before we start to eat."

She was just getting ready to cut into her fish. So far, they had never prayed before a meal or discussed religion. "Are you okay, Mr. Maurice?" She was surprised.

"Just let me do this." They bowed their heads. "God, it seems that we need you at this time. This trial that's happening looks pretty rough for Westlake. I don't have to go into details. I just want to make a request. My future wife has a surprise for them. All I ask is that you endorse this surprise. God, I'm leaving it all in your hands. Amen." Maurice unbowed his head and looked at Shadika. He was debating whether he should use the surprise that he had just planned to make sure that Tina and Tyrone didn't get convicted.

"So you think that it's that bad?"

"It isn't a matter of what I think. It's a matter of me letting you know what the people around here are thinking." Maurice was caught in the middle because he was a respected leader and the closest thing to Shadika.

"What matters to me is that you have faith in me." Shadika was a little upset because he had approached her. She would have preferred an intelligent conversation about the matter.

"I have all the faith in the world in you, but it isn't looking good and Diana hasn't testified yet. That's going to be a mountain of evidence against them. I'd like to know what you have on your mind." He was wishing that he'd gone with his first instinct about kidnapping Diana.

"If you knew about what I have on my mind, you wouldn't be worried at all. So just relax for me. And don't do anything gangsta that you and I'll regret for the rest of our lives." Her appetite had come back.

Darrell Debrew

"I promise that I'm not going to do anything gangsta that we'd regret." He didn't say that he wouldn't do anything.

"So can we eat? I got this thing on lock. You just watch what I do to them." She cut a piece of fish and placed it in her mouth.

******

Tyrone told me to relax about ten times today. Hearing our conversations and letters being put on display scared the hell out of me. I could tell by the looks on the jurors' eyes that they soaked up every bit of it.

I was actually counting the times that my heart beat. That's how hard and fast it was beating in my chest. Tyrone and I wished him death and celebrated his death like it meant the world to us. The only thing that we didn't do was claim that one of us had something to do with it.

Tyrone told me that if he hadn't been in jail that none of the letters or conversations would have been admitted into court. Now he tells me this after we talked the man's death up.

I also understand that my man and Shadika have a plan that's supposed to turn the case all the way around.

All I can do is hope that they are absolutely right.

I'm still thinking about what lies the other witnesses are going to tell. That means that whatever Shadika and my man have planned has to be da bomb.

I'm so stressed that I have to get some rest.

Chapter 18

It was nine-thirty a.m. when Joann took the stand. Coppedge and Shadika had to get a few matters straight on a stipulation. It concerned whether DEA Agent Larry Atkins was on duty when the murder occurred. Shadika wouldn't stipulate until she was shown conclusive proof. This was one of the major elements of the offense.

It took about fifteen minutes to introduce Joann to the jury and the audience. She was sounding and looking the best that she could. She was part of the background.

"Are you personally familiar with one of the defendants?" Coppedge had covered that she was being held for murder.

"Yes. I'm right across from Tina Thompson. We talk through the bars each and every day." She wasn't expecting much for her testimony and would have done it for free.

"Was there ever a time that y'all talked about her criminal case?"

"Yes, we talked about it several times."

"What did she tell you?"

"She told me how much she enjoyed killing Atkins and how much she hated him."

Tina looked around the courtroom and almost jumped out of her seat. Tyrone was the only thing that kept her from standing all the way up. "She's lying. She's lying. She's

213

lying." She was pointing a finger at Joann. People started talking amongst themselves.

Joann jumped a little just to make it look good. Shadika had stood when Tina stood. She was trying to get her to sit back down.

Tina calmed down when a marshal put his hand on her shoulder. Clyde was barely able to keep from laughing out loud.

Judge Grumpfree regained order after she banged on her gavel about eight times. She didn't say anything directly to Tina because she felt that she had been embarrassed enough.

"Mr. Coppedge, you may finish if you like."

"I'm finished your Honor," Coppedge said with a sly smile.

"It's your witness Ms. Jones." Judge Grumpfree had a feeling that it was time for Shadika to turn it up.

Shadika stood and checked the appearance of her dark purple outfit. "Thank you, your Honor." She also had a few documents in her hands.

"Joann," she started out with authority in her voice. "Did you inform Mr. Coppedge that you are a crack addict before you took the stand?"

"I'm not a crack addict."

"May I approach the witness?" The court stated yes by shaking her head. Shadika went over to the witness stand. While she was there, she took a whiff of the air as she was giving Joann some documents.

Joann looked at the documents as if they were ghosts or something.

"Isn't it true that your parents sent you to a program in Pennsylvania for your crack addiction? Isn't that where those documents are from?"

"Yes, they are. But--"

"Let me ask the questions." Shadika smiled knowing that she had more than just a deer in the headlights. "Isn't it true that you've been a crack addict for at least eight years?"

"Yes. I've been smoking crack for that long." She fidgeted as she admitted this. Coppedge knew that there was no way that he could make Joann look good after that answer.

"Isn't it true that you are charged with murdering your boyfriend for two ounces of crack?" Shadika had the newspapers searched to find this information.

"I am charged for murder." She was giving long answers to maintain her credibility as much as possible. Really, her pride.

"Aren't you charged for murdering your boyfriend?"

"Yes."

"For crack cocaine."

"Yes."

Shadika had to take it a little further because she could. "Tell me this truthfully, Joann. You don't want to get caught in a lie do you?"

"Objection. She's trying to intimidate the witness." Coppedge could see that Joann was about to fall apart.

"Mr. Coppedge, Ms. Jones hasn't done anything to intimidate her. She already knows that she's supposed to tell the truth." Judge Grumpfree was a little agitated that he had interrupted. "Please continue Ms. Jones."

"Were you smoking a cigarette before you came up from your cell?"

"No, I was not."

"Your Honor, if you wouldn't mind, would you send your bailiff over to the witness to see if she smells like cigarettes?" It was one of those moments that caused many to ask someone about what she had just requested.

"Objection." Coppedge hollered and looked at Shadika with contempt in his eyes. "What kind of request is that? What does that have to do with the case?"

This was extremely good to Judge Grumpfree. She

looked towards Shadika.

"Your Honor, I think that her smoking in a federal building will shed light on her credibility. The jury is entitled to know about her breaking rules of that nature, especially since someone has to give her the cigarettes." She cut her eyes at the jury and Coppedge. The jury looked hungry.

"I'll do it myself." Judge Grumpfree wanted to know first hand. Coppedge prayed as he watched Judge Grumpfree make her way over to Joann. He wanted to holler at Clyde as she sniffed around Joann. "Yes, indeed, she's been smoking cigarettes."

A smirk came to Shadika's face. She waited for Judge Grumpfree to take her seat before she asked her next question. "Are you aware that it's illegal to smoke in the jail that you are in?" It was humiliation time.

"I didn't know that." She still had a little bit of attitude in her voice.

"But you do know that they aren't sold on the commissary where you are at? That is true."

"Yes." That deflated her a little bit. Clyde wished that he could snatch her off the stand. Coppedge didn't feel too bad about her testifying. She was just one witness.

"So that means that a guard or somebody has been giving you cigarettes and it has not been for free?"

Now this presented a problem for Joann. She would have loved to say "no" and say that she had found the cigarettes. If she said "yes", it would lead to another question. She stayed silent for a few seconds.

"Your Honor, would you order the witness to answer?" Shadika was sure that her credibility had been crushed. But she had to take it further.

Judge Grumpfree gave Joann one of her patented mean looks. Please answer the question."

"Someone gave me the cigarettes." She wasn't about to name any individuals. She had been thinking she should have said "just one."

"So what kind of favors have you been doing to get these cigarettes?" Shadika was counting on her saying something to make herself look bad.

"I haven't done anything."

"So somebody has just been giving you cigarettes to be nice to you?" Shadika was satisfied with the attitude.

"If that's the way that you want to put it." Joann would never throw a name out there while she was on television.

"So you are testifying here today because they gave you some cigarettes?" This was all that it took to make her look the worst that she could look.

"No." Joann felt like she was saying the right thing.

"So you expect us to believe that you volunteered to testify because you feel like it was the right thing to do?"

"Yes, it's the right thing to do." She knew that no one believed her, but what else could she say or do.

"Thank you and I have no more questions."

Tina, along with everybody else, felt that Shadika had done a wonderful job of crushing Joann. Tina was hoping that Joann would be there when she got back to the cell. Tina at least wanted to be able to say a few words to her. She'd find out later that they had moved Joann that morning.

At the Elks Lodge, they were having a small celebration. They had been wanting to see something that seemed favorable. Many others around the world felt the same way.

"Mr. Coppedge, are you ready to call your next witness?" Judge Grumpfree was expecting much more excitement to come.

"Yes, my next witness is ready." Coppedge was feeling that he had made the right decision by having Diana testify last. He wanted to go out with a nice bang.

Diana was looking like a business woman with her dark blue, skirt outfit and pearly white, silk blouse. With her hair pinned up and eyeglasses, she looked like she should be somebody's secretary. Her grace and beauty had everybody's attention.

Coppedge felt like this is where he put nails in the coffin that couldn't be removed. He took his time with the preliminary questions to sort of charm the jury with her presence. It was almost theatrical. They had practiced that much.

He had played her up to be a welfare mother that was doing the right thing to help the system. They even made it known that she had to go into the witness protection program.

With the setting just the way he liked it, it was time for the kill. "Are you familiar with either of the defendants that are here?"

"Yes I am, sir." She got a little more comfortable in her seat.

"Which of the defendants are you familiar with?" He turned to look at the defendants.

"I'm familiar with Tina Thompson. The young lady to the left of Tyrone Taylor." She made eye contact with the defendants just as she had been trained.

"Are you also familiar with the murder of DEA Agent Atkins?"

"I'm very familiar with that also." She felt like she was a natural born actress.

"Please tell me how you are familiar with his murder." Shadika made eye contact with Tina to make sure she was staying under control.

"I saw Tina shoot Officer Atkins in the head."

A small wave had gone across the courtroom. An eyewitness' testimony had been given. What could be considered by some as the strongest evidence that could be presented. People were still talking amongst themselves thirty seconds later. Coppedge didn't want to ask another question until that affect of this had sunk in. Judge

Grumpfree was looking at Diana to determine if she was telling the truth.

Thirty seconds later, she was ready to hear more. "Order in the court. Would you please continue, Mr. Coppedge?" Her instinct told her that this pretty young lady was lying. Judge Grumpfree was ready for Shadika to do her thing.

"What time of night was it when you saw this occur?"

"It was late at night. I'm sure that it was past twelve o'clock."

"Were you scared to come forward with this information?"

"Yes, I was." That was the finish to make her look like a heroine. Just a little reemphasizing.

"I'm through with this witness, your Honor.' Coppedge almost broke a smile. Clyde had been smiling since she had said she saw it occur.

"Ms. Jones, it's your turn." Judge Grumpfree leaned back in her chair and crossed her legs. It was like the bottom of the ninth inning and a homerun was needed to tie the score.

Shadika pulled a folder out of her briefcase. Clyde had his eyes on the folder as if Shadika had pulled an atomic bomb out. Coppedge was looking just as well. The look in her eyes kept him from acting cocky and arrogant.

Shadika had a calm look that seemed capable of anything. "How are you doing, Diana? You look wonderful in that outfit." Tina was in a rush for her to smash Diana.

"Thank you very much." She had the politeness down to a science.

Shadika was thinking of what part would be the best for her to start at. Just last minute thinking.

"You say that you saw my client shoot Atkins in the head?"

"That is correct."

"You say that you saw this happen at about twelve o'clock at night, correct?"

"That is correct."

"Did you know that the pathologist timed the murder as occurring between one-thirty and two o'clock?" This was meant to test her and throw her off?

"No. I didn't know that." She had made up her own time for seeing the crime. Something that Coppedge had taken for granted.

"So how do you remember that it was twelve o'clock at night or just a little later?"

I had just finished watching BET Nightly News. She had to make that up also. She knew that it came on every night at eleven-thirty.

Shadika opened the folder and took out a three-page document. She looked back at Diana. "Do you remember the date that your lease in Westlake apartments started?"

"Yes, I do. It started some time in January of 1982." They had expected this question.

"Does January 17 sound correct?" Shadika had looked at the document to fake like she didn't know the dates.

"I'm not sure." She knew, but didn't want to say. Coppedge was starting to get a little nervous.

"May I approach the bench please?" Judge Grumpfree nodded her head. Shadika handed her the document and walked back to the defense table. "Does that refresh your memory?"

"Yes, it does. The lease started on January 17, 1982." Diana sensed that Shadika was about to get funky on her.

"So you say that the murder happened at about twelve o'clock to twelve-thirty?"

"That is correct."

"Did you look at your watch to make sure of this?" This was a step-up question. Coppedge knew that he had messed up.

Diana felt like this was a test of her acting skills. "No, I remember that I was looking at BET News at this time." She left herself no room to switch the programs to change the time frame.

"I imagine that your son was in the house and he was asleep at this time?" Shadika had taken a risk with this question because she didn't know the answer.

"He's always asleep by nine-thirty." She smiled to make herself look good.

Shadika had taken the right gamble and won. It was time to start slapping her up. She pulled another document out of her folder. "Your Honor, may I approach the bench?" Judge Grumpfree shook her head to say yes expecting to see something really good happen.

"That document says that you didn't have your lights cut on until the twenty-first of January. Isn't that correct?"

Diana looked at it. She looked over at Coppedge for a second. She wasn't thinking that the jury noticed this. "Yes, that is what it says," she stated trying to sound as confident as possible.

"So you were able to watch BET without any electricity?" Tina didn't mind people seeing her shaking her head.

Caught. Busted. Embarrassed. Saying "yes" wasn't a possibility. Stretching her imagination and saying that she had another source of electricity didn't enter into her mind because of shock. "Though my lights weren't --"

"Please answer the question with a yes or no. You didn't have any electricity, did you?"

"No, I didn't." She had tried her best to clean it up.

"That's okay Diana." Shadika smiled like she could be a friend. "We're going in another direction for a minute." She wanted Diana to get comfortable for the next round so she could play with her like a yo-yo. "Are you familiar with Deputy Sheriff Clyde Atkins?"

"Objection." Coppedge hollered as he stood up.

Judge Grumpfree looked at him like he had interrupted her favorite television program. "What Is the basis of your objection?"

"He isn't relevant to her testimony."

"Overruled." She looked back at Diana to make sure that she didn't miss a thing. Coppedge sat back down feeling defeated on several fronts.

"Did Sheriff Atkins approach you about testifying in this case?" It was the beginning of the second set-up. This had to be done precisely.

"No, he didn't." This was a lie. She was positive that she could get away with it.

"But you did meet with Mr. Coppedge on several occasions."

"Yes, I did meet with Mr. Coppedge."

"Did you meet with him on several occasions to discuss things about the case?" This extended question was part of the set-up.

Diana had been prepared to answer this. "Yes, we met several times to discuss what I knew and things of that nature."

"Was Sheriff Atkins at any of these meetings to check the status of the case?" This question was pertinent to her first surprise move.

"No. He wasn't there to check on the status of the case, at least not that I know of." She hadn't been prepared to answer this question, but she instinctively knew that she shouldn't put Atkins out there.

"So you never met with Sheriff Atkins for any reason?"

"No, I've never met with Mr. Atkins."

"So you just called the U.S. Attorney's Office to collect the reward and to do your civic duty?" This was just an extra question to make her make another commitment.

"Yes, that's what I did." This is what Coppedge had trained her to say.

Shadika opened her folder again and pulled out eight

pictures. "Your Honor, may I pass these pictures to the court, the witness, the jury, and the prosecution?" She didn't mention for the press because that was being taken care of while she spoke.

Judge Grumpfree just put her hand out. Shadika gave her a set first, then to Diana, then to the jury, then to Coppedge.

Coppedge wished that he could call for a mistrial. Clyde just shook his head and turned red.

"Diana." Shadika had a grin that she didn't care to hide. Diana tried her best to smile. "Isn't that you and Sheriff Atkins meeting at a hotel in Pennsylvania?"

Diana took a deep breath. "Yes, it is." She was thinking that she did her part and planned to argue for the other half of her money.

"Is it correct that y'all met there twice?"

"Yes." She had no choice but to say yes because she was dressed differently in both pictures.

I have no more questions for the witness." Mission accomplished.

They were celebrating at the Elks Lodge. Maurice was also smiling, though he had already set another plan in motion. This was a situation that called for no chances being taken. Gangsters do what gangsters do.

Coppedge tried his best to clean up her testimony. It seemed that the more questions that he asked, the further he got from his objective. Finally, he stated the prosecution rested its case. He felt that he had no choice by the bored look on the jury members' faces.

Judge Grumpfree wanted to stop him before he started. "Ms. Jones, will you be calling any witnesses for the defense?" She figured Shadika didn't want to ask Diana any more questions.

Shadika stood up. "I prefer to start in the morning. I think that'll make it more convenient for all parties concerned."

"Let it be done." Judge Grumpfree felt that she had been thoroughly entertained for the day. Waiting for the next surprise was delightful.

******

"So, Mr. Sellers, what about the quick verdict that you had been talking about?" He was the last one to make it into the jury room.

"That doesn't mean that they didn't have that cop killed. What they said on those tapes and in those letters still has a lot of weight. We can't forget that." He was extremely disappointed that Diana had been impeached and embarrassed.

"You seem to forget about that thing called a reasonable doubt. Or should we follow your rules?" They had argued on every occasion that they had the opportunity. The rest of the jury didn't mind just listening. They had already voted Mrs. Smith to be their forewoman.

"I still think that she did it. It's a matter of time before the truth comes out." He didn't care what happened. He planned to find them as guilty with the hope that they be tried again.

"What do you think that she's going to do for a defense in the morning? I can bet that she's about to drop the bomb." It had come to the point that the jury felt that they were just watching a show.

"Did you think that the girl might be getting ready to get away with murder? Sure those witnesses got caught lying on the stand, but does that mean that Tina didn't do it?"

He had made a serious point. There are circumstances that give that feeling that a person did something. Those letters and phones calls were also lingering in their minds. To go along with that evidence, they were still thinking about how only one person from the projects stepped forward to give up some information. They also had information about how Atkins used to terrorize Westlake Projects.

"All I know is that the standard is reasonable doubt. What I heard today gave me plenty of reasonable doubt. Plus, think about what is going to happen tomorrow." Mrs. Smith headed towards the door.

The jury members were split on whether Tina had or hadn't done it. They hadn't really thought about Tyrone because there wasn't much evidence against him.

******

When Shadika arrived at the Elks Lodge, there was a crowd in the parking lot waiting for her.

It was a matter that called for a pre-celebration. She had come and represented for the people. They had gone to the point of rolling out a red carpet for her. She was ushered out of her car like she was royalty.

On every radio station and television station, they were talking about what Shadika had done to Diana. They tried their best to get a comment from her as she left the courthouse. Shadika kept telling them "no comment."

Naturally, Shadika felt great about the work that she had just put in. She didn't want to start celebrating so that she could keep her focus. There were a few more steps to be made before the situation was fully wrapped up.

Shadika felt seventy percent sure that she was about to get them acquitted. With her surprise move, she'd feel that the chances were an easy one-hundred percent.

What she planned to do would make history because it had yet to be done and would blow the government's case off the map. When she pulled it off is when she'd celebrate.

"So how do you feel?" Maurice was happy to finally have a private moment with his future wife.

She had some shrimp in her mouth. "I feel that you have these people extremely excited."

Maurice giggled a lot. "I think it has to do with all that work that you put in at the courthouse. I mean you really did your thing."

"I have to admit that I couldn't have done it if you hadn't gathered all of the information." She kissed him on the lips.

"So does that mean that we're a great team?"

"It means that after I do what I'm going to do for the defense, we are going to all be able to get married together." She felt good that so many great things were happening for her at one time. She had a great man and she was feeling that she'd paid her debt to her people. Making history wasn't such a bad thing either.

"So when is his trial scheduled?" Maurice wished that he could tell her what he had in mind. She'd find out soon enough.

"I think that they are going to let him have time served. The Atkins' name is not worth much. How can he lose his trial?"

"With the best lawyer in the world, how can he lose?"

"Thank you baby. I'm ready to start working with you here on a daily basis. I need those ladies to recognize that you are my husband." She just wanted to be saying something.

"I think that people already recognize that. They're treating you like a queen around here. What do you think?"

They kissed. "I must admit that I can't complain one bit. Do you think that these people are going to let me go home and rest?"

"They are going to let you go. They know that you need your rest. Plus, we have some serious love-making to do." He was also thinking how things changed in just one day.

"I love you Maurice."

"I love you Shadika."

Chapter 19

"You look like you haven't been to sleep. And, all I smell is alcohol." Coppedge was expecting Clyde to be in his office.

"What the hell happened?" Clyde had been up all night drinking and socializing with prostitutes.

"Let's go in my office and get some coffee in you. You can't show up in the courtroom looking like a drunk." They went into Coppedge's office. In a sense, Coppedge was relieved that the case was almost over.

Clyde slid down in the chair. "So what happened with Diana? She looked really bad yesterday."

Coppedge handed him a cup of black coffee and sat in his seat. "It might not be as bad as you think." He didn't want to admit that he hadn't thought about a few questions that Shadika asked. These were things that he had taken for granted.

"What do you mean?" He looked up at the ceiling and starting thinking about other ways to get his revenge.

"I think that the jury still remembers what was said in all those letters and in the phone calls." He sat up straighter in his seat. "A few members of the jury seem to still feel that they did it."

"So what does that mean?" Clyde didn't really feel like asking questions and listening. He was mostly curious.

"What we have to hope for Is a hung jury." Coppedge

planned to play up the letters and calls and admit that he picked bad witnesses to testify.

Clyde laughed a disgusting sounding laugh. "So what does that mean?"

"It means that we'll get another chance to get it right. We should have left the witnesses out of this." Coppedge had plans on finding his own witnesses – what he should have done in the first place.

Clyde stood up and looked at him with a sardonic look.

"Whatever. I'll see you when the courthouse opens. I'm hoping that you'll be able to score a few points when she puts on her defense." He headed out.

"I can tell you what she's going to do for her defense." Coppedge was feeling responsible and like a failure. Instead of acting like a mad man, he was looking for ways to still win the trial or salvage it.

Clyde turned around and gave him another bad look. "What do you think that they are going to do?" He was also thinking about all of the work that he had done.

"Tina is going to take the stand and I'm going to tear her up." Coppedge was hoping to see Clyde back into the spirit of winning the case.

Clyde opened the door. "All I can say is that I feel like you messed this case up. I'll see you in a few hours."

Coppedge took himself a drink to deal with the inevitable loss that he felt he was about to suffer. If he could pull a hung jury, he planned to be far better prepared the next time. He figured that his chance to redeem himself would come when Shadika presented her defense. Since they hadn't asserted a certain defense, he didn't have an idea what Shadika planned to present. He felt that his best guess would be that Tina or Tyrone took the stand to tell their sides of the story. There might also be a few character witnesses. Both would fit his purposes just fine.

******

Tina

A month from now I plan to be part of a double wedding and starting a career as a paralegal with Shadika.

It means the world to me to be able to see their case unravel before their faces. It makes me feel like a complete man to know that my legal research has something to do with this. I'll admit that some of the looks that I've seen on Clyde Atkins' face have something to do with this.

I feel like I'm getting my revenge with my lady by my side. It may seem silly, but I needed my lady to see me standing strong. I've been holding her down the entire time throughout this entire trial. All of that makes me feel like I'm a man that she has to respect.

Ya see, a man never wants his lady to see him in a weak position. It doesn't matter if it isn't his fault. Call it what you may, but that's just the way that a man feels.

What we have in store for them is going to make history. We put a lot of work into this. For my other trial, I'm planning to take time served and skip trying to sue them. They offered it the other day.

******

It had been a beautiful night for Shadika, though Maurice kept trying to question her about what she had planned. She kept telling him to wait. She had slept for maybe an hour because of being anxious and excited. Over and over, she kept thinking about what she had to do.

Shadika, Tina, and Tyrone were at the defense table and dressed in all black. From the looks on their faces, they didn't seem to be at a trial that held the death penalty in the balance.

All the reporters had arrived early to try to get Shadika to tell what she had planned. "No comment," was all that she would say. Anticipating what she was about to do caused it to be the most exciting trial day. Many from around the world that didn't care about the case had taken an interest and were tuned in to have a first-hand account. Debates had been a plenty.

There was standing room only in the courtroom. Coppedge showed up at five minutes after nine. He smiled when he and Shadika made eye contact. This was only because of the cameras. Clyde showed up a few minutes later. He purposely didn't recognize the presences of anyone at the defense table. He sat on the opposite side of Coppedge.

Shadika and Tyrone grinned at his behavior.

Just like clockwork, the jury was seated. "All rise for the Honorable Judge Grumpfree." They rose.

Judge Grumpfree came out with a smile on her face. "Are we ready to proceed?" She was looking directly at Shadika.

"Yes, the defense is ready to proceed."

"The prosecution is ready to proceed."

"You may all be seated, except for defense counsel." She gave them a few seconds to get comfortable. She was still standing. "Ms. Jones, is your first witness here?"

"Yes, my witness is in the courtroom." Shadika loved the energy that Judge Grumpfree was exhibiting.

Judge Grumpfree sat. "Would you call your witness to the stand?"

"Yes, I will." She turned toward the prosecution table. "I call Deputy Sheriff Clyde Atkins to the stand." Clyde looked her in her eyes. "That's correct. I call Clyde Atkins to the stand." Then she looked Coppedge in the eyes.

It was the kind of shock that caused everyone to remain silent. The looks on Clyde and Coppedge's faces made them look like they had heard what everyone had heard and were reacting just like the rest of the audience and jury. No one knew what to say or think. Everybody decided to look towards Coppedge and Clyde for their responses. Even Judge Grumpfree was staring at them like they had been tarred and feathered. The moment was such a surprise that the reporters hadn't started writing on their writing pads. They didn't want to miss the next thing.

Tina

All the people at the Elks Lodge got closer to the television. Maurice was so surprised that he dropped a glass.

"Objection, your Honor," Coppedge hollered out of slow instincts and because he had no other momentary alternative, as he stood, after about four seconds of letting Shadika's voice echo through his mind. "She can't do that."

It seemed that his voice was a call for the rest of the courtroom to start making noise. People were asking each other if it could be done. Some said it could be. Some said it couldn't. None of them had a clue and were talking just to be talking because of the situation. None had ever imagined that a cop could be called to the witness stand as a witness for the defense. Some were arguing that she could do it because his name had been mentioned several times during the trial.

Judge Grumpfree was satisfied with the situation that had been created. She let them make noise for a few seconds before she said, "Order in the court," and started banging her gavel.

"Your Honor," Shadika stated with pure confidence in her voice, "there's plenty of case law that says I'll be able to do this."

"No, there isn't your Honor." Coppedge felt that he was correct because of what he had read about prosecutors not being able to be called to testify, unless there are unusual circumstances.

Judge Grumpfree couldn't recall ever dealing with the issue. She was also curious and intrigued. It was the kind of action that she had been hoping for. She had thought on a few occasions that Shadika would make him part of the case because she had alluded to his name on several occasions. Judge Grumpfree couldn't figure out how though.

"Mr. Coppedge, would you be able to cite any cases to support your position? I'd like to hear them." She was positive that Shadika had come prepared.

"Your Honor, I motion that a hearing be conducted outside the presence of the jury and after an hour recess." He was partly confident that they could stop her from calling him to the stand.

"Does the defense have a problem with that?"

"That's just fine with the defense."

******

Clyde was so close behind Coppedge that Coppedge just had enough room to breathe. "What is she trying to pull and what are you going to do about it?" Clyde had just followed him through the side door.

Coppedge was heading for the law library. "I don't know what she's trying to prove. I just know that I don't want you on that stand." He had no idea what she planned to ask him, but it wouldn't be a pretty scene if she wanted him on the stand.

"Tell me if she can do this." Clyde felt like it was a state of emergency.

"I've never dealt with the situation. I know that it's hard to have the prosecuting attorney testify." He had just entered the law library and started taking his jacket off. His assistant had called in sick so he was on his own. He grabbed a book off a shelf and sat down at the table.

"You need to find something in those books that's going to stop this." Clyde sat at the table with him. "Can't I just take the fifth?"

"You'll only be able to take the fifth if you tell the judge what crime you want to protect yourself from." Coppedge had correctly figured that Shadika would be prepared to argue this.

"Damn. How in the hell did this all fall apart?" Clyde stood up and started walking back and forth. He was thinking to himself that he couldn't let it go down like this.

Tina

"We should have never tried this case." He had written down about ten cases to look at that dealt with Compulsory Process.

"Well, you shouldn't have insisted that we find witnesses. These witnesses made us look bad."

"It's too late to think about that. I need to read these cases so that I can present an argument to keep you off the stand. So if you don't mind." Coppedge knew that he was in a rather difficult position that had many disadvantages. He had been ambushed. Letting himself look like a total idiot is what he wanted to prevent.

Clyde stormed out the door. It was time for a drink.

******

"So, Mr. Sellers, what do you think about the trial? I can't wait for Clyde Atkins to take the stand." Mrs. Smith planned to push as many buttons of his as he had tried to push of hers.

"I still think that they did it. Do you see how they are all hugged up and stuff? I'm telling you that they did it." There were other people on the jury that still agreed with him.

"Ain't nobody see her do it and the last witness got caught lying through her teeth. So where is the evidence?" There was no changing her mind. She planned to find them not guilty as she had planned from the beginning.

"If this case wasn't going to trial, you'd be hollering that she killed him and deserved it. I understand where you are coming from." He planned to find them guilty because he felt that she had done it. There was no changing his mind.

"So you think that celebrating a person's death and wishing that person death is enough to find that person guilty of that person's murder?"

"I think that you've overlooked how much love she has for him. Wait until we get to the rest of those letters. I know that she loves him that much."

"You just wish that someone had that much love for you. Stop being a hater."

"Whatever."

The rest of the jury was being entertained all the way around. Most of them had made up their minds about the case. So far, they had been well entertained. It wouldn't be right to them if they didn't get the chance to hear Clyde Atkins' side of the story, especially after hearing his name so much. Since they couldn't hear the hearing live, they definitely planned to get a recording of the proceeding.

******

Clyde and Coppedge were the last ones to make it back into the courtroom. Judge Grumpfree was just about to go looking for them herself, just to have some fun.

"Ms. Stephany Jones, would you please present your argument? I think the prosecution is ready to proceed." Coppedge felt it in her voice that things were about to be all down hill.

"Yes, I'm ready," Shadika stated as she stood up. "I'm also passing the court a short brief for this matter and giving a copy to the prosecution." The bailiff walked over and took the briefs from her. Coppedge didn't think to make a short brief just for appearances.

Shadika waited for the bailiff to finish. All were waiting for her to speak. "Under *United States v. Nixon* of the United States Supreme Court, even a senator and a prosecutor may be called to testify for the defense." Judge Grumpfree was skimming the brief and listening. "Certainly, a police officer would also fall under that umbrella. To paraphrase *United States v. Nixon* of the United States Supreme Court: '[I]t is imperative to the function of the courts that compulsory process be available to the prosecution and the defense for the full disclosure of all facts.' The disclosure of all facts is my intention in calling Deputy Sheriff Clyde Atkins." She looked over at him and then to the jury. "His name and picture have come up and it's reasonable to say that he knows things about this case. Things that are cause for reasonable doubt. I think that this is a simple matter." She sat, knowing that Coppedge didn't have a good comeback.

"Mr. Coppedge, are you prepared to make your presentation?" Judge Grumpfree had made up her mind after she had done her own research in her chambers.

"Yes, I am." He stood up after he made that assertion. "I think that Ms. Jones is on a fishing expedition and hoping to find a smoking gun. It's hard to imagine what Mr. Atkins could say that would aid the defense. The case is a matter of whether the defendants wanted Mr. Larry Atkins dead so bad that Tina pulled the trigger when Mr. Larry Atkins was investigating another crime. I think that this court should deny this request. There isn't anything possible that Clyde Atkins could say that would change if she did or didn't pull the trigger."

Judge Grumpfree took about three minutes to finish reading Shadika's petition. While she had the hearing on hold, many thoughts were occurring. Anxiety and anticipation were building up. When she looked up, many sat up in their seats. After she had read over the petition, she took two more minutes to think to make it look like it was a hard decision.

"I have a decision. Mr. Atkins, your name has come up several times in this trial. We even have a picture of you with the eyewitness. These factors deserve to be explained to the jury by the defense for the purpose of creating a reasonable doubt. Mr. Atkins, you are going to have to testify." Judge Grumpfree looked surprised when the courtroom erupted in an uproar. Everybody had started talking all at once. Many reports were satisfied to the point that they left to start writing their stories, not exactly thinking what the testimony would be about. The situation was that unheard of and exciting.

"Order in the court." Clyde had been looking at Coppedge in a manner to blame him. Maurice ordered that fifty of his people make it to the courtroom to hear the testimony live and in person. Shadika, Tyrone, and Tina were smiling.

History had been made. It was the first time that a police officer that had worked on a case had been ordered to testify for the defense – the first time, period. This was one of the things that Judge Grumpfree had pondered while making her decision. But the situation was more than appropriate.

Compulsory Process gives the prosecution and defense the right to call any witness with relevant information. Shadika had made it her business to build up to her surprise. There wasn't a thing that hadn't fallen out of place. She felt so good about it that, if necessary, she wouldn't have been able to find words to describe how she was feeling.

"Please bring the jury back in. Mr. Atkins, would you please take the stand." Judge Grumpfree seemed serious on the outside. Inside, she was ready for the show and hoping that he got bashed. "By the way, Mr. Atkins and Mr. Coppedge, if there's a reason for Mr. Atkins to take the Fifth Amendment, I need to know about it now. We may go in my chambers now, if you like."

Coppedge wanted to scream that she had overstepped her bounds. "No, your Honor. That won't be necessary." Clyde started heading for the witness stand.

"Good morning, Mr. Atkins. How are you doing today?" She started out with a bunch of questions that he could answer in a cool manner. This was to give the jury something to make a comparison with. She also needed to establish his background. Mostly, all he had to answer was yes to the first set of questions.

"The deceased, DEA Agent Larry Atkins, is your father. Isn't that correct?" It was definitely past time to satisfy the jury's curiosity on that matter.

Tina

"Yes, he's my father." Being forced to testify felt like the worst experience of his life. He was developing an extreme dislike for Shadika. So far, he was able to contain it because the questions hadn't gotten that bad.

"Were you upset when you found out that your father had been murdered?" This was the last part of her foundation.

"Yes, I was." This was a forced answer, which everyone knew the answer to.

"Mr. Atkins, you'd love to see the defendants get the death penalty, wouldn't you?" Coppedge thought about objecting; he just didn't want to get embarrassed for not having a good reason.

"I would like to see justice rendered." He felt that he had done a good job of ducking the question.

She liked the answer. "You wanted it so much that you conducted your own investigation." Now it was time to put him in his own quicksand.

"No. I didn't conduct my own investigation." He knew that saying "yes" would sound terrible to the jury and lead to other places.

"But isn't it true that you were the one that arrested Tina in New York City?" She would have asked the same question, just in a different manner if he had said "yes."

"It's true that I arrested her." Lying wasn't an option when you have been been interviewed on the news.

"Isn't it true that when you arrested her that you had bounty hunters with you?" Just the words "bounty hunters" heightened the jury's interest.

He paused before he said "yes." He figured correctly that she had the news clips and tapes from the event. "Yes, I had bounty hunters to help me track her down." He made it sound worse by adding the tracking part.

"So that means that you conducted your own investigation?" He had committed himself and this made for more pressure that she could put on him.

"No. I didn't conduct my own investigation." He turned to the jury while keeping his composure.

Shadika reached in her briefcase and pulled out a court transcript. "May I approach the witness?" Judge Grumpfree bobbed her head. All knew that the document meant a turn of events, which would be serious. She turned to the second page.

"Is that a transcript of you testifying before a grand jury?" She had her right hand on her hip and her left fist on the defense table.

He looked down at the document to check for the second time if his name was on there. "Yes." He had no choice and he knew where she was about to take him. So far, he hadn't shown any signs of breaking down.

"Would you please turn to page ten and look at the highlighted portion?" She was still in the same position. While he flipped his pages, she flipped hers.

"Your Honor, may the prosecution be provided with a copy of that." That was all that Coppedge could do. It also made it look like he hadn't seen the document, which was true. Not the best thing for his image.

Shadika reached in her briefcase and extended her arm to give him a copy. To make him feel dumb, she didn't take her eyes off of Clyde.

"Does it say that your probable cause for this case was Tina's letters to her boyfriend and some recorded phone calls?" She sensed that she was at the point of making him crack. One more question should do it.

"That is what it says." Members of the jury started looking back and forth at each other. People in the audience started murmuring. The reactions caused Clyde to start turning red.

"But you still didn't conduct an investigation?" She was hitting him with this again because he had shown a sign of weakness.

Tina

"Objection. That was already asked and answered twice." He knew that it didn't matter, but he had to try.

"Objection sustained."

It didn't matter to Shadika. He had already made a commitment and the jury had heard him.

"Is it not true that you were the one that acquired all the evidence from the Bureau of Prisons?" This question was in the same vein, but a little more dangerous because it opened more avenues.

"No. I didn't get the records from the BOP." He cut his eyes at the jury after he said it.

"But the records are from the BOP?" She smiled like she was modeling.

"I'm sure that's where they came from." He felt that he was safe because he knew that she had no paperwork to prove differently. There was none.

"We'll get back to that." She was playing a little game with him. "You weren't on the investigation team that investigated your father's murder, were you?"

"No, I was not." He felt good about answering that.

"That was because of the relationship?"

"That is correct." He felt good about answering that.

"So, would you please tell us how it is that you ended up going to the grand jury if you didn't investigate and you weren't on the investigation team?" She had just wanted to throw a few more jabs before starting to throw hooks that had too much power.

He was stuck. He couldn't say that he hadn't gone to the grand jury. He couldn't tell them the reason that he really went. He just sat there and tried to keep concealing that he was angry enough to kill her. The redness of his face and neck told everyone that he was angry.

She was satisfied that he hadn't answered. "Is it not true that you went to the grand jury yourself, along with Mr. Coppedge, because no one else would?" She looked at the jury and Judge Grumpfree. Just as she wanted, they were looking at him with the utmost interest.

"No, that isn't true." He answered that question with authority because he hated the way it felt to not answer one of her questions.

"So, tell me what other person was willing to do." She knew that it had to be an investigating officer that went. She knew that he would be better off being silent.

"I don't know." It wasn't good that he was losing the strength in his voice and had started sweating. He also would have been better saying he hadn't checked.

"Would you tell us what person gave you the BOP documents?" She had saved this for last for a reason.

"I'm not at liberty to say." He almost said that he couldn't recall. That would have sounded just as bad.

"Your Honor, would you order him to answer?" Shadika loved that she had to go there with him. It made him look that much worse as a witness.

"Answer the question, Mr. Atkins." It wasn't as if he had a privilege to not reveal his sources like a journalist.

He let out a deep breath. "I got the records from the BOP." He knew that it was over. He was looking at Shadika with squinted eyes.

"So you investigated Tina because you needed to put the crime on someone?" This was the icing on the cake. Might as well make him look as bad as she could. The opportunity to make a cop testify wouldn't happen until another lifetime.

"No, that's not true."

"So why did you meet with Diana in Pennsylvania?" She had almost forgotten to put that in there. She was certain that she had won the trial or at least had a hung jury.

"She called me and wanted to be a witness." He felt good about answering this question.

"So you didn't have any witnesses? Excuse me, eyewitnesses from an entire housing project that could be an eyewitness?" This would reveal the weakness of the case.

"You'll have to ask the prosecution."

Shadika smiled at the way he had answered the question and made himself look silly by trying to avoid the question, exactly what she wanted out of him. "But isn't it true that you put out a reward and you've followed this case since your father was murdered?" She was still standing in the same position.

Clyde took a deep breath and looked at the jury again. "Yes, I followed the case and I put out a reward for witnesses." He showed a lot of reluctance in his behavior. He felt himself sinking further and further and hating her that much more.

"So, it's true that y'all didn't have any eyewitnesses when you had arrested Tina." She was sure the jury caught the part about the reward.

He looked at Coppedge. This was one of the worst things that he could have done. He was thinking to himself that he wouldn't let her get away with this. "No, we didn't have any eyewitnesses." The sound of his voice revealed the agitation in him.

"So, you really had no probable cause to believe that Tina killed your father?" She just loved the expression on his face.

"Objection, your Honor. That's a question for the grand jury." This was the only thing that he could find wrong with her examination.

"Sustained."

Shadika knew that the jury would make their own inferences and come to their own conclusions. "The defense rests, your Honor." She sat down.

"Mr. Coppedge, do you have any questions for Officer Atkins?" She knew there was no way for him to be able to clean that up.

"I have no questions." What had just happened was the worst thing in a case that he had experienced.

"Excuse me, your Honor," a black male said as he was walking down the middle aisle. "I have something to say." He was speaking loud enough to get everyone's attention. Clyde was walking back to the prosecution's table to sit down. Coppedge had turned around. Shadika, Tyrone, and Tina were too busy looking at Clyde.

Judge Grumpfree was looking at him with a look of surprise. She was just about to ask him what he wanted. She didn't notice the other people in the audience that had also stood up or the few that had also walked through the door. Shadika, Tina, and Tyrone turned around because of the judge and jury staring at the man.

The man had just stopped at the entrance to the court's arena. He had caught the entire court's attention by standing up at the right moment. "I'm the one that murdered DEA Agent Larry Atkins."

A female that was about twenty yards behind him stepped out in the aisle and said, "No he's not. I'm the one that killed DEA Agent Larry Atkins.' Shadika recognized the both of them. She also remembered seeing the others that were approaching. Clyde was looking at all of them with squinted eyes. The rest of the court was looking with amazement.

Another male that was on the right side of the courtroom gave the female just enough time to get her statement out and said, "No, I'm the one that killed DEA Agent Larry Atkins."

"No, I'm the one that killed DEA Agent Larry Atkins," another female said before the last male could finish his statement. Shadika turned to see the looks on the judge's face and the jury members. She only gave Clyde and Coppedge small glances. They had become small players in this matter. Over twenty black males and females had stepped forward to claim responsibility for the crime. They were all just standing there at the threshold of the court arena.

Judge Grumpfree had never dreamed that this would happen in her courtroom. Nothing was said for more than thirty seconds. It was up to her to say something. Everybody had been staring back and forth at each other. Tyrone whispered something in Shadika's ear.

Shadika stood up. "Your Honor, I move that all charges against my clients be dismissed and dismissed with prejudice. There's no need to continue to waste the jury's time and the court's precious resources." It was like the opportunity of a lifetime.

Judge Grumpfree looked at Coppedge. He was stunned to the point that he didn't want to say anything and chance further embarrassing him.

"The defendants are acquitted." She would have done the same thing, no matter what he said. She had been thoroughly entertained. "They're free to go." All of the people in the courtroom started shouting and celebrating. Clyde left out of the side door before anyone noticed.

Tina hugged Tyrone tight like he might get away. Shadika had to make them stop kissing to get them out of the courtroom. Before she left the courtroom, she waved at the judge. With their personal entourage, they made their way out to Shadika's Mercedes.

Paparazzi caused a big scene trying to get a statement from Shadika, Tyrone, and Tina. They headed straight to the Elks Lodge.

It was pure pandemonium at the Elks. Maurice was giving away drinks and food. People had bottles of champagne, running around like they were forty ounces.

It took Shadika thirty minutes before she was able to get to Maurice. Nobody would let her pass without a few words or a handshake or a hug. Tina and Tyrone were getting the same attention. They even had to dance with a few people that were strangers.

"Mr. Maurice, may I speak with you in the back?" Though she had something very serious on her mind, she had a jovial smile on her face.

"We can do whatever you like." He took her into the kitchen.

"So you just had to do something. You couldn't leave it all in my hands?" She had her lips pursed so that they pointed up to the ceiling.

He laughed a little. "What are you talking about? I've been here all day. So what are you talking about?" He had not realized that he repeated the question.

"So you like to play games now? That's like an insult to my intelligence." She had started leaning on her left hip and standing closer to him.

"You know when you be asking questions, you get this dimple in your cheek that looks so cute. Are you sure that you are in your forties? You didn't look it on television." He had his finger under her chin and was just about to kiss her.

"I'm not mad. I just want you to admit to it." She kept moving her lips so that he couldn't kiss her.

"I can't wait for us to get married and have a few kids and things like that." He had missed kissing her by a fraction of an inch.

"All I ask is that you admit to it. I got mine off. Having secrets isn't the way to start a marriage." She stepped away from him.

"I got scared that day and I planned it as insurance. It's something that couldn't hurt you. So there you have it." He just wanted to make her beg to get an answer.

She stepped to him and put her arms around his neck and kissed him. "I know that a gangster is going to be a gangster. I love you Maurice."

Tina

******

I didn't think that I was going to get to be alone with my man. Maurice told us that we could use one of his houses for a few days. We are getting ready to do that.

I was playing with Tyrone's tool all the way over here. I was glad for Shadika to drop us off. I think it's about two o'clock in the morning – not that I care. The only thing holding us up in finding the bedroom – not that I need to be in a bed to get my thing off. We can do it in a closet for all I care. I wanted to do it in the back of Shadika's Benz. Tyrone did a good job of finding the bedroom.

All of a sudden, I'm nervous. He just turned around and started kissing me.

"I love you Tina," he told me in his sexy, masculine voice.

"I love you Tyrone." I wanted to ask him if we are really here together. I'm nervous because I want to please him so bad. I know females are going to be after him after seeing him on television. He does look that good.

"Tina, I'm going to take my time even though it's been years. You deserve to be treated like a queen." He made me sit down on the bed so that he could start taking my shoes off. With a soft touch, he's taking off my panty hose. I feel so special and I want him to hurry up also. My pussy is throbbing, like it has never throbbed before. Now, he's taking off the other one and he's taking his sweet time. This is killing me.

Oh my God, he's licking the big toe of my right foot and it caused me to start having an orgasm. All that I can do is lean back on my elbows, throw my head back, and moan and groan. He must have read about licking toes somewhere. He never did it before. My pussy is so wet that a tampon couldn't stop all of it.

He must have known that I had stopped coming. He stopped licking and kissing when he got to my knees. He also pulled me up so fast that I lost my breath. There was a big smile on my face that I couldn't hide if my life depended on it. That's how good this moment feels to me.

His tool feels good in my hands. I feel like I can't get enough of it. While I'm unbuckling his pants, he's undoing my blouse and skirt.

I have his tool in my hands and I'm caressing his balls like it's so precious. Before he could finish reaching for my bra strap, I dropped to my knees and started moistening the head of his tool with my lips and tongue.

"That feels good Tina." This makes me suck that much harder and start stroking his shaft with my right hand. He tastes so good to me, sweat and all.

"Oh Tina, oh Tina." His voice calling out my name is sending shivers throughout my entire body.

"Mmm, damn Tina." If he asked me to suck his dick all day and night, I'd do it.

To work this thing like a pro, I started sucking his balls while I'm still stroking his shaft. "Don't stop that Tina." That lets me know that I'm the female that he has on his mind. "That feels so good."

I felt his dick get harder in my hand. I'm licking my way back to the top. I have to have all of this. He's starting to shake. "Oh, that feels so good." That made me have another orgasm. I'm not letting a drop hit the floor. This is all mine. "Damn Tina." It was that good to me also. That's how you put your fingerprints on your man and his dick is still hard. It's about to be on tonight.

Before he can do a thing, I stand up and tell him, "I need to have you inside of me," and pulled him on the bed by pulling him by his dick. It's still hard as steel. When my back hits the pillow, I tell him, "Tear my panties off." Oh my God, he did that with ease just like he always used to do. I didn't let him go while he did that.

"You are the only woman for me Tina. I mean that," he said just before he put his head into my love box.

"I love you Tyrone and you are the only man for me." I'm glad that he's taking his time because I'm tight from not

Tina

having sex for all those years. That's right, I waited for my man. Plus, we're making love, not having sex. "That feels so good Tyrone." I have my chocolate thighs wrapped around his back. And it feels better than it has ever felt to me.

"This is the best pussy that I've ever had. Damn, this feels good." If he hadn't said this, the night would not have been complete.

"You have the best dick that I've ever had. Oh, that feels good." He just hit my G-spot. I have to wiggle to get that again. "Oh yeah." I squeezed my thighs a little tighter. I'm squeezing my pussy also every time that I gain a little control of my body. "I just love the way that you are taking your time."

"I'm going to give it to you just the way that you like until the end of time." He doesn't know how good he's making me feel.

"You're the only woman that I want to make love to. I want to be making love to you until we die."

"Oh Tyrone. That was that spot again."

"Was it? I'll do it again."

Damn, he's driving me crazy. He's hitting my spot like he knows my entire body. "Stroke me a little faster. That's it. Oh yes. That's it."

"It feels good to me also baby." This is definitely what is called making love.

"I'm about to cum Tyrone. Stroke me faster and harder." I can barely stand to feel this good.

"I'm about to bust also. Oh yes, it feels so good." His eyes just rolled to the back of his head.

We climaxed at the same time. An orgasm could make a female go a whole year without wanting any ... Not. I got to be with my man all that I can. We just got out of the belly of the beast.

******

I just finished making love to the best woman on the planet. I can't think of a thing to complain about when it comes to our relationship. If a dude has a female that's better than mine, I'd like to know what it is that she's doing and has done. I'm so satisfied that nothing could make me cheat on Tina. I mean that from the bottom of my heart.

I have to spit about this trial for while. When she put him on the stand, I knew that it was all over. She worked him like she was reading his mind. By the look on his face, I could tell that he felt worse than I felt when his father had me on the ground. I feel like a brand new man and I can face the world with dignity.

When Shadika asked me to do some research on putting a police officer on the stand, I thought that she had lost her mind. When I saw the case that said that a senator could be called to testify, I started believing that is was possible. Also, since there were no cases that had rules against it, I felt that there was a great chance in that happening. Just to be safe, we kept that between us. I didn't even consult with any other jailhouse lawyer to see what they had to say.

I have to admit that she's a genius. Because of her, I'm a free man and part of making history. What more could a man ask of a lawyer?

The nicest thing was being able to walk right out of the courtroom, though I have a pending case. All of those people admitting to the crime probably caused one hell of a shock. I wonder what that is called in the law books. It doesn't really matter. What matters is that I'm a free man and my lady is a free woman. We are a free couple.

Let me say this about my lady. If I wasn't with Tina, I may have never met Shadika. Now, Shadika and I are going to start a law firm. It's all going to be under her name until I get a law degree. I'll be the administrator. So that means that I'll be working hard and studying hard and making good money. Along with having the best lady in the world, I'll be thanking God a lot.

******

Four months later, Tyrone was playing the role of an

attorney and making over fifty thousand a month doing it. Every high-profile case in Ohio came to Shadika first. They just took the cases that they liked.

Shadika worked with Maurice about two to three days a week at the Elks Lodge. She had only started the law firm to help Tyrone and Tina get a great start in life. The biggest formality was talking Tyrone into taking time served. Also, out of respect for them, Shadika postponed her wedding date so that they could all get married together. Tyrone wanted to be able to pay for half of the wedding expenses. It was not a problem with all the high-profile cases that they were taking. Maurice also put up some money for the wedding. They told Tyrone that the wedding would cost about $100,000. That was, also, what Shadika paid for her wedding gown.

To hold the wedding, they rented the largest building in Youngstown. Also, if you weren't from Westlake, you weren't invited unless you were really close to one of the brides or grooms. There were very few people outside of Westlake – mostly Tyrone's people.

Everybody was dressed in their best. There wasn't a detail that had been overlooked to make the day that special.

When Shadika said, "I do," she knew that she meant it and that she was with the man of her dreams.

Maurice and Shadika were so happy that the preacher had to stop them from kissing so that he could marry Tina and Tyrone.

Tina was nervous because the wedding ceremony had surpassed all of her dreams and wishes. In comparison with what she had been through, it all seemed like a dream to her.

When gun shots rang out, just before she was about to give her vow, she snapped back to reality. So did the rest of the audience.

Clyde was walking down the aisle with a nine millimeter in his hands. He had it pointed directly at the brides and grooms. "Y'all didn't think that I was going to let y'all get away with murder." He started aiming directly at Tina. Clyde was walking slowly to the front making sure to watch the rest of the crowd, as they moved to the side, with his peripheral vision.

Clyde had picked a moment he felt that they would be relaxed. He was wearing his Deputy Sheriff uniform to use his position as a cop to his advantage. He only had to shoot two people on the outside that were watching. The silencer had been put away. Everyone that was able made sure that they saw the ceremony.

Tina slowly turned so that she could face him. Tyrone stepped in front of her. People in the audience had all gotten on the walls.

"It doesn't matter Tyrone. I have enough ammunition to kill all three of y'all." He aimed the gun at Shadika. He wanted her to get from behind Maurice. "Get over there with them." He had walked halfway to the front.

Maurice made sure she didn't move. "What are you going to gain from this?" Maurice asked to get his attention. Maurice was also watching his people in the crowd to see if they were on point.

"It's called revenge." Clyde planned to shoot Tina and Shadika in their heads, and then quickly shoot Tyrone and Maurice – though he didn't know him – then turn on the crowd. He was sure they would be running out the doors. He hadn't gotten his aim on Tina's head correct yet. Just a few more yards. She had to die first.

"You don't even know that she did it." Maurice was buying time and trying to keep him from shooting.

"It doesn't matter to --" A gun shot went off and Clyde fell to the floor. Everybody on the stage ducked when they saw Clyde's body buck because they didn't want to be hit if he fired a bullet.

"What the hell took you so long?" Maurice was talking to the same guy that had approached the court arena first.

Tina

Shadika thought that maybe having a gangster as a husband wasn't such a bad thing. Maurice approached Clyde's body along with his main man. They wanted to make sure that Clyde was dead.

When he took the gun out of Clyde's hands, everybody started yelling and screaming, clapping and celebrating.

Tina went behind the podium and made the preacher stand up. "I'm still getting married. So let's get this over with."

When the organ sounded, all realized that they were still at a wedding.

"I'm still getting married. To hell with Clyde," she said to Tyrone to get him to get back in place.

The preacher waited for the rest of the audience to get back in their seats. They just stepped around Clyde's body like he was a piece of furniture.

******

Okay people, since this is about me and my situation, I'm taking over so that I can end this thing proper-like.

My man is looking so good in his black tuxedo that I feel like having sex with him right now, in front of this entire crowd. I've read about some cultures that do that. I feel that good and liberated when I'm in his presence. When I say have sex, I'm talking about the kind of sex that whenever you think about it, you have no choice but to be turned on. For you ladies that haven't experienced these feelings, I'll say a prayer when I get a chance. That'll be some time after the honeymoon. I promise to not forget. Let's get back to this wedding.

My man just said, "I do,' and it made my heart skip a beat and made me anxious because I'm ready to say the same thing. It seems like this is going too slow because the preacher is now talking to me. Yes, I'm trippin' and it's just my imagination that he's going slower with me than he was with everybody else. I want this to happen before something else happens. The roof might cave in or something. Love can do a woman like that.

Thank God he just finished. I said, "I do," before he was able to get the last sentence out of his mouth. Shame on me for disrespecting the preacher. I'll apologize to him later.

I turned towards Tyrone so quickly that the audience has to know that I'm anxious and nervous. I have to thank God again. Tyrone has the wedding band in his hand. It looks so tacky that I'm shaking and fidgeting and my hand is shaking. Thank God again that he grabbed my hands. I'm still fidgeting and shaking.

This has got to be the most beautiful ring in the world. This wedding band represents the bond that Tyrone and I have. Ooh, ooh, ooh. It feels so good to finally have it on my finger. And thank God again the preacher just pronounced us as man and wife. I have to keep thanking God because that's how good I feel. Now, I can't act civilized by letting Tyrone pull my veil up. I've already torn it off and thrown my flowers out to the crowd. I don't care if a man catches them. For the kiss, I have to give my man all I got.

Oh yes. Oh yes. Oh yes. His lips just touched mine. Oh yes. Oh yes. Oh yes. Our tongues just touched. Oh yes. Oh yes. Oh yes. We're kissing like it's the first time that we kissed and acting like we're all alone. We go at it harder when the crowd starts cheering us on. Oh yes. Oh yes. Oh yes. He has his entire body pressed up against mine and I can feel his hardness. If my arms weren't wrapped around his neck so tight, I'd be playing with it.

It's a good thing that Maurice and Shadika stepped up. Though the crowd is clapping and cheering, I feel a little bashful because I was about to lose control. What matters now is that I'm Mrs. Tina Thompson Taylor and I have the best man in the world as my husband.

Since the pages of this book are getting that thin, I have to spit on a few unresolved matters and give a few of y'all a chance to say, "I knew it, I knew it, I knew it."

The next time that this place opens up, they are going to find Clyde's body. Of course, we could bury his body somewhere, but we don't have to do that because not a soul is going to say a thing. If they act like they will, they disappear first. Diana taught us a serious lesson.

Those were just my thoughts on the situation. If I know Maurice like I know Maurice, the body won't be here no longer than necessary and the place will be as clean as most cats' rides on Saturday night at the club. This included getting rid of the car that Clyde drove up in.

The only thing that I don't like about the situation is that I didn't get the chance to shoot him like I shot his father. My entire project knew I that killed Atkins because I was so happy the next day. The only person that I told was Maurice because I needed his advice.

I can still remember that night like it happened last night. I had waited for about a week after my man lost his Rule 33 hearing. I felt that if I couldn't have my man – then Atkins couldn't have his life. I knew he'd come through to get himself some pussy.

I was wearing a black hoodie so that no one would recognize me. When I saw him walking, I started walking towards him. Right after we crossed paths, I turned around and fired two shots in his head. I knew that I had hit him right at the base of his skull. I just kept walking like nothing had happened.

Maurice got rid of the gun for me. Tyrone never asked me if I did it, like a good man should do. Too many questions are a sign of no faith.

If I had the chance to do it again, I'd do it.

About the Author

Darrell J. DeBrew is a North Carolina native. DeBrew's experiences with the criminal world and the criminal justice system drove him to show people the game and educate them; he wants people to be entertained by street life without getting locked up or being adversely affected by the streets. He is the author of Stacy, Keisha and Trina.

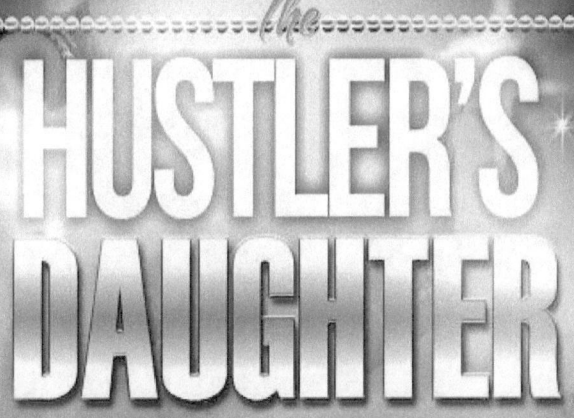

The
HUSTLER'S
DAUGHTER

BY
PINKY
DIOR

A BEAUTIFUL SATAN II

NATASHA'S WRATH

By

RJ CHAMP

Order Form

DC Bookdiva Publications
#245 4401-A Connecticut Avenue, NW
Washington, DC 20008
dcbookdiva.com

Name: _____

Inmate ID: _____

Address: _____

City/State: _____ **Zip:** _____

QUANTITY	TITLES	PRICE	TOTAL
	Up The Way, Ben	15.00	
	Dynasty By Dutch	15.00	
	Dynasty 2 By Dutch	15.00	
	Trina, Darrell Debrew	15.00	
	A Killer'z Ambition, Nathan Welch	15.00	
	Lorton Legends, Eyone Williams	15.00	
	The Hustle. Frazier Boy	15.00	
	A Beautiful Satan, RJ Champ	15.00	
	Secrets Never Die, Eyone Williams	15.00	
	Q, Dutch	15.00	

QUANTITY	TITLES	PRICE	TOTAL
	Dynasty 3, Dutch	15.00	
	Tina, Darrell Debrew	15.00	
	A Beautiful Satan 2, RJ Champ	15.00	
	A Hustler's Daughter, Pinky Dior	15.00	
	A Killer'z Ambition 2, Nathan Welch	15.00	
	The Commission	15.00	

Sub-Total $ _____

Shipping/Handling (Via US Media Mail) $3.95 1-2 Books, $7.95 1-3 Books, 4 or more titles-Free Shipping

Shipping $ _____

Total Enclosed $ _____

Certified or government issued checks and money orders, all mail in orders take 5-7 Business days to be delivered. Books can also be purchased on our website at dcbookdiva.com and by credit card at 1866-928-9990. Incarcerated readers receive 25% discount. Please pay $11.25 per book and apply the same shipping terms as stated above.